THE POOR GENTLEMAN

THE POOR GENTLEMAN

IAN HAY

WILDSIDE PRESS

TO
F. S.
TO WHOSE UNFAILING CRITICISM OF ALL HIS WORK
THE AUTHOR OWES THE FACT
THAT
FOR FIFTEEN YEARS
HE HAS CONTINUED TO TAKE
THE SAME SIZE
IN
HATS

Originally published in 1928.
Published by Wildside Press LLC.
wildsidepress.com

CHAPTER 1

TWO NOBODIES

My morning walk is a matter of routine, and quite unambitious. We live, my mother and I, in one of those small squares which abound in South Kensington, at a distance which makes it possible for me, at my rate of walking (which is well under two miles an hour), to get to Kensington Gardens in twenty-five minutes.

I usually sit in the Gardens for some time. I like the smell of the grass and the sound of the trees, and it is pleasant to hear the children's voices. I am rather fond of children, I think. After that I walk home again, and report myself all present and correct for lunch, to the secret surprise and relief of my parent, who has no confidence whatever in my ability to take care of myself, though it pleases her to simulate entire indifference to my welfare. But, after all, why should anyone worry about me? I am well under forty and in perfect condition; and I always have a surprisingly large number of friends and counsellors upon the route.

Moreover, the route itself is quite easy to follow. On leaving the house (down five steps) you turn to the left, and proceed to the first corner. There is a pillar-box there, so there is no excuse for your passing the turn in a fit of absence of mind. Here you wheel to the left again, and keep straight on until you come to the junction with Queen's Gate. There is a policeman on point duty here—an affable soul. As a matter of fact, there are three of them altogether, and they take duty in turns. They are all affable, though, and I know their names. One of them, Beelby, is on visiting terms with our cook.

After passing the time of day with whichever of the three happens to be there, and having received any necessary cautions as to pavements under repair or railings newly painted, I climb the steep ascent of Queen's Gate and arrive in the Kensington Road. Here I encounter the one serious obstacle of my daily path—the river of traffic which rolls between me and the Gardens opposite.

However, custom makes all things easy. I turn to the left at the top of Queen's Gate and proceed with caution along the now crowded pavement until I arrive opposite the entrance to the Broad Walk, where the policeman on duty arrests my progress and engages me upon seasonable topics until the time is ripe to hold up the traffic and send me across the road with the next convoy of perambulators. After that I am in the Gardens, as much at home as in the old days in Regent's Park.

Of course I can compass more adventurous expeditions than this. On two afternoons a week I lunch at my club and play bridge. The club is situated in Dover Street, and is sadly old-fashioned in its tone: I doubt if you could find a single member of it who is really interested in the Russian Ballet. But it has the best swimming bath in London—sometimes, when I feel like it, I have a swim before luncheon—and one can hear all the athletic gossip one wants, which is very convenient for persons like myself who do not read the newspapers.

My mother always sends me to the club in a taxi, and she believes, poor soul, that I am conveyed home by the same agency. For her peace of mind's sake I do not tell her that I frequently travel most of the way by Tube. It is not a difficult feat, really. Thus:—

On leaving the club I cross the street, turn right, and walk a hundred yards or so until I come to the Dover Street Tube Station. I have a friend at the entrance, with one leg, who sells flowers; he is almost as fatherly as a policeman. Inside the station, just on the left as you enter, there is an automatic ticket machine, which I prefer to patronise rather than join the queue at the window. For some reason people buying tickets for anything, even a half-mile train ride, are never quite so considerate or so observant as at normal times.

I knew Dover Street Station well in the old days, and have elaborated my knowledge since; so I have no particular difficulty in finding the platform when I leave the lift.

I often wonder why Tube platforms are so far from the lift. Take Dover Street. On emerging at the foot of the shaft—about eight-five feet down, I should say—you turn to the right and walk twelve paces. This brings you, as it were, out of the station and into Dover Street again. Then you turn to the left and step out for fifty-seven paces. This means that you have walked out of Dover Street and right under Piccadilly. You now turn to the left once more, go down nineteen steps, and the platform for South Kensington is on your right. I calculate that it is exactly beneath the Ritz Hotel. I wonder if the Ritz authorities know about this. They ought to have a private lift down to it; only people who stay at the Ritz may not travel by Tube.

Having reached the platform in question, I always station myself in the same spot, beside the penny-in-the-slot weighing-machine; then all I have to do is to wait until the train comes in, take five paces forward, and I am right inside the car. (Tube trains have this virtue, that they always stop in exactly the same place.) After that I count stations, and get out at the third—or fourth, according as the train is announced to stop at Brompton Road or not. They always shout this out, and I understand the language quite well now.

South Kensington itself presents no difficulties. It is one of the few Tube stations in London with its upper and lower strata correctly superimposed. There is your lift, right on the platform. Having arrived above-ground again, I take a taxi home. Of course, I could walk—it is no great distance—but my mother always seems to be at home whenever I come in. Fortunately there is no infallible means of distinguishing between a taxi which has come from Dover Street and a taxi which has come from South Kensington Station, except by looking at the amount of fare on the clock; and my mother, bless her, has not thought of that yet.

But I have strayed into an irrelevant and rather boastful treatise upon the way to travel by Underground. What I really set out to describe was an adventure of mine in Kensington Gardens, an adventure but for which this narrative would never have been written.

II

It was a warm spring morning, and the smell of the fresh young shoots was wonderful. I sat in my favourite seat near the Round Pond and listened to the stirring medley of sounds around me. The cricket season opens early in the Gardens, and a game of an unscientific but exciting nature was in progress about fifty yards away. Two nurses, with perambulators, were sitting under the next tree to mine, taking away their employers' characters with extraordinary gusto. Somebody was throwing sticks into the Pond, to be retrieved by an intensely excited dog—a water-spaniel, I should say.

Once or twice I was approached by some seeker after information upon what appears to be the one burning question in the lives of small children and nursemaids—namely, the exact hour of day. I am much employed in this capacity; in fact, I may call myself, without false pride, the unofficial timekeeper of this part of the Gardens. For one thing, I am a regular and reliable figure: the children and nurses all know me well. They even have a name for me.

"Ernie," commands a shrill and authoritative voice, "just you give over 'itting little Dorothy with that bat, and go and ask the Poor Gentleman the right time. You don't want your dinner to get cold, do you?"

Thereupon Ernie desists from the audible chastisement of Dorothy, and runs pantingly over to me.

"Please could you tell me—" and the inevitable query follows. (I wonder why they always ask for the right time. Surely it would never occur to anyone to tell a child the wrong time.)

In reply I bring out my watch and show it to him. This form of procedure is much appreciated, because it implies that Ernie is able to read the time for himself, which is not always the case. If I gather from his demeanour that I have tried him too highly, I proceed to my principal and most popular accomplishment. The watch is a repeater, so I make it chime the approximate time of day for us both, and my small friend hurries off to impart the information before it slips from an unreliable memory.

I had just obliged one of my patrons in the usual manner, when the strains of a military band, faintly audible from the direction of the Bayswater Road, came drifting across the gardens.

In a moment all was changed; military ceremonial of any kind is an unfailing lure for children of every age—and their attendant females. All my neighbours struck camp simultaneously; dogs ceased to bark beside the Pond; chairs tumbled over; perambulators got under way; cricket operations were indefinitely suspended. Everybody "raced across the grass, just to see the soldiers pass," as they used to sing at the Gaiety long ago; their eager voices died away, and I was left derelict. I pulled out my pipe and began to fill it.

Suddenly I was conscious of a human presence at my right elbow, introducing itself by a gentle cough.

"Would I be trespassing too much on your indulgence, sir, if I was to request you to be so kind as to accommodate me with a match?"

"I have a patent lighter, if that is of any service to you," I said, somewhat taken aback by these flowers of rhetoric. "Do you know how to work it?"

"I'm afraid not, sir. They come a bit high for chaps like me."

I performed the necessary conjuring trick with my thumb, and the flame sputtered into life.

"There you are," I said.

"After you, sir."

"All right." I lit my pipe, and my companion then ignited an unmistakable Woodbine.

"Won't you sit down?" I continued. There was a chair beside me. Parkkeepers, who appear to be sentimental fellows, always leave them in couples.

"You are very gracious, sir," announced my new friend.

"You are very ceremonious," I rejoined.

"Am I really, sir? Thank you for noticing of it." He appeared genuinely pleased.

"Are you cultivating the lost art of conversation?" I asked.

"That's it, sir; I am. Between you and me—you and I, I mean—I'm taking a course in it. Trying to better my address and manner of speaking, and so forth. In fact—I'm not taking a liberty, sir, I hope, talking to you like this? I can see you're a gentleman—"

"Go ahead," I said. "Why are you doing all this? A girl?"

"No, sir, there's nothing of that kind. I want to establish a career before I begin looking in that direction. I've always been ambitious, and of course if a man that wants to rise to bigger things is common in his talk there's no denying it's a—handicap." The aspirate of the last word troubled him for a moment, but he blew it out manfully.

"I got the idea a few weeks ago. I ran across an advert. in a paper"—he named a Sabbath organ with a vast circulation and a rather gullible *clientèle*—"and it set me thinking. I've got it here, if you'd care to cast your eye over it." There followed a thin rustling. "It starts just there, sir."

"I have the misfortune to be blind," I said. "Would you mind reading it to me?"

Needless to say, my companion was quite unable to do anything of the kind. In fact, he was stricken dumb. Concern and embarrassment radiated from him: I could almost feel the heat. Of course, one is used to this: people seem to be as incapable of comporting themselves naturally in the presence of the blind as they are in the presence of the clergy—and any parson will tell you what that means.

Gradually he recovered his equanimity, and with it the power of speech.

"I'm sure I humbly beg your pardon, sir…! No idea at all…! I 'opes as 'ow I 'aven't 'urt your feelings in any—"

"On the contrary," I said, "you've paid me just the sort of compliment I appreciate. You've shown me that I don't look blind, and that's half the battle with us, you know."

"I see," said my companion quickly. "Sort of proper pride, like—eh?" Then he added, respectfully:

"War, sir?"

I nodded.

"I was lucky," he said. "I stopped a bit of H.E. at Third Ipray"—no soldier below the rank of sergeant-major ever called Ypres "Wipers"—"but they got it out all right."

"Infantry?" I said.

"Emma Gees—Machine Gunners—Suicide Club. I was Number One of our six."

"You carried the tripod, eh?"

"*And* fired the gun! That was what made up for the tripod. What were you in, sir, if I may presume for to—"

"A Sapper, nominally; but I was with the Intelligence part of the time. We must have a pow-wow about those days presently. Just now I want to hear about this course of yours. By the way, I think it's time we exchanged names. Mine's Barry Shere; what's yours?"

"Alf Noseworthy, sir."

"Not in the Army now, I suppose?"

"No, I'm back at my old trade—electrician. I'm a good craftsman: wireless apparatus, and all that. You'd be surprised if I told you the number of valve-sets and crystal-sets, and amplifiers and everything that I've turned out in the last year or two."

"I have a valve-set," I said. "It's indispensable to me, almost. My newspaper, in fact."

"What make?" asked Alf quickly.

I told him.

"No good, sir. That make is just one long hallelujah of atmospherics, unless you're an expert. I must come round and fix it up for you, if you'll let me."

I thanked him, for he was right about the atmospherics. "Now let's get back to you," I said. "Tell me about this course. I like your enterprise in taking it up."

Mr. Noseworthy gave a gratified little cough.

"Well, a man has his dreams," he admitted. "But I've got sense enough to know that if you want to get to the top you've got to start at the bottom. That's why I noticed this advert., I suppose. Fairly jumped out at me, it did."

"Tell me what it says."

The dreamer cleared his throat, and began, in a husky, self-conscious monotone:

"What are your mistakes in English? They may offend others as much as these offend you."

"What are 'these'?" I inquired apostolically.

"I'm coming to that, sir. Here they are: *'You was'; 'It don't'; 'Can't hardly.' If someone you met for the first time made these mistakes in English, would he inspire your respect? Would you be ready to make a friend of him?"*

"Yes," I said.

"They don't think so in the advert.," said Alf gloomily. "And there's worse coming, sir."

"Perhaps, however, you too make mistakes of which you yourself are quite unconscious. For example: 'Those sort of things'—"

"I'm never quite sure about that one myself," I said. The conscientious Alf ploughed on:

"'All this talk don't affect me at all.' 'I already met Mr. Jones.' 'I don't hardly know what to say.' 'Will I open the window?'"

"That one's all right," I said. "Ask any Scotsman."

"'So you made twenty sales this month?' 'She don't act like she's happy.' 'I ain't speaking to him no more.' 'It seems like it's going to rain.'" Alf paused for breath.

"Who started all this trouble?" I asked.

"You mean, who put in the advert., sir?"

"Yes."

"His name is Mr. Homer P. Keedick," said Alf reverently.

"Aha! And what part of America does he operate from?"

"America, sir? It don't—doesn't say anything about America here. Mr. Keedick lives in the Fulham Road."

"A branch establishment, I expect. I think our friend is American, both in body and soul. Well, did you answer his advertisement?"

"Yes, sir; and he wrote back, by return, enclosing his System. *The Homer P. Keedick Hundred Percent. Self-Correcting System. No Hard Study. No Useless Drudgery. Get the Habit of Correctitude!*" quoted Alf sonorously.

"I suppose Mr. Keedick doesn't do all this for nothing?"

"Oh no, sir. There is a small—honorarium. I've sent him that, and I receive an examination-paper once a week."

"Have you got one about you?"

"Yes. I brought it out here to study. It goes in tomorrow, and I'm not too sure about some of the answers."

"Let me hear the questions."

Alf produced a crackling sheet, and began:

"*Which would you say: 'Just when was you married?' or 'Just when were you married?' 'I laid on the porch' or 'I lay on the porch'? 'Benefishery' or 'Benefisheery'? 'Shedool' or 'Skedool'?*"

There was a good deal more like this, and he read it to the end. Then, with my faltering assistance, he wrote down some answers.

"I'm very grateful to you, sir," he said when we had finished. "I do want to improve myself, and that's a fact."

"I'm here nearly every day about this hour," I said. "Bring your stuff along any time you like, and we'll tackle it jointly. It may improve my English, too."

"Thank you kindly, sir. Of course this is just elementary stuff—starting at the bottom, like I said—and that's why I want to get it over and done with. When I've qualified, Mr. Keedick's got another course ready for me. *Poise and Personality.* That's what I'm after, really."

"Mr. Keedick seems to be an all-round man," I said. "Have you ever seen him?"

"No, sir. *Apply by Letter Only*, it says. Do you think I shall qualify for the second course?" he asked rather wistfully.

"I haven't the slightest doubt of it," I replied.

"The trouble about me," remarked Alf frankly, "is that I haven't never stuck at anything long enough to make any difference. I've got my ambitions, mind you, but I don't never seem to 'ave got put on to a job that my 'eart was in. Machine-gunnery was nearest, but you can't 'ope for a war all the time."

"What about your wireless job?"

"I'm a good practical electrician; I understand induced currents and electrostatics better than most; but my 'eart's not there. Shall I tell you something, sir?" Apparently he had told me nothing so far.

"Go ahead."

"I'll tell you my real ambition—my real dream. It's to be a comedian—a comic in Variety. That's why I'm spending my savings on Keedick's course."

"I don't think correct English is absolutely indispensable in the music-hall profession," I observed.

"No, sir; but it's this Poise and Personality course I'm after, and he won't give it to you until you've taken the other. Personality—that's what gets across the footlights. And that's just what I 'aven't got!"

"How do you know?"

"Because I've tried, sir! In the war, at sing-songs and concert parties, back in billets. You know—the sergeant-major presiding, and 'alf a dozen officers sitting on kitchen chairs in the front row. Oh, I've *tried*!"

"And you weren't a success?"

"I was a rotten failure. They laughed all right; one or two in the back row laughed fit to kill themselves; but I 'ad a kind of nasty instink all the time that they were laughing at me and not at my entertainment; and when I met them in the canteen after, I knew it. No Poise; no Personality—that was my trouble. Everything else was all right, I think. My songs were good: I wrote them myself. The best one I ever wrote, though, I never sang. I wasn't going to waste it on that crowd; I was saving it up. I've got it still; and when the right moment comes along I shall release it!"

"What was it called?" I asked. Evidently I was expected to do so.

"*'The Lips that Touch Kippers Shall Never Touch Mine'!*" replied Alf Noseworthy, with simple pride. "I'll sing you the first verse," he added, in a fit of generous abandon; "I know you won't give it away." He shuffled his chair a little closer, placed his right hand upon my right knee, and sang the verse through, in a voice which entirely filled Kensington Gardens.

"Do you think they'll listen to it?" he asked when he had finished.

"They'll have to," I replied, with perfect truth.

"Thank you for saying so, sir." Alf withdrew his hand and was silent. Then he sighed; evidently his mercurial spirit had drooped again.

"I don't know, though," he said. "It'll probably come to nothing. Perhaps my old father was right. He used to sit in his armchair by the fire, smoking his pipe, and say: 'Young Alfie, you're a stay-at-home—a stick-in-the-mud—that's what you are. You won't never see much of life. Just a nice, decent stay-at-home!' Of course he was wrong in one way—Third Ipray, and all that—but you couldn't expect anyone to foresee a thing like the War. 'E was right in other ways, though. Barring my service I've never 'ad an adventure nor an experience worth anything in my life. And yet that's just what I dream about. Life—people—human nature—that's what interests me. I want to see life; I want to meet people; I want to study human nature; and then make funny songs about all three—songs that would get 'ome to people. I'd like to prove my old man wrong. I'd like 'im to sit in a plush stall, and see my number go up and me come on and play on my audience like a—a instrument. 'E might think something of me then." Alf sighed again.

"Is he still alive?" I asked.

"No, sir; he's been with mother for about ten years now. The air-raids finished him. Still, he wasn't often wrong about things. I expect he was right about me. A stay-at-home! A stick-in-the-mud! Electrostatics and broadcasting apparatus—that's Alf Noseworthy, forever and ever! Adventures ain't on my ticket; nor yours neither, sir, nowadays, I suppose. We're both on the shelf."

"You're right there," I said soberly—little knowing that I lied for both of us.

CHAPTER 2

BEHIND THE CURTAIN

I used to be a great theatre-goer, and am still. But naturally there are parts of the entertainment which appeal to me less than they did. Spectacle, for instance. If I go to a revue, I enjoy the jokes and the songs as much as ever—perhaps more—but if there is too much dancing or display I abandon my stall and seek more profitable company.

Occasionally I penetrate behind the scenes, where I have a number of hospitable friends. I never go, though, unless I am invited.

People ought to think twice before visiting an actor in his dressing-room; he is so completely at their mercy. They enjoy an unfair advantage. They cannot be told that their victim is out of town, or on a journey, or sleeping; the programme and the bills outside proclaim, sometimes in capital letters, that he is within the theatre and wide awake. He can only get rid of his visitors by inviting them to go to the devil; and, after all, those of us who live to please must please to live.

Consequently his dressing-room is the natural resort of artistic gentlemen who want a play read or a song tried out, of laudatory gentlemen who want a drink, of adhesive gentlemen who want a couple of pounds till Saturday, and of susceptible gentlemen who want an introduction to a lady of the chorus. And their host, with the inborn bonhomie of his race, welcomes them all with cries of delight, though he may hardly know one from the other.

The actress, so Maudie informs me—I will introduce Maudie in a moment—is in slightly better case, for she can always eject a caller on the ground of a change of raiment, and keep him standing in a draughty passage, where men in heavy boots tread on his feet and haughty houris withdraw their skirts from him (if they possess any) as they pass; until the actress's dresser, peeping cautiously forth, is able to report that the unwanted one has abandoned his vigil and gone back to his stall.

Maudie is the wife of my friend Hal Horner, who earns, I believe, about three hundred pounds a week and a percentage of the gross (whatever that may mean) for making London laugh louder than anyone else can. I first encountered Hal in a Divisional concert-party somewhere at the back of Poperinghe in early nineteen sixteen.

I have forgotten what the party was called, but it was probably The Whizz Bangs, or The Duds. They were all called something like that. Anyhow, Hal's associates were six in number, and their task was to maintain in a reasonably cheerful frame of mind men who, week in and week out, were enduring mud, blood, and oblique shell-fire in the trenches about Sanctuary Wood and Hill Sixty in the Salient of Ypres. They were sufficiently successful in this enterprise to be perfectly justified in labelling their entertainment "A Hooge Success." (Hal's idea, I fancy.)

Of the sextet, two were vocalists of the sentimental brand, constantly Keeping the Home Fires Burning or extolling Tumbledown Nests in the West; one was a pianist, another was a regrettably vulgar but very amusing female impersonator, and a fifth recited and gave imitations of celebrities whom he had never seen.

Hal Horner was the out-and-out humorist of the band. He was a natural comedian of the first order, though obviously without any technical experience. He had been involved in the original German gas attack in the previous spring, but being in the reserve line at the time had got off more lightly than some hundreds of other poor fellows.

On coming out of hospital, though he could have obtained honourable exemption from further service, he volunteered to remain in Flanders on light duty, and was accordingly, on the strength of a certain reputation earned in a hospital ward, assigned to the concert party, which was how I came to make his acquaintance.

I was in Poperinghe for the night, waiting for the leave train which set out on its tortuous way to Boulogne at five o'clock every morning; so I patronised the Hooge Success. The officer in charge of the proceedings was an old acquaintance of mine, and he presented me afterwards to Hal, whose performance had reduced me to tears of pure joy. Hal proved to be a London City clerk, still a private in rank and a little inclined to jump to attention whenever addressed by an officer, even over a glass of Belgian beer.

However, hearing that I was going on leave next morning, he overcame his natural diffidence sufficiently to ask if I would do him a favour. His wife, it seemed, had not been getting her separation allowance, and circumstances in Balham were dangerously straitened in consequence. Could I possibly get the right string pulled?

I was ultimately able to perform the service required, and was rewarded with the friendship of two really great-hearted people. I visited Maudie in Balham. In appearance she was indubitably plain, and she assures me that she is now, if anything, plainer. (In fact, only Hal's undoubted prestige in the theatre keeps her in the chorus at all—back row.) But I fell in love with her sudden and cheerful smile and the sturdy, Cockney courage with which she was enduring semi-starvation. I never saw either her or Hal again, and never shall, but whenever they see me the occasion has to be celebrated.

I ought to add that after the Armistice Hal was not required to return to his desk in Aldermanbury, for he was offered a quite fabulous salary to appear as leading comedian in a West End revue, and accepted the same, subject to the provision that his wife should be admitted to the theatrical profession with him. They do not live in Balham now; they have a flat in Knightsbridge and a little house at Maidenhead. I have visited both.

One evening I found myself at the Elysium Theatre, drawn thither by the lure of Hal Horner's name and escorted by my young friend and relative, Nigel Dexter. I had spent the afternoon with Mr. Alf Noseworthy, and was feeling the need of a little mental relaxation.

Since our first meeting, three weeks before, we had become quite intimate. Together we had ploughed through Homer P. Keedick's Hundred Percent. Self-Correcting System. Together we had pondered the great man's questions, and sent in our highly speculative answers. Happily they had met with his approval, and so far as I could judge Alf was in a fair way to win the cherished diploma which would entitle him to proceed to the course in Poise and Personality. Best of all, Alf had visited our house and adjusted my broadcasting set, and the hallelujah of atmospherics was now nothing but a discordant memory.

Nigel and I sat in the end seats of our row—I prefer to sit here, as it saves clambering over other people's legs and is handy for the door. Shortly after the curtain went up Master Nigel stirred suddenly in his seat, and I heard him emit a gasp of surprise.

"Barry, old man," he said—his age is just twenty, and when he calls me an old man he means it—"you seem to have clicked with one of the chorus. She's giving you the Glad!"

"Are you sure it isn't you?"

"Quite. Shall I wave to her, or throw her a stern look?"

"I'll wave myself," I replied with dignity, and did so. Nigel was obviously a little shocked.

"She saw you," he reported; "and she's fairly chucking herself at you. Have you known her for long?"

"Has she a turned-up nose?" I inquired.

"Turned right up."

"And a big mouth?"

"I can't see all of it; she's got her ears covered. But—"

"That's Maudie," I said.

"Maudie? Do you know their Christian names?" There was an entirely new note—almost of respect—in Nigel's voice. "A bit of the old pre-war stuff, eh?"

"Very nearly," I said. "She's Hal Horner's wife. Would you like to meet her?"

"Not much," replied Nigel, with the frank brutality of youth. "But there's a bit of goods nearer the end of the row—"

"On second thoughts," I said, "perhaps I ought not to encourage—"

"You can cut out that grandfather stuff," Nigel warned me; then added grandly:

"Do we stroll round to the stage door after the show?"

"No, I shall probably slip through the pass-door during the interval."

"It can't be done. They keep 'em locked," replied Nigel, rather naïvely.

"Wait and see!"

Sure enough, when the interval came, a programme girl asked me if I were Captain Barry Shere.

"Yes," I said. (The Horners are the only people left who still accord me my military rank, long relinquished.)

"Mrs. Horner will be very pleased if you will step through, sir," said the girl.

"Thank you," I said, and rose to my feet. "Are you coming, Nigel," I added carelessly, "or would you rather stay here?"

Nigel affected to consider.

"Well—"

"All right," I said. "Very sensible of you. I'll be back soon. You can read the jokes on the last page of the programme."

Nigel was on his feet in a moment.

"Barry, old man, don't be a cad!"

"All right. Give me your arm."

Maudie met us at the pass-door, and greeted me in a fashion which shocked Nigel again, I fear. Theatrical people kiss so readily. She led us across the stage, keeping close to the curtain to avoid a tumult of men changing scenery at express speed, and presently we found ourselves in Hal Horner's big dressing-room, which, as usual, appeared to be full of people.

Next moment Hal was shaking me by both hands, while he pressed me down into a seat.

"This is marvellous," he said. "I was wondering when I should see you again. Sam, wash this glass for the Captain. Talking of glasses, have you heard this one? An absent-minded professor went into Aitchison's—you know, spectacles and things—and said to the shopman: 'I want a signifying glass.' 'What?' says the man. 'A signifying glass.' 'We don't keep them,' said the man. 'Never mind,' said the professor; 'it doesn't magnify!' Silly, isn't it? Is this gentleman a friend of yours?"

I introduced Nigel. Hal welcomed him with his customary enthusiasm.

"He has just lost his heart to one of the ladies of your chorus," I said.

"Which row?" asked Hal briskly.

"Front," said I.

"Second from the end," added Nigel.

"Blonde?"

"Quite."

"Shingled, I suppose?"

"Absolutely."

"There's a whole bunch of them outside in the passage now," said Hal. "Go and give them the once-over, old boy; and if you can pick her out, I'll bring her in here for you to smoke a cigarette with. Now I must change for the Dutch Doll scene. Excuse me a minute. Captain Shere, let me introduce you to Miss Lil Montgomery. She's sitting just beside you. Talk to the Captain for five minutes, Lil dear."

I heard his husky voice whisper something. There came a clash of curtain rings, and I was left, apparently alone, with an overpowering aroma of Chypre, of which I had been conscious ever since I entered the room. Hal had retired into his inner shrine with the faithful Sam, who had just placed a sizzling tumbler in my hand, and Maudie had doubtless gone to her own dressing-room. Master Nigel presumably, was out in the passage, enacting the *rôle* of Paris on Mount Ida.

From her breathing I took Miss Montgomery to be a well-covered young woman of thirty-five or so. Except for the feminine babel down the passage, the room was quiet.

"Are you in this piece, Miss Montgomery?" I asked.

"Oh, no!" she replied. As a matter of fact she said "Ownow!" and she said it in the constrained and artificial tone which one employs towards afflicted persons. (I am quite used to this.)

"You have just looked in to see Hal, like myself?" I suggested.

"That's right. I'm expecting a gentleman friend to call for me presently. I was in the profession once, though."

"Let me think," I said. "Lil Montgomery? I remember now. I saw you in something just before the war. Was it 'The Banana Girl'?"

"Well, you have got a memory!" said my companion, obviously gratified.

"Some people," I observed, "are easier to remember than others. You led the Grand March of Tropical Fruits. You are tall, aren't you, and fair?"

It was a long shot—I should be ashamed to say how long—but it came off.

"You're quite right. Only my hair is a sort of bronze colour now. But I think you're quite wonderful." I had made a friend.

"And you've left the stage?"

"Yes. I'm doing film work."

"That must be interesting. By the way, talking of the stage—Hal!" I called. "Are you there?"

"Speaking!" replied a muffled voice.

"Can you find a job as a comic singer for a young friend of mine?"

"What sort of face has he got?"

"I don't know: I've never seen it."

"Sorry, old boy. What about his voice?"

"Well, it's a good loud one, anyway."

"Has he had any experience?"

"Only in sing-songs on the Western Front. But I don't think he was very successful." And I related Alf Noseworthy's sad tale. "He's willing to learn, though. In fact, he told me himself that the only way to achieve success in any undertaking is to start at the bottom."

"How about swimming?" asked Hal, in a flash. ("Don't let me forget that one, Sam. I might work it in somewhere.") "He doesn't sound too hopeful, Captain. What's his real job?"

"He's an electrician."

"An electrician?" said Miss Montgomery suddenly.

"Yes, a wireless expert—and a pretty smart one, too. But nothing matters to him now except to be a successful comedian. You know how it takes them."

"How would he like to be a screen comedian?" suggested Miss Montgomery. "I believe I might get him a trial there."

"Could you really?"

"I'm almost certain. Of course, on the screen he wouldn't be able to use his voice."

"I don't think that would really matter," I assured her; "but I should be extremely grateful to you if you could find some opening for him. I have a feeling that the screen would satisfy his ambitions quite as well as the stage. All he wants is an opportunity to express himself. May I send him to you?"

The telephone on Hal's dressing-table gave a purr, and Sam came running out from behind the curtain. Presently he reported:

"Stage door, sir. A gentleman calling for Miss Montgomery. Mr. Prawn, it sounds like."

"Mr. Flawn," corrected Miss Montgomery.

"Ask him to come along and have something," came the ever-ready invitation. But Miss Montgomery was on her feet.

"I think I'll go to him, Hal, dear," she said. "You don't know him, and he's not accustomed to places like this."

Hal thrust back the curtain and emerged, presumably as a Dutch Doll.

"I'll take you along," he said. "It's across the stage, and the route's tricky. I'll be back in a minute, Captain."

"Good night," said Miss Montgomery, taking my hand and shaking it. "I should like to help any friend of yours."

"Thank you ever so much," I replied. "Where ought he to apply?"

"The Secretary, Mayfair Movies. The London office is in Golden Square. They're in the telephone book. Good night! That's a great make-up, Hal!"

They left the room together, and Nigel entered.

"Have you found her?" I asked.

"Yes. A total loss. About four feet high, and rather runs to teeth. I suppose it's the stuff they put on their faces that does it," concluded Master Nigel bitterly.

"That's it. That and the distance. If you'll keep those two facts firmly in your mind for the next ten years, old son, they'll save you from making scores of kinds of fool of yourself."

"The curtain is up," rejoined Nigel, with dignity. "I'm going back to my stall; I suppose you're going to sit drinking here."

And he stalked out. Sam and I exchanged a sympathetic chuckle.

Presently Hal came bustling back.

"Well, Lil certainly does find them," he observed, referring apparently to Mr. Prawn, or Flawn. "Give me a glass of water, Sam." (Water is Hal's sole beverage during business hours, and indeed at most times.) "How much time have I got?"

"Seven minutes."

"Good. Now we can talk, Captain. What about this comic of yours? What does he call himself?"

"Alf Noseworthy."

"What a name for the top of a bill!" Hal spoke almost reverently. "Why does he want to go into the show business?"

"He's suffering from a common complaint—the craving to do something that will render him a little less of a nobody, if only for five minutes, than the rest of his fellow-creatures."

"I know," said Hal. "I was a nobody myself once, and how I hated it! It frightened me, sort of. I saw myself living all my life in the same street, with the same neighbours—every house in the street and every neighbour just the same as me—forever and ever till I died and was buried in a grave the same as a thousand others. I used to say to Maudie: 'If only I could do something that would get me into the papers just once!'"

"And what did Maudie say to that?"

"She said the job of respectable people was to keep out of the papers, and if ever I got into one she'd die of shame. But then Maudie's old-fashioned."

"She certainly is. But the craving for publicity seems to get most people nowadays. I expect the psychologists have a name for it. It's the reason why the rich employ press agents—"

"And it's the reason why the poor write testimonials for patent medicines which have never done them any good. Just to get into the papers! It makes people commit murders, I believe; and to some of them it's worth it. Think of living all your life in a back street in Camden Town, and then suddenly having your photograph on every front page, and columns of print as well; and yourself sitting in the dock at the Old Bailey, as if you were in a box at Drury

Lane, with every eye in Court on you and half the swells in London sitting on the bench to get a thrill out of having seen you! That's almost worth getting bumped off for. Why, I once knew a man who went and confessed to a murder he'd never committed, and never could have committed, just on the off chance of getting into print over it. And they very nearly hanged him, too!"

"Well, Alf Noseworthy's programme is less heroic," I said. "He only wants to make his mark as a comedian. I don't think he expects to get to the top of the tree: all he wants is to rise out of the ruck an inch or two. Cinema work will do as well for him as anything else: that's why I accepted Miss Montgomery's kind offer just now. By the way, will she be as good as her word?"

"I'm not so sure about Lil as I was," replied Hal thoughtfully. "She's a very old friend of Maudie and me, but—well, you know how people go. They take up with some odd crowd or other, and after that you are never so sure of them. And it's a rum business, the film business. It's a new, raw business, and it's an international business, and the international view of what's fair and square seems to be different from the other. And I didn't much like the look of Mr. Flawn just now. He's a film man of some kind."

"What does he look like?"

"Like one of those fellows you see in Hyde Park on Sunday afternoons. Not one of your loud-voiced spouters, but one of the muttering, fanatical sort, that stands under a tree away from the crowd and whispers his stuff into the ears of small groups. Fishy eye—ragged moustache—hate in every quiver of him!" True to his trade, Hal was on his feet, impersonating the absent Mr. Flawn.

"And he's the man that's going to find a job for Alf Noseworthy?"

"Looks like it. I know he and Lil are very thick just now."

There came a smart rap on the door, and the voice of the call-boy:

"Mr. Horner, please!"

"Coming!" Hal rose to his feet. "I wish I could have shown you more hospitality than this," he said; "but I'm on for the rest of the act now." He took my arm and led me to the door. "By the way, have you heard the one about the Scotsman and the Jew who went to church? The parson announced a collection unexpectedly. The Scotsman fainted—and the Jew picked him up and carried him out! Silly, isn't it? Sam will take you back to your seat. Good night. God bless! Come again."

CHAPTER 3

BEHIND ANOTHER CURTAIN

Next day I put Alf Noseworthy in touch with Mayfair Movies, and in due course he made his report, at our old rendezvous in Kensington Gardens.

It was a chilly morning, and my mother was a little reluctant to let me go out.

"It must be done," I said firmly. "I have an appointment in the Gardens."

"It is the spring, I suppose," remarked my mother. "Is she dark or fair?" (My mother and I rather specialise in these little pleasantries.)

"I don't know her well enough to ask her yet," I said. "But she smokes Wild Woodbine cigarettes, and was once a machine gunner."

"Oh! your wireless friend?"

"Yes. I'm trying to get him a job. Fate hasn't been too kind to him."

My mother said no more, but gave my arm a little squeeze, and opened the front door for me. I can quite easily open doors for myself, but one likes to humour people.

Half an hour later I was in my usual seat under the big chestnut tree, and after communicating the right time to two applicants, and listening to a stimulating fight between a fox-terrier and an Airedale, was conscious of the deferential presence of Alf Noseworthy.

"Is that you, Alf?" I asked. "Or am I addressing Douglas Fairbanks?"

Alf was much gratified.

"Well, sir," he said. "I can't say as I have got as far as that; but I've made a start."

"Sit down and tell me about it. Have you been to the offices of the Mayfair Movies?"

"Yes, sir."

"What sort of place is it?"

"Small, sir, but high-class. Plate-glass partitions, and new varnish all over the place."

"And you saw Mr. Flawn?"

"Yes."

"What is he like?" I asked, thinking of Hal Horner's description.

"A foreign-looking gentleman, sir. Dark, with funny eyes, and looks over your shoulder at the wall behind you all the time he's speaking. He's only the agent of the company, he tells me. He's been commissioned to engage a cast for a new big film that they are going to make at the studio. All British, of course."

"Where is the studio?"

"In Essex, sir."

"That might be anywhere, from Leyton to Colchester."

"It's not in London, sir; it's right out in the country. They're converting the whole place into what is called a Location, where they can stage dramas of English country life. Hunting and shooting, and things like that. But they won't be able to open for a bit yet."

"Why not?"

"I understand they haven't quite decided on a story. And then, of course, there's the cast to engage. Besides, their electric power plant isn't entirely—"

"Alf," I said, "the Mayfair Movie Corporation sounds to me a rather unready concern."

"It's a case of more smoke than fire so far, sir, I'll admit; but a beginner like me can't expect too much. And another thing—" Alf hesitated.

"Well?"

"There was a young lady in the office—working the typewriter—"

"Ah!"

"She made me feel that the job would be worth while, anyhow, in a manner of speaking."

"Pretty?"

"Yes, sir: absolutely lovely. Would you like to shake hands with her?"

"Is she here?"

"Yes, sir." Alf Noseworthy raised his voice.

"Edna!" he called.

I heard a light footstep on the grass, and was immediately conscious of a faint aroma of Jockey Club.

"This is Miss Edna Butterick, sir," announced Alf—as one might say, "This is Helen of Troy." I rose and shook hands.

"How do you do, Miss Butterick?" I said. "Won't you sit down?"

The young lady accepted Alf's chair, and we conversed. I took her to be about twenty—small, alert, a practically-minded little Cockney in most things, but of a sentimental disposition.

"I hear you are a tremendous swell in the Mayfair Movies," I said.

"I'm the whole show at present," replied Miss Butterick, frankly confirming an entirely facetious suggestion. "There's just me and Mr. Flawn in the office. The Company only started a few weeks ago, and there's not much doing so far. I got the job through an advertisement in the paper; and jolly glad I was to get it. It's no catch being out of work in London, with nobody to support you."

"Are you alone in the world?" I asked.

Alf breathed affectionately.

"I was when I tried for the job," replied Miss Butterick. "I couldn't even give Mr. Flawn a proper reference. Luckily, he didn't seem to mind."

"Does he work you hard?"

"So far, there's practically nothing doing. I've typed a few letters and copied out an old scenario. And it's my belief that Mr. Flawn gave me that to keep me occupied."

"It looks as if he didn't want to lose you. Can it be that you have got a film face as well as Alf?"

"Alf thinks parts of it are like Mary Pickford's," replied Miss Butterick modestly.

"And you hope one day to appear on the screen together?"

"That's the idea, sir," confirmed Alf. "But we're quite prepared to wait."

I ventured upon a leading question.

"Have you a definite offer, Alf, or a contract of any kind from these people?"

"Nothing definite as yet, sir. But we've come to an agreement mutually acceptable to all parties. Mr. Flawn pointed out to us that seeing we was— were—entirely without film experience, we should have to undergo a course of training. Facial Expression—Registration of the Various Emotions—Gesture—"

"I know. And Personality and Poise. Alf, you've got hold of another Mr. Keedick."

"I don't think so, sir—if I may take that liberty. Mr. Flawn has entirely waived the question of fees—"

"That's very handsome of him. But I can't help feeling there's a catch about it. You're not going to pay a premium, I hope."

"Oh, no!" said Miss Butterick. "We haven't got the money, anyway. We're going to take it out in work—me in typing and Alf in electrical jobs."

"They're putting up a big power-plant on the Location," explained Alf. "For studio-lighting, and all that. I'm going down there in a few days' time. And in return for what I do I'm to have a free gratis course in film acting. Edna will get hers in return for"—he braced himself for a Keedickism— "clerical assistance."

"But you ought to have a contract," I persisted.

"We're going to have, sir; it's all drawn up. But it can't be signed until Mr. Spargo returns from abroad."

"And who is Mr. Spargo?"

"The managing director of the Company, sir. At present he is on the Continent, arranging for—"

"An All-British film? I understand."

"I'm afraid you aren't altogether in favour of our little dream, sir," remarked Alf, with a touch of reproach.

"I'm not sure that it sounds absolutely as safe as the Bank of England. Are you, Miss Butterick?"

Edna's answer came pat.

"No, sir, I'm not. But people in our position have to take risks. Most film stars have started at the very bottom." (I thought suddenly of Hal Horner's dictum about swimming, and choked foolishly.) "But anyhow," she concluded definitely, "I can't go on typing office letters all my life."

"And we've got each other, whatever happens now, sir," added Alf simply.

Plainly it was vain to argue with people in such a condition. So I dismissed my two innocents with my blessing, charging them to notify me immediately if the Mayfair Movies Corporation got rough with them.

II

The same day I fulfilled a luncheon engagement with my uncle, Sir Gavin Dexter. He is my mother's half-brother, and the father of my young friend and relative Nigel. You who read this have never heard of Gavin Dexter, but the world knows nothing of its greatest men.

Some day we shall erect a monument to the Permanent Official. At present we merely make jokes about him. Governments and Cabinet Ministers may come and go—good or bad, we greet their coming with enthusiasm and hail their going with relief—but the Civil Servant stays on forever. His very name is usually unknown to the man in the Tube; but it is he who strengthens the unready hands or restrains the untutored enthusiasms, as occasion may require, of each succeeding batch of Secretaries of State. He is inclined to be hidebound; he is wedded to precedent; yet times without number his hoarded experiences and hardly-earned wisdom have steered our titular governors through an awkward crisis or saved them from a disastrous leap in the dark. We associate him in our minds with red tape and a soft job, and the evening papers are always shouting for his abolition or reduction; but he is one of the few indispensable factors in our national existence. He makes for continuity, which is the only possible corrective and antidote to that endless campaign of conflicting purposes and mutually destructive legislation which we call Party Government. Though you closed the Houses of Parliament for a term of years, and took away everything save a few anonymous mandarins in Whitehall and the policemen at the corners of our streets, the British Constitution would still contrive to function.

Gavin Dexter is such a one. He has done the State some service, but only a chosen few know about it. Periodically his name appears in the Honours

List as having been awarded this or that Order or Decoration, or gained permission to wear a Star or Cross bestowed by some foreign Government. The British Public, who imagine—sometimes rightly—that decorations accumulate upon a Whitehall official much as barnacles accumulate upon a stationary hulk, would be surprised if they realised that in Gavin Dexter's case each of these distinctions signalises the gratitude of a King or Constitution for some international mystery unravelled or some international complication smoothed out.

He is about sixty years of age, and when I last saw him, more than ten years ago, his hair was even then snowy white; but his bright blue eyes twinkled youthfully behind gold-rimmed spectacles. He still wears a cavalry moustache, for he was once a Lifeguardsman.

Besides being my mother's half-brother he was a close friend of my father, and I have always suspected that it was through his influence that I was transferred, willy-nilly, after two years of active service in the war, to a "cooshie" staff job which landed me in Egypt in 1917, and was directly responsible for the loss of my sight.

But for the moment I am not concerned with that episode. I want to describe my luncheon with Sir Gavin, or rather, the conversation which followed it.

We had returned from his club—a whispering gallery of diplomats in Piccadilly—to the greater privacy of his lair in Whitehall. He gave me a cigar and set me in a deep armchair while he rustled papers and engaged in a *sotto voce* conversation with an intensely private secretary. At last we were alone, and he joined me by the fire.

"How's the world?" I asked.

"Very evil, lad—and the times are waxing late. The whole habitable globe seems to be seething with sedition and agitation and downright incitement to rapine and disruption. And the damnable part of it all is that we have to fight it with our hands tied."

"Now construe," I said.

"Don't be a cheeky young dog, then."

"Sorry! Do tell me."

"There's nothing to tell, really, that most people don't know in their hearts—only they won't admit it. Our national disposition instinctively dodges such unpleasant exercises as facing the worst. We prefer to hope for the best, and muddle on. But it comes to this. There is a movement on foot in the world today for the overthrow of civilisation. It is not called that, of course. It is disguised—very skilfully disguised and very plausibly presented—as a movement for the abolition of war and the creation of a loftier standard of international relationships. These ends are to be achieved by doing away with such little artificialities as pride of race and love of country, and merging all nations into a sort of benevolent brotherhood, in which everyone will be free and equal, and nothing but mutual affection will prevail—and an indeterminate body known as the Proletariat will make things excessively unpleasant for another equally indeterminate body known as the Bourgeoisie.

"The truth, of course, is that a very astute gang of rascals, mainly residing in Moscow, are out, for their own ends, to take away from the world the one thing that really matters in life, and that is the personal liberty of the individual. They have decided, with absolute correctness, that the one strong tower which stands between them and their amiable ambitions is the British Empire, where personal liberty prevails as nowhere else. Therefore the British Empire must go."

"That is a tremendous compliment to the British Empire."

"It is; but it rather accentuates the responsibilities of those who have to defend it. However, these gentry have concentrated on us, and there we are."

"In China, for instance, not so long ago?"

"Exactly. And not only in China. India is hopping with their propagandists, too, because it is India that they are really after. But they are not only busy in India; they are wherever the Flag flies. In South Africa, in Egypt, in Canada—"

"And in this island home of ours, too, by all accounts."

"They are; and busy as bees. They're in the factories, in the shipyards, down the pits, and in all places where men are easily stimulated to a sense of grievance over their present lot—and who isn't, these days? The marvel is that they aren't more successful, considering present-day conditions. Do you know what the country expended in cash during the five years of the war? Eight thousand million pounds, right down the drain! No wonder the trade machine creaks! No wonder unemployment is rife! No wonder the country is haunted by distress and distrust! You would have thought that the first breath of subversive propaganda would have finished us. But it hasn't. We function, we actually function; and we're going ahead again! We're an appreciable way back to national prosperity and contentment, in spite of them all. I often wonder why. What do you think?"

"Providence, first. Second, the fact that you can't stampede a British crowd very easily. Uncle, you comfort me exceedingly."

"Oh, don't you be too comfortable," replied my uncle. "Things might be worse, of course, but they're serious enough. Thanks to the two influences you mention, the enemy has failed to win any major operation, but he's dug right in here in our midst, and it's going to be the devil of a job to get rid of him. He's got the Labour Party by the tail—the extreme tail, but an appreciable handful of it—and once or twice the tail has succeeded in wagging the dog. Practically every foolish and violent act which Labour has committed during the past five years has been instigated from Bolshie headquarters. And you feel comfortable about it! That's just the trouble! People like you today are walking on the edge of a precipice, and we can't tell them."

"But for goodness sake, why not?"

"There are two reasons. The first is the British workman—the average British workman, not the extremist. He's a great fellow. We don't want to insult him, and he would be insulted if we told him the truth. None of us likes to be informed that he is a mug—a dupe—that he is being exploited for other people's private ends. If you told the actual facts to the man I am speaking of he would call you a liar and despise you for fighting with unfair weapons. There's nothing for it but to let him get wise to the gang by himself; and that is going to take time. The other reason is the British Nation as a whole. We are a peculiar people, with an ineradicable affection for martyrs. If we were to string up a few of the most poisonous of our native sedition-mongers— and I have got a list of them that would surprise you—we should automatically create public sympathy for them, and, with it, incredibly enough, for their doctrines. So we have to walk warily and wait."

"Trust in God and keep your powder dry—eh?"

"Yes. The only sure course in this sort of fight is to give your enemy sufficient rope. He nearly always ties himself up in the end. Look at the General Strike of a year or two ago. What a gorgeous piece of luck that was for us, who are fighting this crazy underground battle! It suddenly revealed to the British workman what we couldn't tell him—that he was being exploited, that he had been sold a pup by the apostles of freedom whom he had been taught to worship. And, moreover, it brought it home to the ordinary easy-going citizen that there was such a thing as a Moscow menace, and a pretty active one. Roubles from Russia! Blessings from the Bolshie! They couldn't explain *that* away! It pulled the country together as nothing else could have done. For ten whole days John Bull sat up and spoke with a single voice; and that, as they say further west, is some squawk. My only regret is, and always will be, that the General Strike didn't last for twenty days instead of ten."

"You mean you could have turned a defeat into a rout?"

"Exactly. We might have been able to tear up sedition by the roots, while the country was in the mood for it. As it was, we could only shave off the top dressing."

"It went really deep, then, did it?"

"Deep! Barry, the General Strike was intended to be the prelude to a revolution. The country didn't know it. The strikers didn't know it. The respectable old gentlemen who preside over the trade unions didn't know it. But the crowd who are holding on to the tail of the dog knew it—and meant it! And they thought that they had got us; they really did! They were thundering well organised, and their plans had been laid for months. The General Strike was to be the jumping-off point. The idea was that if transport ceased, and the Press were completely muzzled, communication of every kind would come to an end. Rumour would take the place of news; and when people are in the dark about everything, they will believe anything they are told. Moreover, if production ceased, food supplies would cease. Then starvation would set in. Public *morale* would crash; there would be organised rioting; then stark revolution. That was the programme, my boy."

My uncle rose, and I heard him shake himself like an old war-horse. Then he continued:

"Fortunately the Government were in full touch with the situation. We had seen to that. All this trouble had been threatened in the previous autumn, when the coal situation first became acute. The Government weren't ready then, or they would have fought. They wanted time to prepare a defence scheme for the whole country. So they gained a respite of six months—by granting that coal subsidy. Do you remember?"

"Ten millions, wasn't it?"

"Nearer twenty-five, and the cheapest bargain that this country ever got, though, of course, there was a howl at the time. Then they set to work and prepared for the storm. They organised a system of transport and food supply for the whole nation, and the following May, the very morning after the Bolshies had forced the strike, they were able to set their emergency machine running. Food depots sprang up overnight, transport was available everywhere, and the British Constitution continued to function. Of course it wasn't all plain sailing. Bloomers were made: our official excursion into yellow journalism was the worst. But the way in which the possibilities of Broadcasting were utilised as a means of steadying the public pulse made up for a lot. I have often wondered what we should have done without Broadcasting in those days...."

The old gentleman slowed down, and fell into a muse. So did I. The mention of Broadcasting had brought my mind round to Alf Noseworthy; then to our talk of the morning. I broke in upon Sir Gavin's reflections.

"To descend from the momentous to the trivial," I said, "are you acquainted with any plain, ordinary crooks? Does your job bring you in contact with the professional London swindler at all?"

"What do you mean?"

"Well, for instance, in your rogues' gallery is there a man of the name of Flawn?"

"Not to my knowledge."

"Or a man called Spargo? Do you know him at all?"

My uncle was fairly startled this time.

"Spargo? Most decidedly I know Spargo! But do you?"

"No; I never heard of him till this morning. He appears to be managing director of a concern called Mayfair Movies, in which a humble friend of mine is trying to get a job."

"Oho! Moving pictures! What sort?"

"My friend talked vaguely of some project to make All-British films. But the whole affair sounded so shady to me that I thought I would mention it."

"I am glad you did. This is interesting. Your friend didn't happen to have heard any mention made of something called the Dodekadelphi?"

"No. What is that?"

"A rather dangerous secret society of twelve of our native sedition-mongers, of the so-called Intellectual type. They issue revolutionary literature for British and American consumption, and they are connected with a Continental organisation which specialises in revolutionary films. 'Mayfair Movies' may mean that they are going in for home production."

"Then Spargo is one of the Dodekadelphi?"

"Yes; but he is a much bigger fish than all the rest put together; in fact, he is the most dangerous agitator of the Intellectual brand alive today. He has brains and—forgive the expression—guts. Most of the Intellectuals are entirely lacking in the latter. They talk a lot, and create a new heaven and a new earth every time they get their legs under a table, but they are never anxious to risk their precious necks. They have been the same all through history. Look at Camille Desmoulins and his lot. Look at Miliukoff and Kerensky. The Dodekadelphi are the same. They are an odd menagerie. There are two or three quite prominent British novelists and playwrights among them—the idols of our suburban Intelligentsia. I suppose it tickles their fancy to be connected with this sort of thing; or perhaps they have a vague idea that it may save them from the tumbril one day. You'd be surprised if I mentioned their names; and they'd be more surprised still if they heard me do so. But Spargo is different: he is a genius. Did you ever read 'La Peur'?"

"I seem to connect it with the War."

"And well you might. He wrote it then. It purported to be the experiences of a common soldier in the trenches in Flanders. It was the most sickeningly realistic stuff you ever read—enough to give a conscript nightmare for weeks. It was circulated all over France and Belgium. It was translated into English, and sold like hot cakes in America. The highbrow and pacifist reviewers there simply ate it up, and said that if this was war, war ought to be stopped. As if war were a kind of undesirable theatrical show that could be closed by the censor! The joke was that the whole book had been ordered and paid for by Germany, in the hope of scaring us into a premature peace. It was a brilliant piece of work. Still, it was short-sighted on Germany's part, because that kind of propaganda was bound to get round to their own people sooner or later, and react the other way. But Germany was desperate in those days: all was fish that came to her net. (You remember it was Germany that sent Lenin to Petrograd in the first instance.) Well, Spargo wrote 'La Peur.'"

"For Germany? Is he a German?"

"Oh, no. Nobody quite knows what he is. But he's a high-up Leninite now; and the Dodekadelphi are expecting a visit of ceremony from him at Easter. Well, they won't receive it."

"Why not?"

Sir Gavin chuckled.

"Because he happens to be in jail. I had him arrested at Southampton this morning as he came off the Havre boat."

"What for?"

"Aha! That's where the amusing part comes in. For murder!"

"For murder?"

"Yes. It's an extradition case. The American Embassy has applied to the Home Secretary for our friend's person. He's wanted in Butte, Montana. There was a big meeting there last year of the I.W.W.—the so-called Industrial Workers of the World. Certain patriotic citizens tried to get them run out of the town. The citizens' leader was thereupon murdered in the open street—by Spargo. You see, I said he was something more than an Intellectual."

"And you are going to send him back to America?"

"Rather! But I have warned the Ambassador that there'll be a first-class row about this."

"Why?"

"Because his friends can't afford to lose him. He's one of the three really big noises in the revolutionary world, and in many ways the most penetrating of the lot. The other two live in Moscow: Spargo travels all over the world. They simply can't do without him."

"But what case have they? The man's a murderer."

"They'll deny that: they'll call it a case of political persecution. They'll say the murder charge was trumped up. Political offenders aren't subject to extradition in this country: you'll see there will be a campaign started over here to prevent his surrender to the American authorities. There'll be meetings in the Park and Trafalgar Square—a 'Hands off Spargo!' movement, and all that."

"But you're going through with it?"

"I certainly am. It's the chance of a lifetime. He ought to have been put out of business years ago. Unfortunately, he escaped during the war; and you can't do anything to gentlemen of his type in time of peace, unless they play into your hands by blundering into something frank and straightforward, like murder. Yes, Mr. Spargo is going to America. We'll manage it as quietly as possible. With an Easter weekend just coming on, and everybody holiday-making, the news of his arrest won't get round at first. He'll be brought up before a magistrate quietly tomorrow morning, then remanded until Tuesday. On that day he will be dealt with among a consignment of ordinary Bank Holiday drunks, and will be deprived of as much limelight as possible. Anyhow, he's going to spend Easter in jail instead of with the Dodekadelphi, and I'm afraid your humble friend will have to get someone else to sign that contract. By the way, where are you going to spend Easter?"

"Your sons and daughters have very kindly invited my mother and myself to Le Touquet for Easter," I said. "Shall I meet you there?"

"I'll run over for a day or two, if possible. A little golf and an hour or two of chemmy, eh? Demoralising, but refreshing. Yes, I must arrange that. You can find your way to the lift, can't you? Au revoir."

CHAPTER 4

CORRIE LYNDON

The Dexters are a high-spirited family. In fact, as McRory, senior (of *Irish R.M.* fame) once remarked of his own, "God help the house that holds them!"

They have no mother, so my own mother is much employed by them as a chaperon, or perhaps I should say as a confederate; for my parent, when she gets among the girls, has a habit of giving free rein to an incredibly frivolous disposition. Anyhow, when you find yourself an inmate of Cœur du Bois, Sir Gavin's jolly little retreat at Le Touquet, you must look out for squalls, practical jokes, and unrestrained criticism of your appearance, habits, and point of view.

I may say that I, by reason of my infirmity, am exempted from the extremist rigours of the Dexter sense of humour. My firm ally, Vivien, the youngest of the gang, usually takes me under her personal direction; and with my hand upon her slim, vigorous young shoulder, I find my path through the forest of Le Touquet both easy and pleasant.

I may as well describe the rest of the family now, and get them off my mind. Sir Gavin himself you know; also Nigel, his younger son. The other son is Arturo—Lieutenant-Commander Arthur Vigors Dexter. On board his destroyer, H.M.S. *Swallow* (which his irreverent family pronounce "Wallow") he may be the complete Commander; but when he is ashore on what he describes as "a bit of leaf," he is very much of a Lieutenant, and a junior Sub-Lieutenant at that.

The elder daughter, Enid, has now reached the great age of twenty-one, and is, I am told, a beauty. That is probably true, for she was a most attractive little girl. All I can guarantee now is that her beauty is not of the languishing type. Vivien is a tomboy of eighteen, with a sleek dark head, cropped in the prevailing mode, a small turned-up nose, and a tongue which enables her to hold her own, with something over, in battle with her brother Nigel. But, as I say, they are all very good to me.

Cœur du Bois stands among the pine trees, in surroundings suggestive of Lob's Wood in "Dear Brutus," on the edge of the golf course, not far from the fairway leading to the sixteenth hole. When you wake on a fine spring morning and lie waiting for someone to bring you your shaving water, the combination of sounds and scents outside enables you to visualise most of the scene—blue sky, yellow sand, pale green grass, dark green pines, and, commanding all, the big white crescent-shaped hotel, with its red roofs. You can smell the pines and the needle-covered earth; you can feel the warm sunshine, tempered by the sharp salt flavour of the sea; you can hear the shrill and distant babble of the caddies, comprising most of the infant population of Etaples, as they rage furiously together in their pen beside the club-house, pending a professional summons. They sound exactly like sea-gulls on a rock. Overhead, the first big passenger aeroplane of the day is droning its way from Croydon to Paris.

I can remember another Le Touquet—a very different place. That was in 1915. There were no caddies then, though there was still a golf course, of sorts. Not much golf was played thereon, for men had other things to do, and the greater part of the landscape was occupied by a machine-gun school. (The Instructional Hut stood somewhere near the fourth green.) The Golf Hotel was a Canadian base hospital. The Hermitage Hotel, which stands opposite the Casino on the road which runs through the forest to Paris Plage, was a French military hospital. The Casino itself, once the nightly scene of exhilarating but disastrous competition with the Goddess of Chance, was filled with cots and wounded men, tenderly cared for by an English duchess and her staff.

Those days are over now—forever, one hopes. The hotels and the Casino are all performing their normal functions. Le Touquet has become an intensely popular spot. It has been discovered. Chalets and villas have sprung up through the length and breadth of the forest, and the sandy beach of Paris Plage, which separates the pine trees from the restless Channel, and whose two white lighthouses are the most conspicuous mark from Grisnez to Cherbourg, is occupied all the summer by voluble matrons of the French bourgeoisie, directing a shrill chorus of admonition and reproof towards a horde of youthful and not particularly adventurous bathers.

All round the sandy, pine-fringed golf course, from dawn till dusk, the players hew and slice their zig-zag way, accompanied by stolid little girls in blue check pinafores and black felt slippers, handing niblicks and replacing divots. During the Easter weekend of which I am speaking, eighteen hundred balls were driven off the first tee, to fall to earth one knows not where.

My recollections go farther back still. Fifteen years ago Le Touquet was visited only by golfers with a knowledge of French and an urge for overseas adventure. The forest was a real forest. Cœur du Bois stood solitary amid its pines, and just a little new. Lady Dexter was still alive. Arturo had recently gone to Dartmouth Naval College; Master Nigel had recently gone into knickerbockers. Enid was a leggy little girl with big eyes and a flaxen pigtail. Vivien was a toddler of three, with a mop of dark hair and a coy glance for all male visitors. And—my golf handicap had just been reduced to four. Ah me!

II

Breakfast at Cœur du Bois is at eight-thirty, a most unusual hour for Le Touquet. Indeed, I believe that gentlemen returning home to bed at that hour, in what the Casino authorities call *tenue de soirée*, are not an altogether unfamiliar spectacle.

Still, there are some people to whom Casino life is not indispensable, and of such are the Dexters. Arturo, to be sure, occasionally goes and makes a night of it, but then Jack ashore misses nothing. Enid, who is rather serious for her age and generation, can get no kick, in her own words, from dropping her dress allowance down a slit.

Nigel and Vivien, though more adventurous, have not yet achieved a tale of years sufficient to qualify them for admission to the jealously guarded Salle de Baccara. Their nocturnal dissipations are limited to dancing in the outer precincts, or indulging in an inexpensive but hopelessly one-sided game called *boule*. But in the main they are an open-air family, and are usually content to go to bed before midnight and rise, if not with the lark, at least with early tea.

On Easter Monday, then, we breakfasted betimes and at full strength, except for our host, who had been recalled to Whitehall by a mysterious but not unusual telegram the previous evening. He had said no more to me about Spargo, but I imagined that his business might be connected with that hero and the Dodekadelphi. Anyhow, he would tell me in his own good time.

"What are you children all going to do with yourselves today?" inquired my mother, who likes pretending that she is a young matron again.

"Oddly enough," replied Nigel, adjusting the creases in his plus-fours, "I am going to play golf."

"Tennis, me." This from Vivien.

"Arturo?" pursued my mother, as the nautical member of the family attacked his porridge.

"I'm going to hunt the herring, Aunt Sylvia." (There is a drag-hunt at Le Touquet, complete with several red coats and a resplendent official with a hunting-horn, which he wears round his body like a lifebuoy.)

"By yourself?" inquired Vivien suspiciously.

"Well, not quite. I met some rather pleasant Americans in the Rooms last night. They—"

From all round the table came a single resonant hand-clap, delivered above the head, followed by a short, sharp, concerted howl of "Wow!" This is a tribal custom of the Dexters. Whenever one of their number succumbs to the passion of love (which happens pretty regularly) the others greet the event with the rite described.

"What is her name?" demanded Vivien.

"Helen Something. I don't know the other one yet."

"Hunt, I expect."

Arturo fell in the trap. "Why?" he asked.

"Never heard of Helen Hunt, dearie? One Sunday morning she picked up a purse outside the church. She was a good girl, so she told the curate about it; and the curate climbed into the pulpit and said that if anybody had lost a purse they could go to Helen Hunt for it."

"Vivi, darling!" said my mother, as usual.

"Have you heard the one about the Three Bears?" inquired Nigel indulgently.

"Sailors don't care!" quoted Arturo good-humouredly. "Anyhow, this Helen and I ran a bank together. It went down wallop at the fourth coup. That established mutual sympathy, and we agreed to try our luck with the drag this morning."

"Very well: that accounts for Arturo," said my mother placidly. "What about you, Enid, dear?"

"I must do a little marketing in Paris Plage."

"Why not play tennis, too, and let me market?"

"Would you mind?" asked Enid doubtfully.

"I should revel in it. It would be good for my French, too."

"The market women nearly all speak English now," said Enid.

"Or American," added Vivien; and I could almost feel that bluff mariner Arturo blush. "Don't you mind the smell of fish, though?" she continued.

"Not particularly."

"I should hate to be a live hen at Paris Plage Market," said Nigel irrelevantly. "You lie on a hot pavement all day, with your legs tied together. Every now and then a fat woman picks you up to test your weight, and then drops you on your head to show her contempt for it. It must be a relief to become chicken broth at supper-time."

"Animals don't mean a thing to a Frenchman," said Arturo. "They don't intend to be cruel: it's just indifference, that's all. Now, the Levantines do it for fun. I once saw a wretched calf in a sack outside the railway station at Athens, and a—"

"That will be all at present, dear," intimated Vivien gently. "We are having a meal."

"Good heavens!" said Enid suddenly. "The railway station! That's what made me think of her."

"Who?"

"Corrie Lyndon. I'd absolutely forgotten. She crosses today, and she's due here for lunch."

"Who is Corrie Lyndon?" I asked.

"A nice, sensible girl," said Nigel. "A school friend of Enid's. It's a pity about her face," he added.

"What's the matter with it?"

"The question has never quite been decided; but nothing can be done about it now."

"Don't be idiotic for a moment, child," said Enid. "Some one must meet Corrie."

"She's your friend," Vivien pointed out, in true family fashion.

"Why not drive the car into Boulogne and meet her there?" suggested my mother. "It's a lovely day, and Etaples station is always a scramble."

"A bright idea," said Enid. "Barry, would you like to come with me?"

The Dexters are a casual race, but they always seem to contrive to include me in their arrangements. I accepted Enid's invitation, and an hour later found myself by her side in the big family touring-car, heading for that seaport of mingled odours and memories, Boulogne-sur-Mer.

"I thought I had heard of most of your friends," I said, "but Miss Lyndon is a new one on me."

"She's a Canadian. We were at school together in Paris. Then she went home. Now she's over here for a few months paying visits. She's a dear."

"And a nice, sensible girl?"

"That's only Nigel. He thinks anyone older than himself must be a back number. As a matter of fact, Corrie is twenty-three. Her father was killed at—some place at which the Canadians did a lot."

"That might be almost anywhere. Was it Vimy Ridge, by any chance?"

"Yes, that was it. Corrie lives with her mother in Montreal now."

"And she's coming over here alone?"

"Yes. She always could look after herself."

"She sounds rather modern to me. What did young Nigel mean about her face? Is it as bad as all that?"

Enid laughed. "You'd better ask Corrie herself. I'll put you in the back seat together going home."

III

The Folkestone boat was just arriving as we bumped along Boulogne pier. True to her promise, Enid transferred me into the back seat, and then left me in charge of the car outside the *douane* while she plunged into the turmoil round the gangway.

I sat in the warm spring sunshine, inhaling the odour of yesterday's fish and wondering what was the matter with Miss Lyndon's face, and why Master Nigel should have been so regretful about it. At last I heard Enid's voice again, uplifted in encouragement of a stertorous but voluble Gaul bearing a burden. A crushing weight—presumably an American steamer trunk—was deposited on the roomy front seat of the car, and I heard the springs creak.

"Little Enid will have no room to drive," remarked a pleasant voice. "Can't we express this old trunk some way?"

"You won't see it for hours if you do, dear," replied Enid. "I'll squash in all right. You climb into the back seat. This is Captain Shere. Barry, this is Corrie Lyndon."

I held out my hand, and found it grasping long, slim fingers, from which I deduced a long slim arm and a lithe body. The pleasant voice announced that it was pleased to meet me, and its owner seated herself at my side. This time the springs of the car did not creak. Enid seated herself beside the steamer-trunk in front, and we bumped slowly off, followed by the benedictions of an overpaid porter.

My companion and I sat silent until we had crossed the bridge and cleared the town.

"It's a fine day for the Channel," I observed at last.

Miss Lyndon gave a little chuckle.

"I can't think of anything to say, either," she replied.

We both laughed then, and the tension was gone.

"Still, I'm surprised," I said. "I thought all American girls could talk."

"Let's get this straight," said Miss Lyndon, sitting up. "It usually has to be done. I am an American in the sense that I come from North America, and proud of it; and I have lots of friends in the States; but from every other angle I am a hard-boiled British subject, like yourself. Have you got that?"

"I have got it," I replied meekly.

"That's great. Now we can be friends. Do you know this locality well?"

"Very well."

"Would it be easy to visit the battle-fields from here, and the military cemeteries?"

"Oh, yes. You can drive to almost any point on the old Flanders front in a couple of hours or so. It's odd to think how close the Hun was all the time. I suppose you are going to Vimy Ridge?"

Her voice softened. "Yes. Did Enid tell you?"

"Yes."

Miss Lyndon was silent for a while; then she asked:

"Did you meet our boys when they were over?"

"I certainly did. They lay beside us in the Salient during the winter of 'Fifteen. A stout crowd. Did you ever hear the story of the lonely Canadian sentry and the Army Chaplain?"

"No. But I'll bite."

"One night the sentry was on duty at a cross-roads behind the line: Kemmel, I think it was. He had just been taught to challenge passers-by in a proper manner, and he was waiting for someone to practise on. He was thoroughly homesick and blue, and the night was very cold. At last someone came along—a regimental chaplain going up to the line. The sentry called out: 'Hey! Halt! Who goes there?' The Padre halted, and called out, 'Army

Chaplain!'... 'Now what do you know about that?' shouted the sentry. 'Pass Charlie Chaplin, and all's well!'"

"Now tell her your other story," remarked Enid's clear voice.

"Don't take any notice of her, Miss Lyndon," I said. "The Dexter family are cursed with a critical and intolerant disposition."

"You can't tell me!" replied Miss Lyndon feelingly. "You attend to your driving, Enid. Captain Shere, we are passing through a village now: the sign-board says 'Pont-des-Briques.' Have you any line of information about that?"

"Yes. Napoleon stayed here for nearly two years, with the Grand Army camped all round him, waiting to invade England. He had got a bit closer than the Kaiser, you see. He even brought Josephine and the Court along. But Nelson and Trafalgar put the bowler hat on that scheme."

"You seem to know this part of the country well. Were you here during the war?"

"Yes. I suppose I passed through Boulogne a score of times, like every-one else. I spent three weeks in Le Touquet once, in the Casino. It was a hospital then. I'll take you there one evening and show you the exact spot where my cot stood. A fat croupier sits there now. Do you play *chemin-de-fer*?"

"No, not yet; but I hope you do."

"A little; but I need a chaperon these days. You and I will form a syndicate, and we'll make our fortunes."

Miss Lyndon made no reply, but I knew that she was regarding me curiously.

"I'm just dying to ask questions," she said at last, and I knew what she meant.

"Go right ahead," I replied. "We're not so sensitive as people think. It's part of our training. St. Dunstan's is a wonderful place."

"Tell me!" I began to find myself liking her little eager, impulsive manner.

"The first thing they teach you at St. Dunstan's," I said, "is to cut out all the pity-the-poor-blind stuff. A man newly blinded is a mass of self-commiseration."

"Naturally."

"Naturally. Well, they drill that out of him; they almost bully it out of him. He can't resent it, coming from other blind men. (That is why the head of St. Dunstan's has to be a blind man himself.) After that he is taught to live just like other people. We blind used to be herded together in an asylum: now, as soon as we can fend for ourselves, we are turned loose and allowed to find our own way about. It's a wonderful adventure."

I heard my companion draw an odd little breath. Then she continued:

"Is it true you develop a sixth sense?"

"I don't know that it is. We learn to rely a little more on the senses that we have got left, that's all. If you and I were to pass a horse standing in the street you would know it was there because you would see it; I would know it was there because I might hear the clink of its bit. You would hear the clink of the bit, too: but you wouldn't be listening for it, so you wouldn't notice it. It's the same with scent. We are passing a farm now. You can see it, I can smell it."

"I can smell it, too," Miss Lyndon assured me. "Now, tell me about getting around. Is that difficult?"

"Not in a place that one knows."

"You mean in your own home?"

"Yes; and my club, and a few of my friends' houses, and various familiar streets. You soon get to know a place by heart; and once you have learned it, you don't forget it, because your memory is not being constantly confused by a superfluity of things seen. The place I remember best of all, though I haven't been there for ten years, is where I first learned to get about, after—I got like this."

"Wasn't that St. Dunstan's?"

"No, I went there later. This place was a big country house in Surrey, not far from Chobham, and Woking, and those places. It was called Bramleigh Chase, and was used during the war as a hospital. I had my first experience of finding my feet there. I was all bandaged up in those days, and I hadn't undergone the St. Dunstan's regime, so things weren't too easy. I used to creep about passages and up and down staircases, feeling the walls and flinching from the next bump. I was like that then—until St. Dunstan's cured me of such foolishness. But I shall never forget Bramleigh Chase. If you were to put me down there again tomorrow I should know I was there, and I could tell you which room I was in."

"But supposing you were in a perfectly strange place? Walking along this road, we'll say?"

"Ah! there I should welcome a little assistance. Not too much, because we dislike being made to feel helpless—"

"You mean, you would hate to be armed along?"

"Yes. Just a word or touch, if I am walking into anything. I have a little friend in Le Touquet who understands the art perfectly. She is a golf caddie normally. Her name is Marie Thérèse. I will introduce you: she's rather a character."

"Does she go around with you all the time?"

"Oh, no! She just relieves my friends of a certain amount of trouble. One doesn't like to be a nuisance. But round about Cœur du Bois I can usually look after myself. It's not so easy as at home, of course. By the way, I overreached myself at home the other evening. To be perfectly frank, I was showing off. I say, am I boring you?"

"She's loving it," replied the voice of Enid. "Corrie, my child, you are getting things out of this man that the whole Dexter family have failed to get out of him in all history. The old fable of the Wind and the Sun, I suppose. Carry on, Sergeant-Major!"

"How did you overreach yourself?" asked Miss Lyndon, very properly ignoring the interruption.

"A man came to dine with me—one of the 'Oh, my poor fellow!' kind. When dinner was announced, he took me by the arm and tried to lead me into my own dining-room. During dinner he talked in a sort of hushed whisper, as if someone were lying dead upstairs. When the time came for him to leave I fairly sprang at the job of bidding him good-bye. His hat, and coat were hanging on some pegs in a little passage up a short flight of stairs and round a couple of corners. I bustled up the stairs and round the corners as quick as I could, just to show him—to learn him, rather."

"Of course."

"I could hear him puffing after me. When I got into the passage I pointed and said:

"'Your hat and coat ought to be hanging up there, old man.'

"'Perhaps they are,' he said; 'but I must take your word for it. I don't happen to be able to see in the dark.' I'd forgotten to turn the light on!"

"The joke was on you," pronounced Miss Lyndon gravely. "What is that big cemetery that we are passing?"

"Etaples, I expect. There are over ten thousand men buried there—British, Canadian, Australian, even Chinese. Most of them died in the base hospitals about here. You can't see the full extent of it from the road. I am told the best view is from the race-course, on the other side of that river down to your right. Can you see the river?"

"Yes. What is it called?"

"The Canche. That is Paris Plage at the mouth, with the two lighthouses. The forest of Le Touquet lies farther inland, and Etaples itself should be a little ahead of us. (Our Tommies always called it Eatables.) We haven't far to go now."

Ten minutes later we had crossed the Canche and were running through sweet-smelling pines along a smooth, straight road. My companion turned to me.

"Captain Shere?" she said.

"Yes?"

"If your little friend Marie Thérèse should require a day off at any time, I think I could provide a substitute—not so efficient, but honest and willing."

"You are extraordinarily kind," I said.

"It's not kindness at all; it's self-interest. I want to explore this place, and I like the line of talk that you hand out about it. Is it a date?"

"It is a date," I said solemnly.

But I did not feel solemn. My heart was singing—my heart, schooled these ten years to the grim acceptance of what must be. I found myself wondering what this girl's face was like—and then I found that I did not much care. For the first time in my groping, twilit existence I realised that beauty can be embodied in a mere presence, utterly independent of pink cheek or bright eye.

CHAPTER 5

HAZARDS

"Golf—the game that is not worth playing," announced Lieutenant-Commander Arthur Vigors Dexter, simply and suddenly.

His relatives did not allow this bombshell to affect their enjoyment of their luncheon. Only Vivien took any notice of it. She looked up and smiled seraphically.

"Never mind, dear," she said. "I can't hit the nasty little ball either."

As a matter of fact, Arturo is quite a fair golfer; but he is given to the conception of sudden and usually untenable theories on matters connected with sport; and he likes to argue these. The family has not yet forgotten the time when he took up the question of amateur-professionalism in lawn tennis. Vivien refers to it as the "Can We Do Without Suzanne?" week.

"There are two insuperable objections to golf as a ball game," continued Arturo invitingly.

"But as a first step to the Charleston it has much to recommend it," supplemented Nigel.

"This is serious." (Arturo said this in his quarter-deck voice, before which we all quail.) "In the first place, you are hitting at a stationary ball, which at once places golf in the same category as croquet. Isn't that the case, Barry?"

"My Sergeant-Major used to call golf ' 'Ockey at the 'alt,'" I conceded.

"Exactly. And, in the second place, you and your opponent have a ball apiece. That's all wrong, because your opponent can do nothing to make your shot more difficult to play—"

"Let him try!" suggested Vivien darkly.

"And *vice versa.*"

"How about stymies?" asked Nigel, who always leads the opposition on these occasions.

"Stymies are the final absurdity. They reduce the game to the level of chess."

"Why?"

"It's obvious."

"It isn't; but no matter."

"The long and short of it all is," concluded Arturo, "that golf simply cannot be compared to polo or cricket, or any game where opponents compete for the control of a single ball. If it could, it might be a game worth playing."

We sat silent, respectfully contemplating the picture conjured up—of knickerbockered gentlemen in the middle of a smooth fairway contending with niblicks for the "control" of one dented sphere.

"Well," said Nigel cheerfully, "what are we going to do about it?"

"We can't do anything about it. That's why it's a rotten game."

"But why take it lying down? That was never the Nelson way. Engage the enemy more closely, Commander! Listen, I've got a brain-wave. I challenge you to a one-ball match this afternoon, under Cœur du Bois rules. The rules will be drawn up by old Barry here. Are you on?"

"Don't talk bilge. It can't be done."

"It can be done," I said suddenly. Miss Lyndon had gone to Vimy with Enid, and here was a way to get through a dull afternoon. She had been with us for three days now, and her absence created a surprising gap.

"And an Englishman should do it!" concluded Nigel. "Get down to it, Barry."

Thus encouraged, I began.

"Arturo, you object first of all to the stationary ball; secondly, to the fact that you can't do anything to your opponent's ball? Very well then. This afternoon we will go to some quiet spot on the course, midway between two greens. There you and Nigel shall take alternate shots with the same ball—in opposite directions, of course—and the player who holes out first on his appointed green shall be the winner. What about that?"

"But neither of us would ever get to his appointed green."

"I'm not so sure. Anyhow, you can try. And to get over the difficulty of the stationary ball I will bowl it at you—from some safe spot in the neighbourhood of cover-point."

"Barry, this is genius," announced Master Nigel. "How many holes will constitute a match?"

"I think one will be enough," I said. And I was right. It took Nigel exactly one hour and a quarter to score the winning hit.

However, I anticipate. After coffee, Arturo, Nigel, Vivien, my mother and myself set out for the scene of the conflict. The course was quiet, for the Easter rush was past, and we had no difficulty in appropriating a suitable stretch of fairway with a putting green at each end—the eleventh and thirteenth, in point of fact.

I had attached to me as tender one Marie Thérèse, whose name has already been mentioned in this narrative. She is a pinafored young person of about twelve. She first came into my ken last year, when she volunteered, in response to an inquiry broadcast by the caddie-master, to act as prop and stay to "le monsieur aveugle" during his walks abroad. Her own grandfather is blind, so Marie Thérèse understands our ways. She does not push or drag; in fact, she rarely touches me. But her shoulder is always there when there is broken ground to cross; and if I am heading for a tree she diverts me by a silent nudge.

Her sense of humour is keen, but easily satisfied. For instance, if I address her as Henrietta Maria or Augusta Victoria instead of Marie Thérèse, she quakes with amusement for the next half-hour, and tells all her friends about it afterwards. She is not a conversationalist, which is a good thing, for her patois is quite unintelligible to me, and I shrewdly suspect that mine is to her, although she always pretends to understand it.

To return to the game. As is usual with great and sudden inspirations when the stage of practical performance is reached, some of our most original ideas had to be modified quite early, but for the first ten minutes the Cœur du Bois rules were unchallenged. I took my stand at right-angles to the line of play, on a patch of fair turf somewhere in the neighbourhood of the intervening twelfth green, and lobbed a Silver King in the direction of Arturo's voice. Arturo made a blind swipe at it and missed it entirely. The ball was then returned to me. Nigel took his stand facing the other way, and I crossed over with Marie Thérèse and bowled him one from the other side.

Nigel also missed.

After each gentleman had played a further series of what are technically known as air-strokes, Arturo at last succeeded in hitting the ball—or rather, the ball hit the shaft of his club, ran up it, and bounced into his eye. The first revision of the rules then took place, and it was decided to revert to the ignominious idea of a stationary ball.

The game having been constituted anew, Arturo drove off down the fairway.

"Good tap!" pronounced Nigel, ever the little sportsman, and we all tramped after the ball, which lay well on the way to the eleventh green. Presently we were grouped round it.

"Don't knock the cover right off, dear," said Vivien, as Nigel prepared himself for the answering blow.

"Wait and see!" I heard Nigel's club-head whistle through the air. Then came the impact, and the ball sang into space. There followed a distant and hollow crack; then silence.

"*Dans la forêt?*" I inquired of Marie Thérèse.

"*Kwah kwee!*" (This probably means "*Je crois que oui.*")

We proceeded to the scene of the disaster. Here another unforeseen contingency presented itself.

"All I can do here," complained Arturo, apparently from the middle of a bush, "is to use up my stroke in chipping this ball out on to the fairway for *you*, Nigel!"

"The fortune of war, my boy," said Nigel grandly.

"Not a bit. It's a fundamental flaw in the conception of the game. It means that the only way to gain ground for oneself is to slice into a hazard."

"Exactly. Like kicking into touch at Rugger."

"But supposing I do it, too? Where will you be, my lad?"

"I hadn't thought of that. We'd better revise this rule. Barry, what about it?"

"If a player put his ball into a bush or other hazard," I announced readily, "his opponent shall be allowed two shots next time, instead of one."

This ruling was graciously accepted. But another difficulty had occurred to Nigel.

"How is anybody ever going to hole out?" he asked. "Every time one of us runs the ball up near the pin the other will simply bang it away. Holing a mashie shot will be the only chance."

I ruled that a ball played to within two clubs' length of the pin should be deemed as holed out; and the battle was renewed. However, as the afternoon sun was warm, and the rules seemed to be now more or less standardised, public interest in the game began to flag. Vivien and my parent retired unashamedly to a comfortable resting-place beneath the trees, where Marie Thérèse and I soon afterwards joined them, leaving the brothers Dexter to persevere in what sounded like a laboured and embittered exposition of the game of hockey. The representative of the Silent Service was particularly audible.

II

Vivien produced the Paris *Daily Mail*, a cigarette-case, and some letters.

"I'm glad we brought these along," she said. "I rather thought we might need them. There's a letter for Barry here, Aunt Sylvia."

"Shall I read it for you, dear?" asked my mother, who acts as my private secretary when I engage in correspondence, which is not often.

"Don't trouble about it just now," I said, and took the letter from Vivien's hand. "Later will do. Let us have something out of the paper instead, Vivien."

"Righto! Here's a perfectly divine story right in the middle of the front page, about a man in Montparnasse who cut off his lady friend's left ear with a carving knife. We'll start on that. A cigarette for you, Barry? I have lighted it."

She set to work, in dulcet tones, upon the gory details....

Through the trees came the hoarse booming of a rather asthmatic motorhorn. I knew it well; it meant that the ancient touring-car of the House of Dexter was returning from Vimy Ridge. I rose to my feet.

"I think I'll take a stroll," I announced. "Marie Thérèse will look after me. This game seems likely to go on forever; but if any more points come up for judgment, Vivien, I nominate you deputy-umpire. Marie Thérèse, *marchons*! We need exercise. *Etes-vous fatiguee?*"

"*Kwah k'non!*"

"*Bon!* Come on, then."

We moved off through the trees in the direction of the house. Behind me I heard a pair of fair hands clap softly together once, while a gentle voice uttered the monosyllable "Wow!"

"The young can be horribly objectionable sometimes, Marie Thérèse," I said. "Don't you agree?"

"*Kwah kwee!*" replied Marie Thérèse politely.

III

Half an hour later Miss Corrie Lyndon found me reclining in my accustomed basket-chair on the veranda facing the golf course. We exchanged greetings, for we met for the first time that day, the car having left at eight o'clock in the morning.

"Did you find—the place?" I asked.

"Yes; there was no difficulty at all. His name was in the book, in the little recess in the gateway of the cemetery, and I was able to walk straight there. It was beautiful."

"They must all be beautiful, I imagine. I have never seen one; they weren't taken in hand until after the Armistice. But simplicity and regularity mean everything."

"Yes. The white stones, so clean and upright, rank upon rank, like soldiers answering roll-call....I took a photograph, for my mother. Now, what have you been doing all day?"

I told her; and she chuckled in her now familiar fashion.

"They certainly have bright ideas, this family," she said. "And now you are resting up?"

"Yes."

"Then I'll leave you."

"No—please stay. I want you to do me a favour."

"All right. What is it?"

"Will you read this letter for me?" I took it from my pocket. To be frank, I had kept it for this purpose.

"Isn't it private?"

"I have to risk that. Blind men have few secrets."

"I suppose that's true," said Miss Lyndon thoughtfully. "Well, if this one is from a girl, I promise to forget it." She opened the envelope. "No, it's not that kind of letter. Anyway, it's not exactly passionate. It's from someone called 'Yours respecfly, A. Noseworthy.'"

"Oh! Alf? This may be interesting. Please proceed."

Miss Lyndon began:

"Sir, I take up my pen for to say that I am still in good health, and am hopping that you are the same."

"That's the regulation military opening," I mentioned. "I read scores of those in the old days, as Company censor."

My deputy secretary continued:

"The weather in London and England, S.E., continues fine, the pressure distribution having undergone little change during the past twenty-four hours. The depression over Scandinavia is moving away south-westward.

For goodness sake, who is this friend of yours? A cipher expert, or the weather man?"

"Neither; he is an electrical engineer. But he is trying to improve himself. A correspondence course in correct English, and all that. I expect he has been warned not to introduce his principal theme too precipitately, but to lead up to it gradually, with a few appropriate comments on the topics of the day. In this case he appears to have copied out the weather report. What does he say next?"

"Eastertide festivities have now passed their zenith—"

"He's in the social column now."

"And society is flocking back to Town."

"Give him time. He'll come to the point presently."

"Touching that film job. Sir—"

"Ah! here is the authentic Alf!"

"I have been to the Studio. I was driven there at night in a closed car, so I am not very sure where the place is; especially as I was driven back in the same car the same night."

"Aha!" I said.
"What is the matter?"
"I beg your pardon. Please continue."

"Mr. Flawn went with me. I did ask him where we were, but he did not seem very sure himself. He said he wasn't familiar with the country round London, coming as he did from the

North; but it didn't matter, because the shover knew his way everywhere. I meant to have a word with the shover, but did not get the opportunity."

"I'm not altogether surprised at that," I said.

"I looked over the electric plant. I don't know much about film-studio lighting, but it seems to call for a big voltage. There was a great new dynamo, just delivered, that wanted assembling. I said I couldn't do it without help; a couple of stout country lads would be sufficient. Mr. Flawn said he would notify the Chief, but it might be a matter of a few days, the Chief being abroad. I said in that case I might as well go back home and wait; so Mr. Flawn took me back the same night. I may add that no mention was made of my proposed course of lessons in film acting, although I threw out a hint or two. However, the Studio itself only appears to be half finished, so I did not press the matter."

"I'll explain about the film acting presently," I said; "but I may mention in passing that Alf is quite unbalanced on the subject."

"Still, I was glad to get back to my young lady, whom I found in good health. I should greatly appreciate the honour of a short interview with you, sir, re the matter in hand. Pending your return to town, we shall participate in the busy whirl of West End life—"

"He's back to the social column. He lives in Brixton, really."

"Theatres, balls, and what not. Having no more to say, I will now draw to a close. Hoping this finds you as it leaves me, in the pink—"

"That's the old Army touch again."

"I remain, yours respecfly, A. Noseworthy."

Miss Lyndon folded up the letter and gave it back to me.
"And now," she asked, "do I come in on this mystery play or do I not? I may say that I shall never speak to you again if I do not."
"Are we close tiled?" I asked cautiously.
"What does that mean?"
"Is there anybody about?"

"Not that I can see."

"Then I'll tell you."

Miss Corrie Lyndon wriggled closer to me, like a small girl of six.

"I am going to enjoy this," she said. "Where is the body buried?"

"That's just what I don't know. I'm not even sure if there is a body—so far."

"Does that mean you are afraid that this Mr. Noseworthy may have to furnish it?"

"He may, if he's not careful. I can't help feeling that Flawn has designs on him of some kind. Have you any opinion to offer?"

"I can't offer an opinion till I hear the whole story."

Nothing loth, I set to work. I am a reticent person, but I cannot imagine any man declining to share a secret with Corrie Lyndon if she asks him to do so. I unfolded the tale of my meeting with Alf and Edna, and the intriguing consequence thereof.

"What do you make of it all?" I asked, when I had finished.

"From your description of these two, I should say that Mr. Flawn was a good picker."

"I think you're right there. And having picked them, he seems anxious to hold on to them."

"It looks like that."

"Now, what can they do for him that no one else can do?"

"I think," observed Miss Lyndon, "that we can count Edna out of this. She's an accident, more or less: just one of those dumb blondes that don't mean anything. Alf has fallen in love with her, so she tags along. Let us concentrate on Alf. What does Flawn want *him* for?"

"As an electrician."

"Very well. Then why doesn't he hire him straight off as an electrician on a salary instead of all this crazy stuff about lessons in film acting?"

"Presumably because he thought the lessons would be a bigger inducement than the salary."

"That sounds right to me. If so, it means that Flawn is out to get Alf at any price. Why?"

"Because he wants to put Alf on to some job that an ordinary respectable trade-union electrician might jib at."

"That's another correct answer, I think. Next, what sort of place is this Studio, which can only be visited in a closed car at night? Do you think it is a film-studio at all?"

"Yes."

"Why?"

I hesitated. I did not want to bring Sir Gavin into the story, at any rate by name.

"I mentioned the matter the other day," I said, "to someone in a position to throw light on mysteries of this kind; and his conclusion was that the Studio is a studio all right, but that it is going to be used for making films of a rather secret kind. Revolutionary propaganda, and so on. There is a great vogue for that sort of thing at present."

"Well, I think your friend is wrong. I'm only a poor unreasoning female, but I have a hunch that there is something else at the back of this. I can't explain why, but I know. Are you going to believe me, or him?"

I hastened to answer.

"That is what I expected—but not quite sincere, I fear. Never mind; I like it. Now, when do you expect to meet Mr. Alf Noseworthy again?"

"When I get back to town."

"When will that be?"

I hesitated again. My visit to Le Touquet had been timed to last a week, and the week was over already.

"Not just yet," I said. "For one thing, I have to show you round Le Touquet. All you have seen so far is the golf course on a wet day."

"But oughtn't you to hurry?" suggested my companion. "What about Alf and Edna? Supposing something happened to them, just because you weren't attending to your business?"

"You are my business," I said firmly.

My companion made no reply for a little. Then she asked, with the air of one starting a fresh topic:

"What is the programme for tomorrow?"

"I thought we might take a stroll in Paris Plage in the morning. There is a row of little robbers' dens—mostly offshoots from bigger dens in Paris—with hats and things in the windows. You might like to look into them."

"I might even go farther than that. What else?"

"We might have tea at the Normandie. It's a little open-air café just off the principal street, with a band. We might dance, if you feel so disposed."

"You dance, too?"

"Rather—if you don't mind steering. In the evening we will go to the Casino, and break other people's banks. We'll go tonight, if you like."

"I think I'll stay at home tonight. But tomorrow night is a bet. How do you play this game, anyway; and why is it called *chemin-de-fer?*"

"I suppose because the shoe goes round and round the table like a railway train."

"What is the shoe?"

"It's a polished wooden box, as wide as the length of a card. The cards are packed in it, and you slip them out with your finger and thumb from one end, one at a time."

"How do you play the game?"

"People sit round a green table—"

"How many of them?"

"Nine, as a rule, with a croupier beside them. The bank—the shoe that is—is slid from player to player. When your turn comes, you put your stake in the middle of the table—a hundred franc chip, we will say. The croupier calls out its value, and your right-hand neighbour says 'Banco!' and stakes a similar sum. Then the fun begins. You slip your opponent two cards out of the bank; he peeps at them, to see what they add up to—"

"What do court cards count as?"

"Aha! I see you have the card brain. Court cards all count as ten—which means in this case nothing."

"Nothing?"

"Yes; Chemmy is a game of single figures. Eleven counts as one, twelve as two, and so on. In this way the highest possible figure is nine. Chasing the nine is the life's work of some people: there is a bungalow down near the Casino with 'Neuf' painted on the gate."

"I have left my opponent peeping at his cards," Miss Lyndon reminded me.

"Sorry! Well, if he has a natural nine or eight he throws down his hand at once, and it is up to you to equal or beat him. But if his hand comes to something smaller—which is much more likely—he is entitled to one more card from you. This may improve his hand, or not."

"Or not?"

"Yes. Supposing he has a three and you give him a seven—what does that make?"

"Ten. Nothing! I see."

"But supposing you gave him a six, what does that make?"

"Nine. He beats me!"

"Not necessarily. You haven't seen your own cards yet. You now turn these up. They may come to nine too. If so, you are equal!"

"And then?"

"You have a fresh deal, until one of you wins."

"This game is going to give me heart failure," announced Miss Lyndon. "Tell me more."

"Of course nines and eights are simple things to handle, when one happens to get them. But supposing your opponent finds that his hand is only worth six, is he going to stand on that, or ask you for another?"

"You tell me!"

"Well, what cards could improve a six hand?"

"Let me think. The ace, a two, or a three."

"Yes; that's all. Anything else would be useless, or worse. A seven, for instance, would reduce the value of a hand to three. So your opponent would stand on a six. On anything below five he would certainly draw."

"But supposing he had a four, and I gave him a seven? I should have ruined his hand."

"Probably, but not certainly. The hand would still be worth one, and you might deal yourself three court cards—nothing!"

"I simply wouldn't do such a thing. The Maple Leaf forever! However, if my bank does go down, the other person takes the stake?"

"Correct."

"And if my bank wins, I take the other person's stake?"

"Yes; but you don't go out of business. You add the loser's stake to your own and run the bank again, twice as big now. Of course you can pass the bank whenever you like, but no one would do that after the first coup. The money only begins to mount up after the third or fourth."

"Supposing I hang on until the fifth, and go down?"

"You lose everything, including your original stake."

"I couldn't bear it!"

"Your own fault for being greedy. The whole art lies in getting out at the right moment."

"How often do you usually run a bank yourself!"

"I am ashamed to tell you: twice! But the croupiers always say it is the best way, and they ought to know. Of course, if I have made a bit I sometimes run on for longer."

"But what are the other people doing all this time? This game appears to be a game for two."

"Oh, they have plenty to occupy them. The bank often gets too big for a single player to stake against; then everybody is allowed to come in to any extent they please. If the amount they put up doesn't equal the amount in the bank, the bit left over is called a *bénéfice*, and the banker receives that, whatever happens. The remainder—"

Miss Lyndon leaned back with a resigned sigh.

"That'll be all for this afternoon," she said. "I'm getting dizzy. Let us talk about something else—something easier. The mystery of your friend, Alf Noseworthy, we will say."

"Certainly. It's a sticky business, this Noseworthy case. Let's discuss it thoroughly: it'll take some time. I think it would be a good plan to have a series of informal committee meetings about it, say, twice daily, until further—"

"The villagers approach," announced Miss Lyndon calmly. "This committee is adjourned, anyway."

The distant voices of Arturo and Nigel were audible through the trees. My fair confederate rose to her feet.

"I must dress for dinner now," she said. "But I'm looking forward to tomorrow. Au revoir!"

Her light step died away. I sat on, thinking.

"You'll be sorry for all this, my son," I said; and I was not referring either to the vice of gambling or to my interest in the Noseworthy mystery.

CHAPTER 6

AMBERGRIS

I spent practically the whole of next day in the company of Miss Corrie Lyndon, and as not infrequently happens when one walks of set purpose into the danger zone, the staid history of my life took a sudden bound.

The morning we devoted to the golf course, seated in a warm hollow of soft, running sand in the side of a hillock looking down upon the fifteenth green. The fifteenth hole at Le Touquet is what is humorously called a one-shot hole, and you reach it (eventually) through a gap in the pine woods, over a sandy ridge, upon the summit of which an intensely officious small boy stands all day long with a red flag, chanting "Jouez!" at intervals, as an intimation to the couple on the tee that the couple on the green have at last holed out.

It is a long carry to the hole—nearly two hundred yards—and Miss Lyndon and I were ensconced at a point which commanded a good view of the place where the niblicks usually got to work. We were also near the sixteenth tee, from which the tigers are accustomed to drive right over the top of a wood, the humbler members of the animal kingdom making a dog-leg of it.

It was a still, hot morning. From where we sat we could faintly hear the sound of club against ball upon the fifteenth tee, followed by a perceptible thud, an ominous crack, or complete silence, as the ball dropped on to the green, swerved into the pine trees, or buried itself noiselessly in the shifting sand. And in this connection we devised a little round game of our own. As soon as the ball was heard to leave the tee, I drew a word picture of the person who had driven it. If, when the individual in question came tramping over the skyline, his or her appearance tallied in any sort of way with my description, Miss Lyndon paid me two francs; if not, I paid her one.

We had been engaged in this pleasant nonsense for nearly two hours, and I was seven francs down. A mixed foursome were holing out on the green.

"The girl with the cigarette has missed her putt," my companion informed me.

"I know; I heard her."

"That loses them the hole. The fat man in the rainbow jumper has the honour on the sixteenth tee. He's going to try and carry the wood."

"I bet you ten to one he doesn't."

"I take you."

"Crack!"

"You win," said Miss Lyndon. "Hallo, another couple are driving from the fifteenth. Good shot!"

Thud! A ball had fallen on the green below us. Next moment came a second thud.

"They are both within six feet of the pin. What are your intuitions this time? No—wait! Here is the third ball coming over."

"I didn't hear it fall," I said presently.

"No: it's out to the left, in the rough. Now, what are those three players like?"

"The first," I replied, "is a man of about six feet three, with a scrubby black moustache and a Zingari tie. The second is a youngish rather chubby man, with prematurely grey hair. He may be wearing an Old Wykehamist tie."

"Now, how should a poor, ignorant overseas—?"

"Sorry. Red, black and yellow in the first case; red, blue and brown in the second."

"Thank you. What about the third man?"

"He is biggish and clean shaven, with a merry blue eye. His caddy will probably be giggling."

"Here they come. And—you can go right up to the top of the class. Still, something tells me that I have been framed."

"You would look very nice framed," I assured her.

"I mean, you have been betting on a certainty," Miss Lyndon explained coldly.

Her suspicion deepened when the three-ball match, on catching sight of us, diverged from its path—to the indignation of the bureaucrat with the red flag—and came over in our direction.

"We have turned aside, Barry, old man," said the voice of my tall friend Rex Fryer, "to bid you good morrow. Warren Scott and Odo Lerwick are also present."

"Go along with you," I said. "I am the excuse: let me introduce you to the reason. Miss Lyndon, these are three bad men." I gave their names, and the honest trio, after a few ungainly gallantries, passed on to the green. All three missed their putts.

"I sometimes wish I could see your face," I said to Miss Lyndon.

"Only sometimes?"

"Well, at some times more earnestly than others. I expect it would explain why I appear to be so popular when I go for a walk with you. It might also explain a cryptic remark of our young friend Nigel when first your name was mentioned in my presence."

"What was that?"

"He said: 'It's a pity about her face.' I thought at the time that he spoke in compassion; I have since realised that he was giving way to our national propensity for understatement. I suppose it is very beautiful?"

"*Jou-e-e-ez!*"

Two balls crashed into the wood, one to the right, the other to the left. I abruptly diagnosed a pair of profiteers in pink hunting-stocks. But I was wrong: the interlopers were Nigel and Arturo.

We declined their suggestion that we should accompany them on the rest of their round, and after discharging a broadside of mingled naval and military repartee, they passed away. We sat on.

"Referring," I began, "to the matter we were discussing—"

"It is half-past twelve," answered Miss Lyndon. "The morning rush seems to be over."

"I can hear voices," I said. "Give me a chance to earn another franc or two."

"No money will pass this time: these people are not playing. They are just roaming around the woods—a rather unsuitably dressed woman and two men in white flannel trousers and white shoes."

"French?"

"I'm not sure. They look foreign—at least, the men do—but of course they might be anything, in a place like this." Corrie Lyndon lowered her voice. "They have sat down quite near us. One man is sallow, with a dark moustache; the other is clean shaven and heavily built, with high cheekbones and pig's eyes."

"Casino hounds, I should say. Perhaps they are members of the famous Levantine Syndicate, who are playing at the top table this week. They go from place to place—Cannes, Biarritz, Deauville, Le Touquet—and work their system."

"What sort of system?"

"Intuition, chiefly. I believe they are marvellous. Each one of them knows in his bones whether he is in winning vein or not, and sits in or sits out accordingly. What is their lady friend like?"

"Nothing in particular. She seems to know you, though. She is staring hard at you."

"And the gentlemen, I presume, are staring hard at you?"

"One of them is—the big one. He gives me the Willies. Let us go away from here. It must be lunch-time."

II

In the afternoon we visited Paris Plage, travelling on the *Allez roulez*—the amusing miniature train that runs through the forest to the neighbourhood of the Casino—an affair of two little open cars and a toy engine.

We strolled down the wooded drive that leads to the sea, past—but not always immediately past—the little *bonneteries* and *bijouteries* which line one side of that seductive thoroughfare. Miss Corrie Lyndon lingered there, to the extent of two hats and an automatic lighter. The latter she presented to me. Then she piloted me down the narrow, busy little main street of Paris Plage to the Normandie.

Here we sat down in an outer courtyard in brightly painted barrels carved into the semblance of chairs, and sipped our tea to the music of a band. Then, penetrating to a hall within, we danced together. Miss Lyndon was pleased to commend my sense of rhythm: I complimented her upon her expertness as man-at-the-wheel, and (occasionally) shock-absorber. We were rapidly slipping into the easiest of companionships. Our minds seemed to jump instinctively to the same topics: once or twice she answered a question of mine before I asked it. My soul expanded: infinite content settled upon me. If I had been a cat I should have purred: if I had had a tail I should have wagged it.

Suddenly, as we sat at our little table in the sun, a shadow fell between us. It passed, leaving behind it a faint aroma of something—something unmistakable and unforgettable. I shivered.

"Has a goose stepped over your grave?" inquired my companion.

"Not a goose. A vulture, perhaps. A vulture smelling slightly of ambergris. What memories one's sense of smell can bring back!"

"You'll have to tell me this one." Miss Lyndon's voice brooked no denial.

"It's a long story," I said, "and not in the least romantic. It has to do with my—my hundred percent disability. It all happened in Egypt."

"I did not know you served there."

"I was sent out in 1917. I had been wounded once, and I think they meant to give me a soft job. They put me into the Intelligence at Cairo. The place was alive with our troops. The Gallipoli show had been over for several months, and by rights most of us ought to have been fighting on some really interesting front. But Enver had announced that Egypt was to be the Turkish Army's next objective, and we had taken his bluff lying down."

"Who was Enver? I know I ought to know."

"I don't see why you should. It happened more than ten years ago. Where were you then?"

"In a school for little girls in Montreal."

"Very well, then. Enver was conducting a school for British Generals in the Near East. He was one of the really great adventurers of the war. He might have been Sultan of Turkey or President of the Turkish Republic if he hadn't been so clever. No one knows where he is now. But in those days we kept Egypt full of British soldiers just to oblige him, and he kept Egypt full of spies and conspirators just to worry us.

"One night my boss, old Brock Wycherley, sent for me, and said that an Australian battalion had had their bomb store raided and two hundred Mills bombs sneaked."

"I'm sorry, but—"

"Mills bombs? Quite. They were hand grenades, a product of that era. Bombs are obsolete now, like Enver, and soldiers no longer receive instructions in their use, which is lucky, for they are tricky things to practise with. Anyhow, the Aussies had lost theirs, and were dancing mad about it. This wasn't the first event of its kind, either. There was a very skilfully organised system of pilfering and sabotage in operation all over the place. Evidently some capable mind was at the back of it. Brock Wycherley had sent for me to say that a little bird had told him that the bombs, and other portable property of ours, had been concealed in a house in a pretty shady part of Cairo. By the way, do you know Cairo at all?"

"Not yet."

"Well, the district in question lies in front of Shepheard's and behind the Eden Palace, and this particular house was a café of rather dubious character. (No doubt about it at all, really, but never mind that.) The old man wanted confirmation of the rumour. One way was to raid the place in force, and the other was to send someone along, quietly to spy out the land. Obviously the second course was the wiser. If the whole affair was a mare's nest, we should be saved from making a public exhibition of ourselves; if not, there would be no harm in collecting more definite information before making a pounce. So I was sent."

"Wasn't it dangerous?"

"I suppose it was; but there was a war on, anyhow. I had to act at once, because Brock Wycherley had it on fairly reliable authority that there was shortly going to be an attempt upon the lives of our brand-new Egyptian Cabinet, and it rather looked as if the bombs had been borrowed for the purpose. It was arranged that I should disguise myself as an ordinary Cairene taxi-man, and drive right up to the door of this particular place about midnight, when its ostensible business would be at its flood, and say that I had been sent to fetch someone or other home. If the man at the door said that the gentleman in question was not there, I was to send him upstairs to inquire; then follow him quietly. If he declined, I was to insist on seeing the proprietor—of whom, by the way, nothing was known except that his name was Manoukian. If and when I penetrated into that gentleman's presence, I was to keep my eyes open and use my own judgment.

"The first part of my entertainment went off all right. I drove up to the house in my Ford, and found a most villainous-looking fellow guarding the door. I pitched my tale about the man I'd come for—an imaginary person ending in 'Bey'—and the doorkeeper turned at once and went along the passage and up a stair. I followed him. It was not difficult, because the ground floor was full of people; in fact, there was some sort of entertainment going on in the room on the right of the passage—musicians chanting, and girls dancing, and soldiers sitting about.

"As soon as I got to the first floor I slowed down. My villainous friend had not noticed me at all, and went up higher. The first landing was quiet, except for some chattering and giggling behind two or three closed doors. I climbed the next stair. The second landing was empty, but on the far side was a door standing open. Through it I saw a man sitting at a table with his back to me—a heavily built man in a tarboosh. The doorkeeper was there, too, delivering my message, I suppose. I had to make up my mind quickly. If the man at the table was Manoukian, should I go in and try a diplomatic conversation with him, or should I pass him by and start on a private exploration of his upper premises? It was a pretty thin chance either way, but I decided on the private exploration. I started up the third stair—"

"I'm getting all worked up over this," announced a small, hoarse voice beside me. Then, with a touch of impatience:

"What is it, please?"

The voice of the waiter broke in:

"A gentleman desires to speak to Mademoiselle a little moment."

"A gentleman?"

"Yes, mademoiselle; an English gentleman."

Miss Lyndon hesitated, and evidently looked round at the person indicated. Then she rose to her feet.

"Anything once!" she said, half to herself. "I'll be right back, Captain Shere." Then she left me.

I could hear her talking to a man a few yards away—or rather, a man talking to her, for she hardly spoke. When she came back to me she was breathing rather rapidly through her nose.

"And what has roused your wrath?" I asked.

"Captain Shere, do I look like the bad girl of the family, or do I not?"

"Has someone been mistaking you for her?"

"He certainly has."

I half rose. "Where is he?"

"Now, don't you get excited too. He was quite respectful. Here is his card, which he did the honour to confer upon me."

"What does it say?"

"'Captain Percy Flawn.'"

"Flawn? That's funny. Any address?"

"No. But he told me that he had once been in the British Secret Service."

"Then I can tell you two things about him. The first is that he is a liar: no man in the Secret Service ever tells anybody about it. The other is that his name is familiar. Do you remember Alf Noseworthy's letter?"

"Why, of course I do. I hadn't thought of that. Still, it may be a coincidence."

"Has this man a black moustache and a shifty eye?"

"He certainly has. How do you know?"

"I have had him described to me twice in the last three weeks. But what on earth did he want you for?"

"He invited me to dine with him tonight—to make a fourth with him and two friends! I'm as mad as a wet hen. Still, it was my own fault for letting him speak to me."

"Did he mention the name of his two friends, by any chance?"

"No, except that one was his fiancée."

"The other, presumably, is a boy friend."

"Yes."

"Then it is evidently the boy friend that you have made a hit with. Is he visible?"

"Oh, yes, and the fiancée. All three of them are sitting over in a corner of the courtyard; in fact, they are the people who came and stared at us in the wood this morning."

"Oho! And you say that the lady seems to know me?"

"She did this morning. She's got her back to you now."

"Has she bronze-coloured hair?"

"She has, as far as I can see. Who is she?"

"Her name is Lil Montgomery. It was she who offered to get Alf Noseworthy a job with Flawn. I wonder who the big boy friend is."

"I don't know; but he never takes his eyes off me. Do you mind if we go somewhere else now?"

III

Half an hour later we were out on the sand dunes, making the most of the failing afternoon sunshine and allowing the Channel breezes to blow away the recollection of our recent encounter.

"You never finished your story," Miss Lyndon reminded me.

"Oh, the bomb story? Let me see, where was I?"

"You had just decided to go up the third staircase."

"Then there's not much more to tell, I'm afraid. I fairly crawled up that stair, on my hands and toes, to distribute my weight and avoid creaks. Presently the stair wound round, and I saw the third landing above me, dimly lit. Up I crept, until my hand was on the very top step. I felt something hard and thin lying underneath it. I picked the thing up. There was just enough light to see what it was. It was the detonator of a Mills bomb!"

"I know this is the climax of the story," said Miss Lyndon apologetically, "and I hate to ruin it—but what is a detonator?"

"A thing to make the bomb go off. Mills bombs are filled with ammonal, which does not explode easily—not from a spark, or anything like that. It requires a real kick. The detonator fits into the bomb. It is filled with another explosive—easy to touch off, and strong enough to get the ammonal to function. For safety's sake, bombs and detonators are usually kept apart until the last moment. This staircase evidently led up to the hiding-place of the bombs, and someone had dropped a detonator on the way up. It was an extraordinary piece of luck for me."

"I wonder! Go on."

"Having discovered all that I wanted to know, I now decided to get out and home, without saying good night to anybody. I turned round to go downstairs again—and found myself face to face with Mr. Manoukian! He was standing on the stairs three feet below me, with murder in his face."

"*Oh!* What happened?"

"Nothing, for the moment. Our meeting was evidently a mutual surprise. He just stood gaping. Then I noticed that his eye was fixed on the detonator in my hand, and I knew I was booked for trouble—trouble early and complete. So I adopted shock tactics: I took a flying leap on to him, and we went down the stair together. We arrived on the landing in a heap, with me on top, and the fight was on. I got my left hand twisted into his collar, and tried to jab him in the jaw with my right. But he was wonderfully quick and immensely strong. In a moment he had grabbed my entire fist in one enormous hand, and was trying to bend my wrist back and break it. The detonator was inside my fist: I had forgotten all about it, but I could feel it there between my finger and thumb. I struggled desperately, but he held me. I remember being conscious of an overpowering smell of ambergris: they use it in the Levant a good deal for perfume, and he was drenched in it. I went on twisting at his shirt collar, in the hope of choking him, and he went on trying to break my wrist. Something was bound to go, on one side or the other. Finally his collar went, and he was free. He let go of me, rolled over, and jumped to his feet. Then I saw his hand go round for his gun. He had put his foot on my chest to keep me down. His boot, a heavy German field boot, was the last thing I ever saw; for at that moment the detonator went off, right in my face. The heat of my hand had done it. It was not an unusual thing to happen; many a careless bomber has lost a couple of fingers that way."

"But you—what did it do to you?"

"Oddly enough, it hardly damaged my fingers at all; but it finished my eyes for good....After that, luckily, everything became a blank, until I felt myself being lifted out of my Ford at the hospital. A military police patrol had found the car standing deserted in a part of Cairo called the Dead City, with me lying at the bottom of it, a pretty bad mess....That's the story. You are only the third person I have ever told it to."

There was a long silence. Then Corrie Lyndon asked:

"What happened to Manoukian?"

"The place was raided next morning—I wasn't fit to make a statement before then—but of course he was gone, bombs and all. I believe he was a pretty high-up official in the German Intelligence. I often wonder whether the detonator damaged him at all. If ever I meet him I shall ask him."

There was a longer silence. Finally Corrie Lyndon said:

"Do you know it hasn't disfigured you at all? There are no marks."

"So I have been told. It's strange not to know any more what one's face looks like—or what other people's faces look like, for that matter. It's a risky business having to depend for information upon people like young Nigel Dexter."

Corrie Lyndon said nothing, but I knew she was watching me.

Suddenly I said:

"I asked you a question this morning, and you did not answer it. May I ask it again?"

"If you like."

I was lying on my left side, resting on my elbow: opposite to me I was conscious of her fragrant presence, a few feet away.

"Is it very beautiful?" I asked. "I'm not trying to be impertinent." I waited.

"You can touch it if you like," she replied simply.

I extended my hand. She took it in hers and led it to her face. The tips of my fingers began their trembling pilgrimage—outlining a round chin, a short, straight nose, a cheek like the petal of a flower. I laid my hand gently over each of her eyes: I could feel her long lashes brush my palm.

"Are they blue?" I asked.

"Yes."

I felt her hair. It was parted on one side, and the back, in the fashion of the day, was cropped as smooth as a boy's. But in front, as she lay on her side, a great waved lock had tumbled over her forehead.

"It feels golden brown," I said. "Is it?"

Her head nodded beneath my hand; but she said nothing.

Lastly, very, very softly, I outlined the curve of her mouth.

"Thank you," I said, almost reverently. "Now I know—and I shall never forget."

The mouth trembled beneath my finger tip, and something warm and soft splashed on to the back of my hand.

CHAPTER 7

THE THREE RESOLUTIONS

My mother, as usual, came into my room before dinner, to make sure that I had tied my evening tie correctly.

"It's very crooked tonight," she said severely, pulling it straight; "and your hair isn't brushed either. You look like an explorer home from the wilds. What is distracting your thoughts, my son?"

She spoke with studied unconcern, which she knows I appreciate, but behind it all I diagnosed maternal anxiety.

"I'm all right," I said; "but I don't seem to be able to find anything tonight. Where is my note-case? I laid it down when I came in, but it seems to have moved itself."

"Here it is on the floor, full of money. How prosperous we are!"

"I looked in at the bank this afternoon: we are going to the Casino tonight. Now I've lost my cigar-case."

"Here you are."

"Thank you. I'm sorry to be a nuisance, but things seem to be all wrong tonight."

My mother never attempts to comfort me when I get into a disconsolate state.

"Come downstairs and have a cocktail," she said. "I can hear Arturo at the shaker now."

"I will," I replied. "How wise you are, dear!" I added suddenly. And I meant it.

Still, it was a subdued and self-conscious explorer who descended the stair. I was angry with myself—the unreasoning anger of a vain man who has just realised that he is no stronger than anyone else. One hates to draw up private and rather pompous rules of conduct for oneself, and then break them. True, I had refrained from the last fatal step, but only by the interposition of Providence. That soft, suddenly trembling lip—that sweet, heaven-born tear—they had almost been too much for me. In another moment my fortitude would have crumpled, and I should have shattered forever, by one wild torrent of words, the thing that now bound me to life—the serene companionship and unquestioning trust of Corrie Lyndon.

Providence upon this occasion had taken the most unexpected and quite unrecognisable form of Captain Percy Flawn, late of the British Secret Service. He had emerged from behind a neighbouring sandhill, ostensibly scanning the adjacent Channel for passing ships, but palpably stalking Corrie Lyndon. Probably the Big Boy Friend had not entirely given up hope of Corrie's company at dinner, and had sent his henchman to make a final effort.

Upon catching sight of the ambassador, Corrie rose lightly to her feet, with a careless announcement as to the hour of day, followed by a *sotto voce* word of explanation to me. She then took my arm, and we strolled back to the Plage, chatting brightly and almost brushing from our path a frustrated and highly incompetent exponent of the art of espionage.

We hailed a car and drove back to Cœur du Bois. It was a silent journey. What my companion was thinking I did not know: my own state of mind I have already described. However, just before we arrived at the house Miss Lyndon gave me a characteristic and comforting surprise.

"Would it wreck my reputation with you for maidenly modesty," she inquired, "if I were to call you from now on by your Christian name—on a fifty-fifty basis?"

I tried to think of a graceful and appreciative reply, but could produce nothing better than a humble "Thank you so much."

But I went up to my room reassured on one point. She suspected nothing: otherwise I should hardly have been admitted at this moment to further intimacy. I had not given myself away after all.

There for a few hours the matter rested. To pursue private affairs in the bosom of the Dexter family is a quite impossible feat, because as a body the Dexters believe in what I will call Community Conversation. It was not until we found ourselves enjoying the comparative privacy of the crowded Casino ball-room that Corrie and I were in a position to indulge, if we thought fit, in the further discussion of intimate topics. For my own part I was content to let well alone; and so, I imagined, was she.

But I was wrong.

"Is there any place here where we can sit quietly?" she inquired, as our epileptic musicians stopped, apparently in the middle of a bar, with the stunning suddenness which appears to be a characteristic symptom of the disease.

"Not that I know of," I replied. "The Salle de Baccara itself is probably the most peaceful spot at this hour."

"Then let us go there."

We complied with the usual formalities at the desk, and in due course were passed into the Temple of Chance. It was still cool and airy, and there was little sound save in a distant corner, where croupiers were calling the game.

"How many tables are going?" I asked.

"Three: otherwise the place is about as crowded as an ice-cream parlour at the North Pole."

"It will be full enough by eleven o'clock."

"Then at eleven o'clock you and I will gamble. But at present I am going to outrage all your British sense of propriety."

We had sat down on a comfortable settee by the wall, and I tried to light a cigar with my new lighter. I bungled it, and Corrie helped me. Then she said:

"You were unhappy about something at dinner."

"Unhappy? I was under the impression that I was the life of the party."

"I know; that was what made me notice it. You were all wrought up. Why?"

"It is no use being reserved and British with you, I suppose?"

"Not the slightest. Tell me."

I was silent for a full minute. Then I said:

"It goes some way back. Ten years ago I had to rearrange my life a little, so I drew up a list of resolutions for myself to observe."

"I know."

"How do you know?"

"The girl has second sight, perhaps: a sure sign of a weak intellect. Anyhow, she knows. Shall I tell you some of the resolutions?"

"If you can."

"The first was: 'I will keep smiling.' Is that correct?"

"It was something like that, I believe."

"It was exactly like that, and you know it. The second was: 'I will never trade on my infirmity to arouse sympathy.'"

"This is all rather embarrassing," I protested.

"The truth is usually embarrassing. Shall I tell you some more resolutions?"

"How many more do you know?"

"At least two; but I'm only going to tell you one. It was: 'I will never be a drag on anybody.'"

She had got home again. I bowed my head.

"Are my thoughts as penetrable as all that?" I asked miserably.

"Penetrable? About as penetrable as an English holly bush! If I didn't happen to have a natural X-ray disposition—! Well, of late you have been tempted to go back on some of these resolutions of yours, and you are disappointed and scared over what you consider your weakness. That is why you behaved the way you did tonight."

"I'm sorry."

"I am not scolding you. I just want you to know that I know, and that it is no use trying to be Up-stage and County, as Vivien would say, with me."

"All right, I won't."

"Then that is settled. Now, turn about is fair play. Do you want to call me down for anything? Tell me off, I mean. What do you think of me, anyway? You have known me for nearly a week. What is your reaction to me, as they say in Boston?"

I considered; then tried to speak judicially.

"You are a strange mixture," I began.

"Most of us are. Give me some of my ingredients."

"Well, in the first place, you are extremely beautiful and intensely feminine—"

"The girl," announced Miss Lyndon, "blushed deeply and covered her features with her fan. Tell me some more."

"And yet in some respects you have just missed being born a boy."

"Not so good! How?"

"You take a boy's keen interest in the mechanical side of things; you want to know what makes the wheels go round. Often in our conversations during this week you have interrupted me—"

"I'm sorry."

"I like it—in order to make me explain some material detail that the average woman would have passed over as dull and unimportant and only of interest to men. When I was telling you of my Egyptian adventure this afternoon you wanted to know all about Enver and his intrigues, and you wouldn't let me go on with the most exciting part of my narrative until I had explained the mechanism of the Mills bomb. Only a boy would have done that. And I heard you talking magnetos and timing-gears with Nigel the other day like a trained motor mechanic. I expect if you were left alone with a car you would take the gear-box down and get covered to the elbows in black oil in five minutes."

"Quite right; I often do. But these are all rather good qualities. Tell me some of my bad ones."

"I'll finish the good ones first. The greatest is your splendid directness of character. Look how you tackled me just now, when I was fretful and crotchety, and straightened everything out. Very few people have that gift; promise me that you will always hold on to it. Directness of character means courage, and courage means everything."

"Well, you ought to know. (That is intended as a compliment, of the grudging British kind.) Now tell me a few faults, in case my halo should sprout too quickly."

"I haven't discovered any yet."

"Well, I'll tell you one. I have no tolerance; I am violent in my likes and dislikes. In other words, I am a woman. Now, you tell me one."

"I know what I'll do instead; I'll set you to play *chemin-de-fer*. They say that's a great agent for revealing defects of character. *Allons!*"

CHAPTER 8

SUIVI

By this time the rooms had filled up. There was a surging chorus of greeting and conversation all round us, almost swamping the mechanical recitative of the croupiers. With Corrie's hand on my arm, we moved easily through the well-dined throng. Presently we encountered Enid and the effervescent Arturo.

"Come and have a *dekko* at the top table," said the latter. "The nobility and gentry of the gambling world are now assembled, chewing their toothpicks. Mr. Guldenschwein, the well-known Scottish deer-stalker; Mr. Hank B. Tutwiler, the Oklahoma philanthropist; La Marquise de Fausse-Tirage, and the Sisters Golly. Walk up!"

"We must get places for ourselves first," I said importantly. "Corrie, do you see a table that looks cheap to play at and almost ready to start?"

"Number Seventeen has a man at it, shuffling cards; but there's no one else."

"Are there things lying on the table to keep places—cigarette-cases, and mascots, and odds and ends like that?"

"Yes. But place five is empty."

"That will do for us. Lay this lighter there, and we'll come back when they call us. Are you going to play, Enid?"

"No: I'm only dancing. Come and have another fox-trot, Arturo, before you start breaking the bank."

We reserved Corrie's place, and presently found ourselves amid the crowd which stood round the roped-off top table. Corrie described its occupants to me. To our regret the ladies and gentlemen so vividly enumerated by Arturo were not present; but there were plenty of equally intriguing sights.

"What a lot of money!" was Corrie's first remark. "Bundles of *mille* notes, and things like flat cakes of soap. What are they?"

"I fancy they are ten-*mille* counters; but I have never owned one. Who has the bank at present?"

"A hook-nosed man with a monocle."

"That is probably Lighter. He is here nearly every weekend."

"He has put up one cake of soap," announced Corrie reverently, "and the woman on his right has *banco'd* it."

"What is she like?"

"She has a carved ivory sort of face, like a mediæval saint. I believe if you pulled off her wig she would turn out to be the Archbishop of something. She has just asked for another card, and Lighter has turned his two up."

"What do they make?"

"Only three. And he's given her a nine."

"That's interesting. I wonder if he will draw."

"Surely!"

"I'm not so certain. Watch!"

"He hasn't drawn....She has turned up her three cards, and they're only worth two! She had a three to begin with, and the nine has busted it. (Pardon my language, but I don't know the technical term.) She doesn't look a bit like an Archbishop now. Why is the croupier putting chips down a slit?"

"That is the cagnotte. Five percent of every *coup* goes to the Casino. It tots up to a nice little sum by the end of the evening. Is the Archbishop going to *suivi?*"

"What does that mean?"

"Have another go at Lighter."

"No; she quits. A baggy-faced man in horn-rimmed spectacles has come in instead, with two cakes of soap....He has looked at his cards, and he won't take any more....Hoo, Lighter has turned up a natural eight!"

"Has he? Good night, Horn-Rims!"

"Horn-Rims declines to go to bed. He's put up some more soap."

"It's the third *coup*. He has a chance."

"Hoo-ooh!" Miss Lyndon gave my arm an unintentional but painful pinch.

"What has happened?"

"Horn-Rims has turned up an eight—"

"And Lighter?"

"Nine!"

There came a muffled groan of sympathy from the spectators. "*Le coup de Landru!*" murmured a Frenchman beside me. Once more the croupier called the stake.

"The bank is getting big," I said. "Nearly eighty thousand francs. I fancy it will be a case of a little bit all round now. No one will tackle this bank single-handed."

But I was wrong.

"*Banco!*" said a hoarse, guttural voice.

"*Banco est fait,*" announced the croupier.

"Who is that?" I asked Corrie.

"Wait a minute: I can't see round this woman. Now I can. He has just sat down, with his back to us. I don't like the shape of his head. I think—I believe"—Corrie gave a wriggle of excitement—"Yes, it is! It is my admirer!"

"Flawn's Big Boy Friend?"

"Yes. And I hope he loses! There, I told you I was only a woman!"

"Has he drawn his cards?"

"Yes; and thrown them on the table."

"*Neuf—et cinq!*" announced the croupier composedly.

"That finishes Lighter," I said. But Corrie did not answer. She was engaged in an animated conversation with a total stranger on her other side. (This, I was to discover, was a habit of hers.) Presently she turned to me.

"He says that the Boy Friend is one of the famous Levantine Syndicate. He has been winning packets of money all the week. Let's stand behind him and see if we can put a curse on him."

But this admirable suggestion was frustrated. Across the room floated the voice of a *changeur*.

"*Table Numero Dix-Sept.*"

"Our table is starting," I said. "Come along!"

Corrie immediately forgot the Boy Friend.

"I'm all excited!" she announced, and fairly dragged me through the crowd.

II

Under my distinguished direction, Miss Lyndon seated herself in place Number Five, immediately opposite the croupier, and armed herself for the coming battle with a thousand francs' worth of chips. I squeezed a chair in beside her, on her right hand—at the table, but not of it.

"The *changeur* has given me ten big blue-and-yellow things," Corrie announced.

"Then give him two back, and ask for some red ones. We are only small timers at present."

The exchange was effected, and I asked:

"There should be a notice hung up about the *minimum du départ*. What does it say?"

"Three louis. What does that mean?"

"It means that you can't stake less than three louis at this table—sixty francs—when you take the bank. I would stick to that minimum for a bit, if I were you."

"I certainly will. I am not even going to punt until I have watched the game for a while."

"What sort of company are we in?" I asked.

"Quite presentable, compared with the top table."

"That is always the way at this game. The higher the stake the lower the type, and *vice versa*. A three louis table should be almost human. Describe them, please."

"A couple of grey-haired old Frenchmen, of the bourgeois type—"

"Beware of them. They usually draw to a five. Who else?"

"A woman who looks like Harry Lauder dressed as a barmaid," announced a hearty voice in my left ear, while a boisterous hand descended on my shoulder. Arturo had rejoined us. He took up the tale. "Item, a retired Major—a bottle-scarred veteran. Item, a man and his wife from Surbiton—"

"And two Casino blondes," continued Miss Lyndon.

"Thank you. Are you going to join us, Arturo?"

"No; your table's filled up. I am just cruising at present; Enid has gone home. I shall return later, Corrie, and torpedo one of your banks. Au revoir!"

He disappeared, with his usual abruptness, and Corrie and I settled down to the game which had just begun.

Play at first was quiet. It was obvious that no one at the table had very much money, and the banks when they ran were passed early. Corrie devoted herself chiefly to note-taking and pithy comment. Once, when a bank had run three times and the whole table were invited to "make their game," she adventured one red chip. The bank promptly won again, and the red chip was gathered up, to her unfeigned dolour, by a devastating palm-leaf shovel.

Presently the bank came round to her, for the first time, and on a word from me she staked three louis.

"Benko!" said a voice immediately on my right. (The gentleman from Surbiton, I gathered.)

The cards clicked from the shoe. Then:

"Another card, please!"

"Turn up your own first," I murmured to Corrie.

"They make five," she said.

"Give him his card, and stand on your five."

The next remark came from the croupier:

"*Sept—et cinq.*" A triumphant arm on my right reached across me and took the shoe.

"Better luck next time," I said. "Banks are doing badly so far. Some one will start a run presently, and then we shall see."

The man on my right—evidently they breed heroes in Surbiton—put up ten louis. But he fared no better than Corrie, and the bank slid on its way.

"Who has it now?" I asked.

"The First Blonde. She has put up one blue chip—all she seems to have. I hope she wins." Corrie, I began to note, was a loyal supporter of her own sex.

Her good wishes brought luck, for the bank ran three times. Then the First Blonde, through caution or panic, pushed the shoe from her.

"*La main passe*," announced the croupier. "*Un banco de trente-neuf louis.*"

"What does that mean?" Corrie asked me.

"Anybody can have the bank, out of his turn, for that amount. The price will come down, though."

I was right. Presently the croupier announced that the bank was "at auction." A dare-devil spirit descended upon me.

"Bid ten louis," I said to Corrie.

"*Dix louis!*" called Corrie bravely.

"*Quinze louis!*" said a high-pitched voice somewhere on my left. It was one of the Frenchmen.

"*Vingt!*" Corrie spoke for herself this time. Evidently her blood was up. There was a brief pause: then the croupier announced:

"*Ajugé a vingt louis.*"

"Now we've done it," I said. "Put up four blues."

"Heavens! All that?"

"Yes; but you stand to win as much. Now, what bids?"

"Benko!" This from Surbiton again. I heard the click-click of the shoe. "No more, thank you!" said an ominously satisfied voice.

"Turn your cards up, Corrie," I said. She did so, and gave a little gasp.

"*Neuf—et sept!*" announced the croupier unconcernedly. "*Un banco de trente-neuf louis.*"

"That's torn it," announced a rueful voice, and my right-hand neighbour pushed back his chair. "And I'll tell you another thing; this is a rotten seat, and I'm off. Come on, Gladys!"

He drifted away, receiving first-aid from his dutiful helpmate, but refusing to be comforted. Some one promptly took his place. At the same moment a voice opposite to us called "*Banco!*" It was the voice of Arturo, on his promised torpedoing expedition.

"Are you going to fight him, or pass the bank?" I asked Miss Lyndon.

"We're going to sink him at sight," replied my colleague firmly.

Click, click; click, click. Then:

"Sorry!" said the voice of Arturo.

"*Huit!*" announced the croupier, and I heard him raking up the money.

"Well, it's still in the family," said Corrie philosophically. She turned to me. "I only had a three. Our capital is getting a bit low."

"Never mind; the evening is early yet. Ah, the shoe is empty. This is where we all get up and stretch."

"I see—the seventh inning," remarked Corrie incomprehensibly. "Well, perhaps business will improve with a new shoe."

It did, but not for us. One or two of our opponents had moved elsewhere. Others eagerly took their places. The stakes began to increase; bidding became higher. Evidently our table was going up in the world. In addition to the

Surbiton contingent we had lost the company of the First Blonde, who had disappeared, overcome with Gallic chagrin at seeing her bank run again—for someone else. Their places had been taken by a naphthaline-scented lady (now on my right) and my friends Rex Fryer and Odo Lerwick, the honour of whose company I darkly attributed to the presence at the table of Miss Corrie Lyndon.

Meanwhile, Corrie herself had scraped acquaintance, in characteristic fashion, with her left-hand neighbour—the Second Blonde.

"She's such a nice little thing," she said to me, "and her luck has been terrible. She can't even afford to say '*banco!*' now when her turn comes."

"Is she French or English?" I asked.

"English—a young actress out of a job. I'm so sorry for her."

The seat on my right continued unlucky. Its latest occupant, who had steadily been staking single red chips with conspicuous lack of success, had now reached the limit of her fortitude. She rose with a dejected sigh, and drifted away, leaving in her wake a waft of frustrated naphthaline. Her place was immediately taken by a gentleman who had recently been refreshing himself with *crème de menthe*. For five minutes he said "*banco*" to everything, to the consistent profit of the bank; then, changing his tactics, bought the next bank for fifty louis. It went down at the first *coup* to Rex Fryer. The newcomer rose to his feet, with a sigh that fairly withered the table, and retired hurt to the bar, which he should never have left.

"That's a bad seat," said Corrie. "I'm glad we didn't pick it."

"There's one at every table," I said. "I wonder who will be the next victim."

The question was immediately answered. The chair was drawn back by an obsequious menial; someone was bowed into it—evidently some Casino god had condescended to visit the three louis region—and a heavy body deposited itself close beside me.

Meanwhile, Corrie was whispering to me again, in her eager, childish way:

"She wants to know if she can come in on my next bank." (The reference was apparently to her peroxide friend on the left.) "She thinks I have a lucky face. May I go halves with her?"

"Oh, yes, of course! Rather!" I was speaking mechanically, for I was half stunned. My thoughts were far away: they had flown back ten years, to a narrow, ill-lit staircase in a disreputable house in Cairo: I was locked in the embrace of a raging giant, and my senses were half drowned in the stale, sickly odour of ambergris. Now the giant was sitting composedly beside me, laying out innumerable chips. In other words, the Big Boy Friend and Mr. Manoukian were one and the same person. (I had been vaguely conscious of the fact when I winded him at the Normandie, but somehow it had failed to register in my mind. I suppose my thoughts were fully occupied in another direction.)

Anyhow, here he was in the flesh, having abandoned the top table and the Levantine Syndicate in order to sit near Corrie Lyndon. Well, I sat between them.

III

A bank had just gone down, and the croupier was paying out all round the table. I touched Corrie's arm. Her head came close to mine.

"Look who's here!" I said.

She leaned forward, then gave a little start. Manoukian, who was evidently on the *qui vive*, elected to take this as a gesture of welcome. He leaned heavily in front of me, and said:

"I hope fortune is being kind to you." He spoke perfect English. ("But Greek, Egyptian, or Armenian," I said to myself.) Corrie laughed lightly.

"It might be better," she replied.

"Would you like to come in with me on my next bank? I am a lucky man tonight."

"No, thank you. I should bring your bank down with a crash. As a partner I am the complete hoodoo."

"I am willing to risk all that. Just a louis or two?"

"No, thank you."

"Alas, then I must play alone! But if I make my fortune, I shall ask you to celebrate it with me later. A glass of wine at the buffet, perhaps?"

Now, under the easy etiquette of a Continental card-table any gentleman may invite a lady to join him in a bank, without offence. But if he follows up this overture by asking her to have a drink with him, it is quite plain that he does not regard her as a lady. I half rose from my chair. But Corrie was quite equal to the occasion. She gave me an imperceptible and sedative pat on the knee, then turned to the Second Blonde.

"Will you join me in my next bank?" she asked. "Something tells me that I am going to be lucky."

"Oh, thank you, dear!" said the girl gratefully.

It was a perfect rebuff. I chuckled, perhaps a little louder than was quite polite, and lit a cigar. The aroma of ambergris is apt to be a little overpowering at times.

As usual, the Second Blonde's own bank went down, smitten to the earth by Manoukian. (Corrie, of course, had refrained.) The croupier slid the shoe along to Corrie's left hand.

"Now give me that last old chip of yours," I heard her say, "and we'll teach it to grow!"

"*Un banco de dix louis,*" announced the croupier. Manoukian said nothing, but tapped it on the table.

"*Banco est fait.*"

Corrie dealt the cards.

"I am afraid I must ask for a third card," said Manoukian smoothly.

Corrie made no reply: the croupier spoke for her.

"*Huit à la banque!*"

"Well done!" said Manoukian. "*Suivi!*"

Again the cards clicked out.

"Once more I must trouble you."

"*Neuf à la banque,*" announced the croupier briefly. "*Un banco de trente-neuf louis.*"

"*Suivi!*" said Manoukian again.

Now, one of the first rules of *chemin-de-fer* is that you should not *suivi* overmuch, if at all. If you do, you are simply gambling against your own money. Yet here was a man from the top table, a shining light in the Levantine Syndicate, playing the game like a callow undergraduate. Plainly, these tactics were symbolical of something deeper. The fight was on, for a bigger stake than lay on the table. I bristled, prophetically.

We had reached the third *coup*—the critical *coup*. I said to Corrie:

"Are you going on?"

"I certainly am." She turned to her partner. "Would you like to get out now? If you like, I'll pay you what you have won."

"Oh, no. I'll stay with you, please."

"Fine!" Click, click; click, click.

This time Manoukian said nothing, but tapped on the table again in true professional style, indicating that he would stand. Corrie turned over her cards.

"Five," she said to me. "Shall I draw?"

"No; stand. I have a hunch."

"I will stand," said Corrie to Manoukian.

"*Egalité!*" announced the croupier a moment later.

There was a little flutter of interest all round the table. Evidently the personal nature of this particular encounter was making itself felt. Corrie dealt again.

"No more, thank you," said Manoukian.

Corrie's head came close to mine again.

"I've got another five," she said.

"Draw then. His hand will probably be better than last time."

Straightway Manoukian rose to his feet.

"I protest!" he said. "In all courtesy I protest—especially to the English ladies and gentlemen present at the table. This man here can look over my hand; yet he gives advice to the lady beside him."

A dispute in a casino attracts a crowd quicker than a street accident in London. In a moment a highly interested ring of spectators had gathered round our table—with them that ubiquitous and imperturbable genius, the *Chef du Casino*. Manoukian, with his veneer of gentility cracking in all directions, repeated his accusation, this time a little more dramatically. I felt almost sorry for him.

"This gentleman," replied the *Chef* icily, "is a well-known and esteemed *habitué* of the Casino. He has the great misfortune to be blind."

"His eyes were done in during the War—by some of your friends' poison-gas," added Odo Lerwick, whose day has never been entirely wasted if he has succeeded in turning a second-class row into a first-class row.

Manoukian, to do him justice, was quick to realise his blunder. He ignored Odo's brilliant flight of imagination, and turned to me.

"I apologise, monsieur," he said, "most sincerely." He sat down.

"That's all right," I said. "Now you'd better draw your card, Miss Lyndon."

Click!

"That makes me seven," said Corrie.

"*Bon!*" said Manoukian graciously.

"*Un banco de soixante dix-huit louis,*" chanted the croupier.

This time Manoukian had nothing to say. He had gone at the bank three times like a bull at a gate, out of pique. Now he sat back and waited: he had reverted to his Levantine Syndicate form. I felt in my bones that he meant to win this bank, but not until someone else besides himself had contributed to it.

Rex Fryer jumped in.

"I'll have a dash at you, Miss Lyndon," he said.

He took two cards, cried out to heaven—there is nothing secretive about his methods of play—and asked for a third. He received it with further symptoms of anguish. Corrie turned up a six, and Rex Fryer contributed sixteen hundred francs to the growing pool.

Next Odo Lerwick had a try, and went down in his turn. Then the bottle-scarred veteran and the lady who looked like Harry Lauder formed a syndicate. Again the bank won. Then came a pause: no one would bid.

"*Faites vos jeux, messieurs et dames.*"

"*Banco!*" said a nasal voice, from among the spectators this time. We had accumulated a gallery as large as the top table.

"*Banco est fait—debout.*"

"Who is this?" I asked Corrie.

"Horn-Rims, from the top table."

"Are you going to stand up to him?"

"I run this bank until it crashes."

"Bravo!" There followed the rustle of *mille* notes, as Horn-Rims laid down his stake, then the click of the shoe. Then the nasal voice again.

"I guess that scoops it."

"*Huit*," added the croupier.

"*Et neuf!*" replied Corrie calmly. The table gave a murmur of gratification: one always likes to see outside punters discomfited.

The *mille* notes were swept into the pile, and the croupier issued his usual invitation. Manoukian was leaning forward with folded arms, all alert. I could feel him. But he made no move.

"*Faites vos jeux*," said the croupier, and I heard chips and paper raining down all round the table. Evidently the public had decided—as the public always does—that the bank must come down this time. I touched Corrie's arm.

"Say '*Rien ne va plus*,'" I murmured. "Safety first!"

Corrie obeyed, and the croupier repeated her warning. The rain ceased. She dealt the cards, and I heard the croupier shovel them up. Then—

"*A vous, monsieur.*"

There was a long pause. Evidently the cards had been handed to someone who could not make up his mind what to do with them. A novice, probably, who happened to have put up the largest stake. At last he spoke:

"*Nong!*"

"Six," said Corrie.

"Five," replied the voice, in a tone which apologised to the entire table. There was an indignant murmur, while the croupier raked in chips all round.

"Why are they so angry with the poor little man?" Corrie asked me.

"When you draw for the table in general you *must* draw to a five. However, that's his funeral: you're on velvet now. You'll have a big *bénéfice*, whatever happens."

"*Un banco*," announced the indefatigable croupier, having separated Corrie's permanent from her precarious winnings, "*de trente-deux mille francs. Faites vos—*"

"*Banco!*" It was Horn-Rims again, throwing good money after bad. But Manoukian sat up.

"*A table!*" he snapped.

"*Banco à table*," said the croupier.

The crowd pressed closer. They had long realised that this was a fight between Corrie and the Levantine Syndicate.

Once more, with absolute coolness, Corrie played out the cards. Manoukian picked his up.

"Another, if you please," he said.

Click! There came an interested murmur from all round the table. Corrie turned to me.

"My hand makes six," she said. "I stand, of course?"

"What have you given him?"

"A six as well."

"Then you must draw."

"To a six?"

"Yes. It's a cruel thing to have to do, but it's your only chance. You're almost certain to have given him a better hand than yours, now."

"Very well."

Click...! I did not need to ask who had won the *coup*, for the crowd almost cheered. They were pro-Corrie to a man.

"*Huit—et sept!*" proclaimed the croupier above the babble. "*Un banco de—*"

But louder still rose the half-hysterical utterance of the Second Blonde.

"I can't bear any more, dear! Let's get out."

"Why, certainly," said Corrie cheerfully. "*La main passe.*"

Ah! The long tension was over. The crowd began to drift away. The croupier raked in Manoukian's final contribution, and issued a direction to the *changeur*. The *changeur* produced a large lacquer wooden bowl—that bowl is a dream which comes true perhaps once in a gambler's life, and more often never—and I heard them piling it high with chips and paper.

"Tip the croupier and *changeur*," I said, "and we'll take this over to the *caisse* at once."

"*Merci bien, madame!*"

"*Merci bien, madame!*" Evidently the tip had been a characteristic one.

We rose from our chairs. There was a rush for Corrie's, but Manoukian was there first. He went over my toes like a tank in action. Next moment he was bidding for Corrie's bank, which was at auction.

"*Cinquante!*" he said, and the bank was his—at last.

Then Corrie committed the crowning audacity of her first (and last) venture as a gambler.

"*Banco!*" she said, and I heard her draw a *mille* note from the bowl and lay it on the table.

"*Huit!*" said Manoukian.

"*Et neuf!*" said Corrie for the last time. "Come along, Barry!"

IV

A polite but entirely unimpressed gentleman at the *caisse* added up the pile in the bowl. It came to about seventy-five thousand francs or, at the current rate of exchange, something over six hundred pounds. He made a bundle of the *mille* notes, and began to pay out on the chips.

"You can't take all this home with you," I said to Corrie. "The Casino people had better give you a cheque for it in the morning—or, rather, two cheques."

"It doesn't seem right, my taking *any* of it!" said the Second Blonde. "I couldn't have won a bean without you tonight, dear. It seems a shame."

"Listen," said Corrie—and there was a curious note of diffidence, almost nervousness, in her voice. "About this money—I should hate—you see, I don't have to earn my own—" She led the girl out into a corner, and a conversation ensued, to which I did not listen.

When they returned the Second Blonde was sobbing, openly and wholeheartedly—the incredulous, rapturous tears of one who has not hitherto realised that angels may occasionally walk this earth.

"It's a fortune!" she was saying, evidently not for the first time.

"A very small one, I'm afraid."

"If you only knew. That was my last hundred francs in the world! If it hadn't been for you— Well, anyhow, God bless you, dear! I can go home now—and by myself! Is there any place," she added inconsequently, "in this old Casino where I can give you a kiss?"

"I'll go and get my hat and coat," I said, and departed forthwith.

Corrie found me ten minutes later.

"Arturo's car is outside," she said. "I'll drive you home in it; he can hire something."

"Have you said good-bye to your little friend?" I asked.

"Yes. She told me all about herself; and—I think that bowl of chips came along at a very fortunate moment. She goes back to London tomorrow morning. I'm ever so grateful to you for steering us through that game."

"And what have you got out of it?" I inquired sternly.

"This." Corrie handed me something round and smooth. "That's the original five louis chip which started the famous bank. She said I must take it for a souvenir. You keep it for me."

I slipped it into my pocket. It is there still.

V

Fate had a final adventure in store for us that night. We were in Arturo's two-seater, and Corrie was on the point of slipping in her gears, when a suave voice emerged from the cool darkness a few feet away.

"Good night, Miss Lyndon. Am I to have my opportunity for revenge tomorrow night?"

Was the fellow entirely unsnubbable? I had been simmering all evening, and now I boiled right over.

"No, you are not," I said. "And good night to you—Mr. Manoukian!"

There was a moment of tense silence. I could almost hear his great frame stiffen. Then Corrie's foot came down upon the accelerator and we raced towards the gates.

Presently we were running homeward along the smooth straight road through the forest. The smell of the pines was cool and sweet, and Corrie was close beside me. I stretched luxuriously. I had almost forgotten Manoukian.

"Tired?" asked Corrie.

"No; I feel unusually wide awake. I have had an eventful day—eventful and instructive."

"Instructive?"

"Yes. I have learned a lot about your character in the last twelve hours, and more still in the last two."

"Good, or bad?"

"Both. You are a spendthrift. On the other hand, you have even greater courage than I thought."

"I shall need it all," remarked Corrie with feeling, "if ever I find myself alone in a dark alley with Mr. Manoukian. And so will you. You should have seen his face when you called him by his name!"

CHAPTER 9

HANDS OFF SPARGO

"What sort of time did you have at Le Touquet last week?" asked Sir Gavin.

"Eventful. Eventful and amusing. We had quite a thrill, in fact."

"We? Were any of my precious family mixed up in it?"

"Only indirectly. Miss Lyndon took a leading part, though."

"Oh, that young lady! I was sorry to miss her. Her father was a great-hearted fellow."

"Some virtues seem to be hereditary," I said.

"This sounds interesting. Go ahead with your story."

My uncle, having lit his pipe, subsided into his armchair on the other side of the fire-place, and remained motionless while I told him the tale of the duel at the tables. To make my narrative more intriguing I kept back Manoukian's name until the finish. The mention of it when it came certainly succeeded in its purpose. Sir Gavin gave a sharp exclamation.

"Manoukian? You're certain?"

"Positive." And I gave my reasons. "Besides," I added, "I fairly knocked him out when I addressed him by name. Miss Lyndon said he looked like blue murder."

"You told him you knew him? You infernal young idiot!"

"It wasn't a very bright thing to do," I admitted; "but I was feeling pretty mad at the moment, and I wanted to get under his skin. Anyhow, the thing is done. Now, tell me more about Manoukian. I know he's on your list. What has he been up to lately? He dropped out of my young life after that evening in Cairo."

"Wait a minute and I will refresh my memory. I have his dossier somewhere." My uncle rose and went into a corner. I heard the creak of a safe door, then the rustle of papers. Presently he returned and sat down again.

"Here we are," he said.

"By the way," I asked, "what is Manoukian's nationality?"

"Nobody knows; but I should say he was fundamentally Greek, with a dash of Egyptian and Armenian thrown in. He's a protean customer. When he had that rough-and-tumble with you in Cairo he was in the German Intelligence Service, and most efficient."

"So I thought at the time. What is his real name?"

"That I don't know either. He was known in Egypt as Manoukian, in Germany as Herbrand. Of course, as one of their spies, he had a number, too; I've got it down here. After the war he was in Ireland for some years, under the official style of Captain de Courcy, successfully complicating an already difficult situation. When we booted him out of that distressful country he betook himself to Russia, which is, of course, his spiritual home. There I think he must have remained, for we have heard little or nothing of him since. I wonder if his presence on this side of Europe has anything to do with Spargo's friendly call."

"Is Manoukian a member of the Dodekadelphi?"

"No. He has many gifts, but he can hardly claim to be a man of letters. He has a persuasive tongue, though. I wonder what it all means." Sir Gavin gathered up the papers and returned them to the safe, then sat down again. "This sudden appearance of all these people—Spargo, Manoukian, Flawn! It looks to me like a regular gathering of the vultures, for some dark business or other. What did he call himself at Le Touquet? Not that it matters."

"I never heard; but we could find out. He was in the company of Flawn and a lady called Lil Montgomery. The Casino people must have been satisfied with his credentials, otherwise he would not have got into the Salle de Baccara."

"Oho! He was with a lady, was he? His old failing!"

"What do you mean?"

"Ladies are his—what shall we say?—his heel of Achilles. That is why he is not higher up in his profession. Years ago he gave away an official secret to a woman in Budapest, and nearly caused a Balkan war. Another time he dallied in Madrid for a week, courting a lady when he ought to have been undermining a throne, whereby a revolution was indefinitely postponed. That is where Spargo scores: he never allows himself to be lured by any bright eyes from the path of duty."

"I ought to say, in common justice to Manoukian, that in this case the lady appeared to be with someone else."

"Ah! Perhaps advancing years have taught him sense. That will make him all the more dangerous. Anyhow, I will make inquiries at Le Touquet about him. Meanwhile I have to report to you that I have been getting after your friends of the Mayfair Movies."

"And what have you discovered?"

"Nothing. The Company is not registered; it appears to consist entirely of a door-plate and Mr. Flawn. Moreover, the offices, when visited by one of my young men, were found to be closed up tight. The door-plate was gone, and so was Flawn."

"He was at Le Touquet, of course."

"Yes; but we didn't know that then. The landlord said that the Company had moved elsewhere—to larger premises, not specified."

"I wonder where the new premises are?"

"Nowhere, I should say. Flawn took that office for the time being, partly as a London *pied-à-terre* for his associates and partly to ensnare a few harmless but necessary adjuncts to his plans like Alf Noseworthy. Probably G.H.Q. has been shifted to the Studio now."

"It would be interesting to know what has become of Edna Butterick," I said.

"That is just what I wanted to ask you. She may lead somewhere. Have you her address?"

"No. Our interviews invariably took place under a tree in Kensington Gardens."

"Romantic, but unbusinesslike. Never mind! Obviously, the next thing we must do is to locate this mysterious Studio. Can you tell me whereabouts in Essex it is?"

"No; just Essex. That was all Alf knew or ever told me."

"Of course it may not be in Essex at all. If they are as anxious to cover their tracks as they seem to be, why should they let slip a gratuitous piece of information like that? Did Alf mention how long it took to drive there?"

"Not so far as I remember. But here is a letter which he sent me." I brought it from my pocket and handed it over. Sir Gavin skimmed through it.

"*Driven there by night in a closed car....Driven back in the same car the same night.* Nothing of any use here. I see he adds that he *would greatly appreciate the honour of a short interview with you on your return.* What about that?"

"I wrote to his address, but had no reply. He's probably at the Studio again."

"Certainly, I should say. And I don't suppose they'll let him out until they've done with him—or for him!"

I sat up.

"You mean poor old Alf is in danger of some kind?"

"I'm sure of it. There's a big plot building up at the back of all this, only I can't get the pieces to fit together yet. First of all, we have Flawn engaging Alf for some mysterious job in the depths of the country, which calls for the service of a skilled electrician. Then we find Flawn in association with Manoukian, who is an international spy and agitator of the most dangerous description. Finally, we have the present hullabaloo over the arrest of Spargo, who is also associated with Flawn, and through Flawn with Manoukian. And you had to go and put Manoukian on his guard! You're a nice diplomat!"

"There is a hullabaloo on, then?" I asked, tactfully diverting the conversation.

"Deafening. You remember, I said there would be."

"You did. What exactly has happened since Spargo's arrest? I have been out of touch with London news."

"Spargo was brought up at Bow Street on the Tuesday after Easter, where the magistrate licensed him for trial in the United States of America; then formally notified the Home Secretary of the fact."

"And has Spargo been shipped to America yet?"

"No. You can't hustle the Law like that in this country. The next move lies with the Home Secretary, who must give an undertaking for Spargo's surrender to the American Ambassador. But a period of fifteen days' grace has to elapse before Spargo is actually handed over. During that time he has the right to pick holes in the indictment—sing a song of Habeas Corpus, and all that. A first-class scrap has been in progress all the week. Our chief difficulty is that Spargo claims to be a naturalised Russian, and declares we can't hand him over to America without the consent of the Russian Government. Normally he would be within his rights there; but as we have severed all diplomatic relations with Russia for the time being, the question does not arise. However, his friends aren't relying on legal niceties; they know that an ounce of sentiment is worth a hundredweight of law. It's the great heart of the British public they're after, and the propaganda machine is working overtime. Capital stuff, some of it."

"What form does it take?"

"The form I predicted—outraged virtue. One of the world's intellectual protagonists thrown into a prison cell by a Capitalistic Government on a trumped up criminal charge! Have you seen the papers this morning?"

"My mother reads me the political summary, the sporting news, and the Service promotions."

"Then you have missed something good today. It comes in the Correspondence. Listen!"

I heard the crackling of a weighty and important sheet; then Sir Gavin read:

"*Sir,*

"*I am no politician, but I claim to be a man of letters; and as a man of letters I call upon all true lovers of intellectual freedom to band together and frustrate the outrage now in course of perpetration upon that great, almost divine figure, Emanuel Spargo.*"

"Who wrote this?"
"I'll tell you in a minute.

"*That such a man—the lifelong foe of war, bloodshed and violence of every kind—should be indicted upon a charge of taking human life would be humorous if it were not so pathetic. The motive of the application for his extradition is clear: the blazing searchlight of his intellect has flashed once too often upon the dark places of the social and political life of England and America. Spargo is making the world unsafe for Bureaucracy: therefore Spargo must be silenced. But how? You cannot throw a man into prison for speaking the Truth and preaching the Gospel of Progress. If you did so, some few unimportant but not altogether despicable persons might object, might cry out, might make things awkward at the next General Election. No! This saintly figure must first of all be smirched, must first of all be branded with some stigma which all men will reprobate. So Emanuel Spargo is accused of murder—murder!—in an obscure town in a remote corner of the United States, and his enemies are now combining to smuggle him away, out of the reach of such protection as the intelligent public opinion of this country can afford him, to be handed over to the refinements of Mob Law five thousand miles away. Sir, is Emanuel Spargo to be taken from beneath the sure shield of the Union Jack and thrown to the wolves at the bidding of the American Ambassador? In other words, is this a civilised country or is it not?"*

"And what do you think of that?" inquired Uncle Gavin.

"The real heart-stuff. Who wrote it?"

"Laxley Spooner." (Laxley Spooner is one of the most enlightened and progressive of our modern school of sociological novelists, and controls a large and rather hysterical public.) "Don't you like that bit about the sure shield of the Union Jack? That was probably what did the trick, and got the letter accepted by this steady-going old journal. And more than that: it has evoked a leading article—something very moderate and statesmanlike, of course, but a leading article—about our ancient tradition of never denying the right of asylum to sincere though misguided critics of existing political institutions, whatever their nationality. He's a nasty little sedition-monger, is Spooner, but as clever as a monkey. He invokes the Union Jack, and actually gets this old paper to sit on the fence in the matter of Spargo! Here's another effusion, in another organ of more advanced views."

"Who wrote this one?"

"Desmond Aynho."

"The dramatist?"

"So he alleges."

"What does he say?"

"He pitches it shorter and stronger.

"If our Mandarins sincerely desire to crucify Emanuel Spargo, let them at least have the common honesty to charge him with the crime that he has actually committed—the crime of creating a

breach in the ramparts of Privilege—and let him stand his trial on that charge, at the hands of a British Jury. Desmond Aynho taking off his hat to a British Jury now! *But there must be no lynch law; no 'lettre de cachet.' Above all, Spargo must not be sent from this country to certain martyrdom.*

You see, Barry—martyrdom! I told you about our national weakness for martyrs. These two intellectual crooks know all about it, too, and they're playing right up to it."

"Isn't it possible that they may be quite sincere in this case? Perhaps they do honestly admire Spargo—for his brains, we'll say. After all, they don't know about his other activities."

"Not know? My dear boy, let me tell you something. Spooner and Aynho are both members of the Dodekadelphi—and in this business up to the neck! These letters are the first shot in a gigantic campaign by the Intellectuals to get Spargo off. It's not his brains they admire; it's his—other attribute. They can't do without him; he's indispensable to them. They plot murder in a high-minded, benevolent, love-your-neighbour sort of way—and Spargo carries it out."

"Personally?"

"He has been the direct instigator of five brutal political murders in the last seven years. Two of them, I believe, he committed with his own hand; only it was never brought home to him. But in the Butte case we have got the goods on him. Not that that will save us from a rumpus. I am afraid Labour—the honest, chivalrous, chuckle-headed section, and it runs into millions—will be bamboozled into investing him with a martyr's crown. Note the invocation of the Union Jack and the British Jury. Not a whisper of subversive doctrine there! There is to be a mass meeting and a procession to Hyde Park on Sunday—they are to be held all over the country, for that matter—and already there is talk of a universal strike for forty-eight hours, as a great national gesture of horror and reprobation of our infamous conduct."

"What earthly good can that do?"

"I'll tell you what it can do. It can paralyse intercommunication throughout the whole country for a definite period. Within that period an immense amount of efficient *sabotage* can be put over. A national panic might possibly be started. The police and troops can't be everywhere, especially if the telegraph and telephone are out of commission and all transport suspended. And of course the people at the back of all this don't intend to stop after forty-eight hours. They will try to do this time what they failed to do in the General Strike last year. If they can make a good start they will follow up their success hot and strong; and the honest, martyr-worshipping working man will realise his mistake too late. Of course, if the Government can keep in touch with the country we shall be all right; but isolation for more than a day or so will be serious."

"They can still broadcast."

"Yes, thank God, they can still do that. Meanwhile, I should very much like to know two things. Perhaps you can help me there."

"What are the two things?"

"First, where is this Studio of Alf Noseworthy's? There's dirty work going on inside it, I'm certain. The place may be an arsenal, a bomb factory, or anything of that kind. Second, I want to know what has become of Manoukian. He's here in Western Europe on business. That business may have been hung up by Spargo's arrest, and in that case it is possible that Manoukian will come to London and lend a hand with the present agitation. If he does, I want to get my hands on him. While we are on the subject, I should advise you to accept police protection, my boy. Manoukian owes you something, and he has the reputation of paying debts of that kind in full. In fact, he may come over here solely on your account."

As Sir Gavin spoke it occurred to me that Manoukian might come over for a different reason altogether—a much stronger and more intelligible reason. But I kept my own counsel. Had I been a little less reticent, or less self-conscious, this narrative might have taken a different course. But there are certain secrets that one does not communicate—even to the official recipient of such things.

CHAPTER 10

THE DAY OF REST

London on a Sunday morning not only sounds different; it smells different.

On a weekday, as I perform my matutinal breathing exercises at my open window, I am usually greeted by the mingled odours of asphalt and petrol-vapour and the steady roar of traffic from Fulham Road, half a mile away. Not that London is an unduly noisy place at any time. While it is the vastest it is also the least blatant of cities. The Englishman appears to be the only motorist in the world who has realised that it does not help in the least to blow one's horn in crowded traffic. Stand in the Green Park about six o'clock on an autumn evening, when the Piccadilly river is running at its swiftest, and you might almost be in Venice.

But on Sunday morning I awaken to a new world. Nothing can be heard save an occasional church bell or the clatter of a milk wagon, and the thin twittering of the birds in the Square garden. You can even catch an occasional and distant bugle-call from Chelsea Barracks. You have a feeling that if anyone were to scratch a match on Cleopatra's Needle you would hear that too. Eight million people—and not a sound!

And there is an entirely new selection of smells—smells which only travel on quiet days. Their nature depends on the state of the wind. Sometimes I can sniff the scent of hawthorn blossom, coming from some garden close by. When the wind is in the south-west I am conscious of the riverside—gas, and coke, and brewery hops, with perhaps a whiff or two from the cargo of a barge moored somewhere for the duration of the Sabbath. And occasionally, on a very clear day, when the wind is in the east, I am conscious of the pungent, not unpleasant, aroma of tan-bark, all the way from the tanyards of Bermondsey.

On this particular Sunday in June I was up early—early for Sunday, that is. I felt no desire to stay in bed. Night and day mean nothing to Us, but I can always tell when the sun is shining. I breakfasted alone—my mother had gone to Torquay to visit her only sister—and I was in Kensington Gardens by eleven o'clock.

On my way I encountered my friend Beelby, P.C., sunning himself at the corner of our connecting street and Queen's Gate.

"Sunday duty?" I inquired sympathetically.

"It's Sunday duty for most of us today, sir. Those that aren't on point duty in the ordinary way, like me, are warned for the special goings-on this afternoon."

"This afternoon?"

"Yes, sir. This Bolshie procession. Some of us has got to go and walk with them—walk with 'em in this sun, all the way from the Embankment to the Marble Arch—keeping 'em in line like a lot of kids and preventing decent people from throwing 'alf-bricks at them! A lot more of us have to stand by in our stations all afternoon, in case of trouble. And they call this the day of rest!"

"I take it you are not a supporter of the Communistic movement?"

"I'd like to give the whole crowd of 'em a pint of rat-poison apiece," replied Beelby simply. "I suppose you aren't going to the Park this afternoon, sir?"

"No fear! Wild horses wouldn't drag me there. Is there going to be a big crowd?"

"The biggest ever, we're told. And all over a fellow that ought to have been turned off at Pentonville years ago! Good morning, sir."

Noting with satisfaction the comfortingly reactionary attitude of the Force towards subversive propaganda, I continued on my way to Kensington Gardens, and presently found myself under my usual tree. The place was very quiet and the morning was warm. I lit my pipe and sat day-dreaming....

"Might I speak a word to you, sir?"

I sat up.

"Good morning, Miss Butterick. I had a sort of feeling that I might meet you here today."

"You've been abroad, sir, haven't you? Alf told me you would be away until after Easter."

"Yes; I only got back three days ago. How is Alf? I want him."

"I haven't seen him or heard of him for nearly a fortnight, sir." Edna Butterick's cheerful little Cockney voice was troubled.

"I say, that's bad luck. Where is he? At the Studio?"

"Yes, sir; he's at the Studio all right. All wrong, I mean! He went off there suddenly, just before Easter—and not a word since!"

"Perhaps they have some rule against correspondence at the Studio. Trade secrets, and so on. Have you asked Mr. Flawn about him?"

"Mr. Flawn's gone too, sir. He told me on the Thursday before Good Friday that I needn't come back till Tuesday. I've been back every day since then, and found the office closed each time." Miss Butterick drew her chair nearer mine. "I'm getting frightened about Alf, sir; I don't mind telling you. It isn't as if I even knew where that Studio was. That's why I came along here: I've been every day for a week, waiting for you. I thought you might be able to advise me."

"I wish I could," I said; "but, to be frank, I came here today on the off-chance of being able to get you to advise me."

"Then we're both a pair of no-uses," remarked Miss Butterick despondently. "What's more, it looks as if I was out of a job again. And with Alf gone—"

And then I heard the voice of Corrie Lyndon, a few feet away.

"Here he is, Nigel. Now, what prize do I get as the Original Girl Scout?"

I rose, my heart bumping foolishly, with extended hand. Corrie shook it first, then Master Nigel. After that, I presented Edna Butterick.

"I'll buzz off now," observed the latter formally.

"Don't go," said Corrie. "I expect you and Captain Shere were talking about Alf Noseworthy."

The laws of etiquette having been duly observed, Edna sat down again willingly enough, and, evidently realising that here was a receptive spirit, got to work on Corrie at once. She gabbled in a steady undertone, growing more and more confidential as she proceeded, for the space of five minutes, helped out by sympathetic noises from Corrie. Meanwhile, Nigel and I made conversation.

"We came to ask if you would like to join us at the Bolshie circus in Hyde Park this afternoon," said Nigel presently. "There'll be bands and banners and a good deal of hot air, and perhaps a scrap or two. Corrie and I and Arturo are going. Are you on?"

I forgot all about the wild horses I had just mentioned to P.C. Beelby.

"Rather!" I said—"if I shan't be in your way."

"Don't be an old ass."

Corrie's voice was audible again: she was bidding farewell to Edna.

"And I was talking to the manager of the Bank of Montreal, on Regent Street," she was saying, "only yesterday; and he told me that he was at his wits' end for a good stenographer. I'll warn him about you before you get snapped up."

"Thank you kindly, Miss Lyndon. Good morning. Good morning, Captain!" and Edna Butterick took her departure, obviously inspired with that new outlook on things in general which comes to those who meet Corrie Lyndon for the first time.

"Corrie," announced Nigel, "old Barry is all for it this afternoon. We'd better take him home to lunch now, and sally forth in a body afterwards—what?"

"I'm sorry," I said, "I'm lunching out."

"Where?"

"With two theatrical friends of mine—Hal Horner and his wife."

"It's all right, Corrie," remarked Nigel reassuringly: "I've seen the wife. Where do they live, Barry?"

"Knightsbridge."

"Righto. I'll roll up in a taxi and fetch you about three. We must see this business through. England has need of us."

II

Sunday lunch at Hal Horner's is a feast which can be (and usually is) consumed by any number of persons. Hal and Maudie are an intensely domestic pair in their off-hours, and the nucleus of the gathering is invariably furnished by a solid phalanx of relatives from both sides of the house. Then come colleagues from the theatre, with perhaps a trio of golfers who propose later in the afternoon to repair with Hal to Wimbledon Park. Throw in a few professional friends down on their luck, a jockey, a professional cricketer, and a stray Cabinet Minister, and you have a gathering fairly representative of Hal's idea of a sociable Sabbath.

On this occasion there were about fourteen of us. At least, I was introduced to that number; there may have been more. To judge from the babble of voices and the thunder of the cocktail-shakers there may have been a hundred.

Luncheon started at last. (Actors, who have to be the most punctual folk alive in the exercise of their profession, are apt to be a little oblivious of time when off duty.) Maudie installed me at her right hand, and helped me liberally to cold salmon and hock. The seat upon my other side was occupied by a radiant young creature—I could almost feel the radiance—a member of a newly-imported American musical comedy, who confided to me that she was just crazy about our historic capital, and proposed on the morrow to "eat" at the "Old Chestershire Cheese," right in "Ben Johnstone's" chair.

"I suppose you didn't get away for Easter?" I said to Maudie, when I had a chance to speak to her.

"No. The show only closed for Good Friday, and we had *matinées* on Saturday and Monday. Where did you go, Captain?"

"Le Touquet. By the way, I met a friend of yours there. Or rather, I was close beside her more than once. Miss Lil Montgomery."

"Lil? You mean to say she didn't speak to you?"

"No."

"That's funny. You made a great hit with her that night in Hal's dressing-room. You see, you remembered her in 'The Banana Girl,' and that was more than ten years ago. I don't believe she's had a job since, poor thing. I'm surprised she didn't make herself known to you again."

"Perhaps she had her own friends to look after."

Maudie made a disapproving noise. "Was she with that Flawn?"

"So I was told."

"I don't like him. I don't trust— What's that, Sam?" The faithful one had inserted himself between us, and was whispering hoarsely and ceremoniously into Maudie's right ear. I turned to my other neighbour.

"Are you going to watch our Revolutionaries walking out this afternoon?" I asked.

"I should say not. We got a big enough bunch of those stiffs back in N'York. Hal and Maudie are taking me riding in their automobile, out to their country home."

"At Maidenhead? You'll enjoy that. Make Hal take you on the river; but don't let him handle a punt-pole, or you'll lose him for a certainty."

Here Maudie interposed.

"You're wanted on the telephone, Captain," she said, "by a lady. And who do you think she is?"

"I don't know, I'm sure."

"The boy knows, but won't tell," remarked my other neighbour.

"Well, you'll never guess. It's Lil—Lil Montgomery! Speak of angels!"

"How does she know I'm here?"

"I may have mentioned it to her the other day; I saw her on Thursday. The phone is in my bedroom; I know you won't mind. Sam will show you the way."

Presently I found myself sitting on Maudie's bed, speaking into an instrument encumbered by chiffon frills.

"Hallo!" I said. "Miss Montgomery?"

"Speaking. Is that Captain Shere?"

"Yes. How do you do?"

But Miss Montgomery was in no mood for social punctilio.

"Listen," she said rather breathlessly. "I've only got a minute or two alone. Take care of yourself. You understand? Look out for yourself!"

"What on earth do you mean?"

"What I say. Look out for yourself! Do you get that?"

"Yes. But—do you mean that—that someone is looking out for me?"

"Yes, that's it. And not only you. He's after her as well—her most of all!"

I was all agog now; there was no need to ask who "he" was—or who "her" was, for that matter.

"Where is he?" I asked eagerly. "In England? In London? And where are you speaking from? Tell me where I can—"

"Number, please?" said a brisk voice.

I uttered a furious exclamation.

"You've cut me off!" I shouted. "Put me back again—quick!"

"Sorry you were disconnected," said the voice placidly. "What number were you—?"

"How on earth do I know? Get it! No—get off the line, and let me hang up! She'll call me again."

But the summons came no more. Evidently Lil Montgomery had shot her bolt; perhaps she had been interrupted. But the bolt had found its mark, and a pretty commotion it had created in the heart of the target.

I returned to Hal's festal board. Fortunately Master Nigel had arrived to take charge of me; in fact, he was occupying my seat, engaged in affectionate dalliance with the young lady from the transatlantic musical comedy.

"He'll be around again presently," I heard her say. "He's just left us, to fix a date with a girl on the phone. No, here he is. Captain, you're looking all blue. Did she fall down on you? Is the date busted?"

Amid such amiable pleasantries as this we took our departure. Hal, having presented me, as a parting souvenir, with a cigar of pantomimic dimensions, accompanied us down the lift in person, regaling us on the way with an improbable anecdote about a man who went to sleep in a Ford car. Presently we climbed into the waiting taxi and drove off.

"Arturo and Corrie are going to meet us in the Park," said Nigel.

"Where?"

"At Gussie's pitch."

Gussie, I should explain, is one of the permanent features of Hyde Park on a Sunday afternoon. He is an elderly gentleman in a panama hat, with a deep-rooted and vehement grievance against the Government of this country. What that grievance is no one has ever been able to discover, for Gussie has never yet succeeded in arriving at the point of his indictment. He takes so long over his introductory tirade, and wastes so much time in rebuking interrupters, that the aim and essence of his oration are to this day wrapped in mystery. He has been there for years. He always speaks from the same spot and at the same hour—three-thirty sharp—and he always employs the same form of words. This is unfortunate, because it has enabled the more regular members of his audience to get some of Gussie's most characteristic passages by heart, which they are accustomed to chant (sometimes in a humorously perverted form) in unison with him, or possibly a bar or two ahead of him—a proceeding which entirely robs Gussie's points of the elements of suspense or surprise, and goads their exponent to senile fury. Nigel and I often spend an hour on Sunday afternoons listening to the Hyde Park orators, and we seldom fail to allot five minutes of our time to Gussie.

My answer to Nigel's announcement was quite mechanical. I hardly heard it. Lil Montgomery's words had thrown me into a fever of anxiety. If only I could have found out from her where Manoukian was! Supposing, as was more than likely, that he was here in London, he might be in the park today. Supposing an organised riot were started round the spot where Corrie was standing? Supposing Manoukian and a bodyguard of hooligans succeeded in hustling her into a quiet corner? Supposing—?

I stopped short, and pulled myself up. My fears were running away with me. We were in the heart of sleepy, peaceful, law-abiding London, on a Sunday afternoon in June. True, a seditious demonstration had been planned, and there might be disorder; but the London police understand these matters like no one else. They would escort the demonstrators to their appointed place, allow them to fulminate to their heart's content, and then lead them tenderly back to the place whence they came. London—an infinitesimal part of London—would have a boisterous but diverting afternoon, and that was all. But I registered a grim determination that as soon as I reached Corrie's side I would stay there. I meant also to stay near a policeman. To kidnap a London policeman in broad daylight in Hyde Park is a difficult feat.

The taxi stopped.

"We've got to wait until a procession goes past," explained Nigel.

"What are they like?"

"Quite a stout crowd, really—working men in their Sunday clothes, with rather amusing banners and sashes. Some of them are wearing war medals."

"The salt of the earth," I said. "I'd take off my hat to them, if I wasn't afraid that the gesture might be intercepted by a Bolshie."

"It's pretty sickening, all the same, to see them in a show like this," grumbled Nigel.

"Oh, it's not so bad as all that. Of course, it's a pity in a way, because they have so many real and legitimate grievances of their own that one hates to see them alienating the sympathy of the community by doing other people's dirty work. On the other hand, they're not of the riotous kind; they'll act as a counter-weight to the hired riff-raff from east of Aldgate pump."

The taxi moved on again towards the Marble Arch. Here a bored but friendly policeman intimated to us that we must get out and walk.

"All space in the Park reserved for distinguished foreign guests this afternoon," he explained.

I took Nigel's arm and we joined the steady stream that was pouring through the gates.

"The Park seems pretty full," I said.

"Absolutely chock-a-block. All the usual Sunday afternoon lot—citizens with wives and babies and perambulators; shop-boys and their flapper friends; the usual mob of cranks spouting away under the trees; and about a million Spargoites on top of that."

"Tell me the minute you catch sight of Corrie and Arturo."

"All right, old man."

"Is Gussie functioning?"

"I can see him over there, standing on his little mineral water case; but I don't think he has begun yet. He's waiting for the procession to get past; they're bound for the open ground behind the trees. There's a ring of twelve platforms arranged for them, with a lovely red flag flying over each."

We made our way slowly past the row of speakers under the trees, the habitués of the place—all discoursing furiously, and most of them quite unintelligible. They are a strange race, these Hyde Park orators. Some are professional propagandists, hired to exploit a political or religious fashion of the moment; others are obvious eccentrics with an *idée fixe*; but the majority are inarticulate, complex-ridden, rather pathetic gropers, suffering from suppressed grievances and suppressed enthusiasms, to whom a wise law has granted free speech as a safety-valve and Hyde Park as a place in which to blow off steam.

Their audiences today did not seem to be so large as usual; the Hands-off-Spargo demonstration was proving a potent counter-attraction. Still a fair crowd surrounded our friend Gussie, and I noted that his well-trained choir of tormentors were all present and in good voice.

Nigel and I had now reached our rendezvous—a beech tree close to Gussie's rostrum. Corrie and Arturo had not yet arrived, so I propped myself upon my shooting-stick and lit Hal's cigar. Gussie was just embarking upon his exordium, which, so far as I know, has not varied since the Armistice.

"What is Life?" he began in a high, piping voice. "Friends, I will tell you. Life is Happiness. What is Happiness? I will tell you that, too. Happiness is Liberty. What is Liberty? Liberty is Tolerance. And Liberty without Tolerance—what is that? I will tell you. It is Licence!"

Here the choir, recognising their first cue, got cheerfully to work.

"Licence! Licence! Licence!" they chanted. "On and Off! Off and On! Wines, Spirits, and Beer! Beer, Spirits, and Wines! Jug and Bottle! Bottle and Jug! A-a-men! What cheer, Gussie!"

"Oh, you're there, are you?" observed Gussie resignedly.

The chorus replied that they were, adding an excerpt from a current ditty to the effect that the more they were together the happier they would be.

"Ladies and Gentlemen," piped the ancient, "I ask you to take no notice of those puppies—"

"Bow-*wow*!"

Gussie tried a fresh tack.

"Citizens of England," he demanded fiercely, "what was the greatest outrage ever known in our national history?"

The answer came, *fortissimo*:

"When Gussie went off without paying his landlady that ninepence!"

"Maggots!" remarked Gussie dispassionately. "Get back to your cheese!"

In the midst of the cheerful disorder which now reigned, I was conscious of Nigel's voice in my ear.

"There's a fellow standing opposite to us, looking very hard at you, old man."

"I'm used to that kind of curiosity," I said.

"I don't think it's that. He looks as if he were trying to make up his mind to speak to you."

"They often do. Sometimes it is to offer me the consolations of philosophy or religion. They seem to assume that one possesses neither. What is this sportsman like? A street-corner preacher?"

"No. He's a slim, dark fellow, in some kind of uniform. Black, with white fixings."

"That sounds likely enough. Is he wearing a peaked cap with a white band round it?"

"Yes."

"Then he's a St. John Ambulance man. They are always about on these occasions. Perhaps he thinks I'm going to faint. First Aid, and all that. Do I look droopy at all?"

"No; but he's coming to speak to you."

A voice addressed me, civilly enough.

"I beg your pardon, sir. Are you Captain Shere?"

"Yes."

"I was sent to look for you. I'm sorry to say there's been a slight accident."

I started up.

"To Miss Lyndon?"

"Yes, sir. Nothing serious. There was a bit of a disturbance just now over there by the gates; the young lady was knocked over in the rush. However, we got her out all right. She's in the ambulance now. She asked me to come here and notify you."

"Where is the ambulance?" I asked, closing up my shooting-stick with a clash.

"In Park Lane, just outside Grosvenor Gate. The police sent us there, out of the way. Shall I lead you to her, sir?"

"Thank you very much."

"Perhaps your friend will hurry on and say you are coming, sir. The police are inclined to complain of obstruction, and—"

"Of course. Nigel, double on ahead, like a good chap, and say I'll be along in five minutes."

"Righto!" Nigel turned from my side and was swallowed up by the crowd.

I took the ambulance man's arm, and the people made way for us. They even stopped baiting Gussie to do so. There is nothing wrong with the manners of the British proletariat, when they act instinctively. We climbed the railings, crossed the broad carriage-road that runs parallel with Park Lane, and turned to our right towards Grosvenor Gate.

"You're sure it's not serious?" I said again.

"Nothing at all, sir. It started with a crowd of twenty or thirty people trying to break the line of a procession, so as to get across Park Lane. The procession didn't like it, and there was some pushing and hustling. The young lady—"

"Was she in the crowd that tried to get across?"

"Yes—with a gentleman." (Arturo, of course! He had probably led the assault. Ass!) "She was knocked over, and her ankle was twisted. However, she will be quite easy where she is."

"What sort of ambulance is it? One of those trolly affairs?"

"Oh, no, sir—a big motor-ambulance; one of our best. Closed, and able to take four stretcher-cases comfortably, besides the attendant. We'll run the young lady to St. George's Hospital in no time."

"It's lucky you were here," I said.

"We have our orders," replied the man shortly.

We were passing out of Grosvenor Gate now. Park Lane was strangely quiet. Afar off I could hear twelve orators getting to work at once.

"Here's the ambulance, sir," said the man. "The door is at the back. I'll lead you round to it. Here we are, officer; I found the gentleman. Ambulance not been blocking the traffic, I hope?"

"That's all right, mate," replied the unmistakable voice of a policeman—majesty and condescension nicely mingled. "Plenty of room; they're all inside the Park by this time. You'll have a clear run to St. George's. So long!" He strode away back to his traffic point inside the gates; and close beside me I heard the chauffeur of the ambulance start up his engine.

My guide took my arm again.

"You've got to step off the pavement now, sir," he said. "Steady! That's right!"

I heard the sound of a door opening. I called.

"Hallo, Corrie! Are you there?"

There was no answer.

"Step inside, sir," said the man. "You can talk to her on the way to the hospital; she's a bit faint. Give the gentleman a hand, there."

I set my foot on the low step at the back of the ambulance, just beside the purring exhaust. A brawny hand took mine and fairly hauled me into the ambulance. I heard the door close behind me; then the footsteps of my guide outside, as he proceeded to the front of the car and climbed up beside the chauffeur. A minute later and we got under way, as softly and smoothly as a canoe leaving a river-bank.

A new voice addressed me; presumably it belonged to the owner of the brawny hand. It was harsh and nasal.

"Sit down—on that chair beside you."

I did so, contentedly enough. Corrie was there, and nothing else mattered. Outside, the chauffeur clicked his gears, and we were on top speed, running swiftly towards Hyde Park Corner. I raised my voice—

"Well, Corrie, how goes it?"

Again Corrie did not answer. The nasal voice saved her the trouble.

"Keep quiet," it said to me, "and stay put! If you speak or move in the next half-hour, you're dead!" Something hard and blunt was thrust into my ribs. "Do you know what that is?"

I bowed my head.

"Yes," I said; "I know."

It was the barrel of an automatic pistol.

CHAPTER 11

A SABBATH DAY'S JOURNEY

And Lil Montgomery had warned me! No wonder I felt foolish.

"Look out for yourself," she had said, in that breathless, plucky little message of hers. "Look out for yourself! And not only you! He's after her as well—her most of all!"

Yet, with her words ringing in my ears—yes, and occupying all my anxious heart as well—I had walked straight into this booby-trap. I had even allowed myself to be separated from Nigel, at once my eyes and my body-guard, and was now delivered into the hands of the enemy, powerless to help either myself or Corrie. I lowered my face into my hands and groaned. Oh, for my sight—my sight for five minutes!

"Quit that!" commanded the nasal voice.

I pulled myself together sharply: to have been rebuked by this ruffian for giving way to emotion was a tonic in itself. But I did not lift my head: I wanted to think.

Our conveyance slowed down, then swung to the right. We were in Piccadilly. Where were we going? Presumably anywhere but to St. George's Hospital. But where? Only time could show—time and observation. I must concentrate for this.

Already a gleam of hope had come back to me. My captors had overlooked something: they believed that as a blind man I could not possibly follow the route of the car. Well, there I had a card up my sleeve. My knowledge of London, like Sam Weller's, was extensive and peculiar. In the old days it had been my hobby, in my decrepit two-seater, to explore the countless channels, great and small, in which flows the life-blood of London town; to master London's entire street-plan, discovering convenient by-ways and avoiding congested arteries. Once, in the summer of 1914, I had raced against my uncle's Rolls-Royce from Ranelagh to Stanmore, and beaten that majestic vehicle, thanks entirely to superior local knowledge, with ten minutes to spare.

With the coming of my blindness, my bump of locality had developed, if anything, and my power of visualisation increased. I had often amused myself while driving in a friend's car by following the route in my mind and announcing the name of each successive cross-road, or public building—or, for that matter, public-house—that we passed. Well, the time had come to put that trifling accomplishment to a stern test.

I sat with my head in my hands, trying to clear my mind. My thoughts clung obstinately round Corrie. Was she hurt? Was she bound? Was she gagged or blindfolded? The last two almost certainly, I felt. But there was little profit in such speculations at present: I could serve her better in another way. With an effort I wrenched my mind from all thought of her, and fastened resolutely upon the task of following the route of our moving prison.

We were at Hyde Park Corner, heading west. Very well; in that case we should have to conform to the motions of the newly-instituted merry-go-round system of traffic. Sure enough we swung to the left, then round to the right again. Then we slowed down almost to a stop. Evidently we were in a block.

A bell tanged sharply, twice. I had forgotten that London ambulances are so equipped. Instantly we began to move on again: perhaps the police-man had given us the right of way. I grinned, despite myself. To conduct an abduction by ambulance had a touch of real genius about it.

Soon we were running on top speed again, presumably along Knights-bridge, right past the block of flats wherein I had lunched an hour or two ago. We should reach Albert Gate in a moment. Here there would be quite a choice of routes. We might side-step into the Park; we might turn south, down Sloane Street; we might bear left along the Brompton Road; or we might run straight through towards Kensington. All four ways would ultimately lead us out of London in a westerly or south-westerly direction. We did not seem to be bound for Essex at all. Ergo, the Studio—for I presumed that the Studio was our destination—was not in Essex. Sir Gavin had been right.

Again we slowed down; again our bell tanged; and again we were waved on through the traffic. I could hear the rattle of the engine of a stationary motor-bus as we slid demurely past it. We sped on again, presumably along Kensington Gore. I should be passing within half a mile of my own home in a minute or two. However, I did not think they would take me there.

Once more we slackened speed—this time abruptly, and with brakes bit-ing hard. We appeared to be in the middle of a crowd of people, filling the road and talking. A flicker of hope leaped up within me. Could this be a rescue party, miraculously mobilised from somewhere—by Arturo and Ni-gel, perhaps? No; I realised that it was only the audience dispersing after a Sunday concert in the Albert Hall.

Now we were in the bottle-neck of Kensington High Street. There was more noise here, more congestion; but we slid through easily enough, aided no doubt by our external suggestion of necessity and mercy. It seemed fairly obvious by this time that we were bound either for Hammersmith Bridge and

Richmond or Chiswick and the Staines Road; assuming, of course, that our journey did not terminate sooner.

But a surprise awaited me here. We had passed, I calculated, the top end of Earl's Court Road, and with Kensington behind us were bowling softly along towards Olympia and Hammersmith, when suddenly the car turned sharply and giddily to the right—across the very bows of an abruptly halted and eloquently protesting motor-bus eastward bound—and shot up a gravelled side-road, with a fair gradient, at right-angles to our previous route.

"Campden Hill," I said to myself. "We are going across to the Uxbridge Road. Are we doubling back, or just zigzagging, I wonder? Well, in either case it shows that this bunch of thugs are not so confident as they might be."

Our sudden change of direction had another effect. Someone, lying apparently on the shelf-like cot above my head, emitted a groan. But it was a masculine groan. Instantly our custodian was on his feet.

"You can cut that out," he intimated.

The groaner turned over restlessly.

"I say," inquired a weak, hesitating voice, "what's all this about? Where are we? I'm feeling deathly sick. Hallo! Corrie? Is that you? What on earth are we—"

The speaker broke off, gurgling, apparently under thumb-pressure from our vigilant day-nurse.

"If you're coming out of the ether, brother," announced that ministering angel grimly, "I guess I'd better fix you so you can't neither holler nor see. Bite on that, while I—"

"Don't be a cad!" protested the voice faintly—and was silent. But I had learned something. Nigel also was with us, and was lying on the left shelf (so to speak) of the ambulance, while Corrie lay opposite to him on the other.

The ambulance took another sharp turn, this time to the left; then proceeded smoothly along a straight and slight declivity. Hastily I recalled myself to my immediate duty.

"Next station, Shepherd's Bush!" I murmured. "Holland Park Rink on the left; the old White City on the starboard bow. Now, are we going to Uxbridge, or are we going to slide back to Chiswick?"

The car bore slightly to the left, then kept steadily on.

"Goldhawk Road," I said. "We were just zigzagging."

For a mile or so we progressed uneventfully along tram lines; I could distinctly hear the kiss of our rubber tyres against the metals. Presently, at a point where I knew these turned off to the left, we bore slightly to the right, and held on. Whoever was driving knew his London. The road which we were now following was a little known and most convenient by-way which avoids the crowded Chiswick Mall and does not emerge upon the main thoroughfare until a mile or so from Kew Bridge.

On we sped, through the sunny summer afternoon, followed no doubt by the respectful sympathy of the promenading denizens of Chiswick Park. Presently our attendant rose to his feet and opened some kind of window or trap behind the driver's seat. A pleasant draught of air was wafted through, dispelling the soporific odour of anæsthetics which pervaded our conveyance.

"Perce," he inquired, "why did we have to go right off of our trail back there in—"

"That'll do, Mike!" said the voice of the man who had accosted me in the Park. (Could "Perce" be the pet name of that late distinguished ornament of the British Secret Service, Captain Percy Flawn?) "Close your face; blind people aren't deaf. The reason was that another ambulance was bearing down on us, and I was afraid they might want to give us some sort of high-sign that we couldn't return. So I told Pucky here to turn off quick. Where am I?"

"Top of the class!" replied Mike affably. "Say, Perce, listen!"

He lowered his voice: evidently a confidential conversation was pending. I seized the opportunity for which I had been waiting ever since I had felt Mike's gun in my ribs. I put up my hand and groped along the edge of the cot on my right. Almost immediately I encountered what I was hoping to find—the hand of Corrie Lyndon. Her fingers closed over mine, in calm and friendly pressure: evidently she was quite conscious, and undismayed. I half rose, and extended my field of research. My hand touched her face. As I expected, she was blindfolded. But she was neither fettered nor gagged. Good! At least she was suffering no actual discomfort.

At the same moment I heard the little window close with a snap. I sat down, with the mechanical promptness of one playing musical chairs, and resumed my attitude of profound dejection. Fortunately our friend Mike had noticed nothing; at least he said nothing, and he had not struck me as the sort of person who would allow any perceptible misdemeanour to pass unrebuked. Once more I concentrated upon my self-imposed task.

Then, without warning, doubt assailed me. The distractions of the last few minutes—most of all the rapture of Corrie's touch—had broken the thread. I was not so certain of our whereabouts now. We seemed to be running along a main thoroughfare again, with trams on it. If so, we must be approaching Kew and Brentford. If I was right in my theories, we must also be approaching the starting-point of the new Great West Road—that broad, eight-mile ribbon of concrete which swings off to the right just before Brentford, across market-gardens and suburban allotments, past Osterley and the outskirts of Hounslow, to join its parent road within a few miles of Staines. If we were westward bound we would certainly take the Great West Road.

I waited and listened; listened and waited. But the car continued monotonously on its way, along a paved thoroughfare. Occasionally we passed a tram, occasionally a motor-bus. We seldom checked our speed, for our bell rang incessantly, and it was evident that the police were with us, or rather, with Captain Flawn and his friends Pucky and Mike.

We covered another mile or so: *toujours* tramlines. Surely we were not going to thread the narrow and tortuous main street of Brentford in preference to the great smooth by-pass? Or had we borne left and crossed Kew Bridge, bound Richmond way?

Suddenly my courage faltered. Why should we be near any of these places? After all, it had been the merest guess-work from the start—blind-man's buff played in deadly earnest. For all I really knew we might be in Lewisham or Streatham. And, oh! so much depended upon my guessing right. Then I remembered the detour to avoid the other ambulance, and how completely my improvised interpretation of that manœuvre had squared with the geography of Campden Hill. I took courage again. Perhaps I was right after all. If only, only I could pick up some recognisable landmark—some definite landmark of sound or sense of smell!

And my prayer was answered. Two minutes later I was inhaling the aroma—the blessed, resinous, unmistakable aroma—of Pears' soap!

"Isleworth!" I almost shouted the word. The factory, I knew, stood close by the road here, just where the road passed under the South Western Railway. Many a time I had sniffed its pleasant fragrance. Even on Sundays, with active operations suspended, it was quite perceptible. God bless the brothers Pears—both Ambrose and Ferdinand, or whatever their initials stood for!

I had found our bearings now. We were practically clear of London, on the main road to Staines and Southampton. That put an end to dead reckoning, and limited further conjecture nicely. There was only one more road fork of any importance ahead of us—the Bath Road, which branches off to the right half-way through Hounslow. If we passed that we were booked for Staines. There is a linoleum factory at Staines, and on most days that ancient riverside resort smells like Kirkcaldy. We might get a whiff going through: it would only be a Sunday whiff, but it would confirm my calculations.

Suddenly the tramlines came to an end: smooth asphalt lay beneath our wheels. We were through Hounslow, past the junction with the Bath Road, and in the open country. Our speed increased: evidently we had a clear road. I could afford to relax a little from my vigil, and think.

Of course, Manoukian was at the back of this elaborate rounding-up expedition. Corrie naturally was the principal objective. I presumably had been taken because I knew who Manoukian really was, and Manoukian knew that I knew. Nigel had been included in the bag because there was nothing else to do with him. But where was Arturo? Had he shown fight and escaped? Or had he been lured off on some fool's errand? The former, I hoped; then he would be able to spread the alarm. If not, what was to become of us—especially of Corrie? I ground my teeth, and cursed myself for being so helpless and useless.

Still, not so very helpless—or so utterly useless. At least I knew where we were, which was probably more than Corrie or Nigel knew. Besides, my captors were plainly underrating me as an opponent. That fact might prove a useful asset later on....

We were in the streets of a town again, full of life and bustle. I sniffed. I could not honestly detect the ingredients of linoleum—the atmosphere on this warm Sunday afternoon was a little too redolent of petrol-vapour for that—but presently the car made an elaborate "S" turn, with a slight rise and fall in the middle, and I knew we were crossing Staines Bridge.

We were nearly twenty miles from London now. Ahead of us lay a stretch of tortuous road, then the main street of Egham, then the long narrow ascent of Egham Hill. That should be my next landmark.

II

Egham Hill lay behind us. We had scaled it not without fuss, having been brought to a dead standstill half-way up—to the audible concern of Mike, who appeared to be of a nervous disposition. Agitated inquiries through the trap had elicited the news that an ascending Ford and a descending char-à-banc had got into mutual difficulties just ahead of us, and that for the moment the fairway was closed.

Presently, to my regret, we moved onwards and upwards again. The char-à-banc, victor in the unequal encounter, rumbled triumphantly past us down the hill, while the Ford's mourners gathered up the fragments and laid them reverently in the ditch.

We came to the summit of the hill, where a vast red-brick college, at once the bequest and the memorial of a benevolent purveyor of pills and ointment, dominates half a county, and began to descend the other side, through country once thickly wooded but chopped bare by sturdy Canadian loggers during the War—dipping down finally into the lovely hollow which contains Virginia Water. We slid cautiously through the throng of parked motors and Sunday loungers which obstructed the road outside "The Wheatsheaf," then quickened for the hill past Wentworth golf course, which starts immediately beyond. There is a road fork here on the right, leading to Ascot and Reading, but we took no notice of it. "Sunningdale Station next," I said to myself. This would be easy to identify, for there is a level crossing there. If that were closed we should hear the train go past; if not, we should at least feel our car bump over the two pairs of rails.

I cast my mind ahead. Beyond Sunningdale lay Bagshot; beyond Bagshot a really crucial road fork. If we bore left there, we should presently find ourselves in Aldershot; if right, we might go as far as Land's End. I began to feel anxious—Aldershot marked the limits of my intimate geographical knowledge of the one road, and Camberley of the other.

But I need not have worried. We were descending the hill that ends at Sunningdale Station. It was not likely, I knew, that the gates at the level crossing would be closed against us on a Sunday; and I was bracing myself for the bump that would come as we crossed the railway lines, when the car slowed down, took a full and deliberate turn to the left, and proceeded up a narrow and resonant side-road on second speed.

"Hallo!" I thought. "Are we aiming for Chobham and Woking, or just zigzagging again?" Then I reflected that it would be interesting to pass through Chobham.

The road now began to dip and wind across a heathery moor, crowned at intervals with pine clumps: I could smell both. I was in familiar territory. Just ahead of me lay a district thick with memories—memories that burn deep into a man's soul, and never leave him though he may have emerged, at long length, victorious from the ordeal with which they are associated. I could follow our route without effort now, by instinct and habit.

Sunningdale golf course lay on our right rear. We dropped into a hollow. I was conscious of the smell of wood-smoke and cooking. Gipsies! This was an immemorial camping-ground of theirs; doubtless they were mobilising for Ascot.

We entered a village; a long, straggling village. It was Chobham. We should be passing the post office now; now the little tobacconist's at the corner.

We slowed down again, and sounded our bell. Then we rounded the corner—the very corner where the tobacconist's ought to be—and struck out to our left. Something told me that we were drawing near to the end of our journey. At the same moment an incredible suspicion—a quite preposterous hope—assailed me. Could *that* be the place to which they were taking me? Could it? No, the thing was impossible. The arm of coincidence was not as long as all that. The age of miracles was past.

Well, a few minutes would tell.

We climbed steadily uphill for a mile or two, then turned right and ran, I knew well, along a sunken road overarched with trees. Then suddenly the car slackened speed, and after a slight swerve to the right, as if to take full advantage of the width of the narrow fairway, turned hard to the left; then stopped. And—I knew exactly where. The miracle had happened.

"They're waiting for someone to open the gates," I murmured mechanically. "I wonder who lives in the lodge now? Not old Mother Rudd, I'll be bound."

Rusty hinges whined. The sound of dogs broke upon us—dogs barking furiously at our vehicle, and snuffing under its doors. I could picture them, savage brutes. Evidently strangers were not welcomed at the "Studio."

We glided forward again, over rough gravel. The gates clanged behind us, and the sound of dogs died away. Only another half-mile now, first up, then down, through flowering rhododendrons.

Mike rose and stretched himself. I heard him close up the camp-stool upon which he had been sitting, and thrust it under a cot. Then he addressed himself to Corrie.

"I guess we can loosen you up now, sister," he said. Apparently he released the bandage from her eyes, for she thanked him gravely. Mike then turned to Nigel. He must have removed his gag, for Nigel began to talk at once.

"Would you mind taking your thumb out of my mouth, sir?" he said. "I'm a vegetarian." Evidently Nigel had recovered.

Mike, who obviously was not quick at repartee, merely recommended his patient not to get fresh; then removed the bandage from his eyes. I heard Nigel sit up and gasp.

"Barry, old man! You here too? Good Lord! What *is* all this about?"

"No use talking just now," I said.

"Or later!" added Mike.

He had the last word, for at this moment the ambulance drew up under a lofty and Homerically resounding portico.

Two minutes later, with my arm in Corrie's, I stumbled, not for the first time, across the threshold of Bramleigh Chase.

CHAPTER 12

THE SILENT HOUSE

I rose from the bed upon which I had been lying, fully clothed, for the last three hours, and softly opened my bedroom door. But first of all I laid a finger upon the electric light switch beside it. It was turned down, which meant that the light was out. (An economical Sister had once mentioned that little fact to me, and I had remembered it for more than ten years). If the passage outside was dark, at least no ray of light from within my room would now betray my opening door.

I waited, listening. It was about two o'clock in the morning, and the house was utterly still. My door, I knew, opened into a passage containing some half-dozen other doors. Was that passage lighted or not, and was any-one watching? Well, I would soon know. I walked gropingly, so as to give the impression of complete helplessness, to the end of the passage, where I knew there was a switch which controlled its illumination. Many a time I had heard it clicked off and on by night-nurses going their rounds. I had slept in this very passage—aye, and in that very room—for more than six months once. And these people thought I did not know which county I was in!

I found the switch. It was turned down, so all was well. I retraced my steps along the line of doors until I came to the one next to my own. Nigel was here; I had heard them lock him in, and I had heard him moving discon-solately about until the small hours. Where Corrie was I did not know, but Nigel might.

As I had hoped, the key was in the lock. I turned it softly, and entered, closing the door after me. Then I turned up the light. I heard young Nigel sit up in bed with a startled exclamation. Then he saw me.

"Barry, old man! Marvellous! How did you get here?"

"I walked. They hadn't troubled to lock me in; in fact, they didn't even close my door when they left me. I had to do it myself. Where's Corrie?"

"Somewhere adjacent, I think. They shoved me in here and led her far-ther up the passage."

"There are only six rooms in it: she must be in one of them. Probably the last; it is bigger and better than the others."

"How on earth do you know? What is this place, anyway?"

"I'll tell you presently. Are you in pyjamas?"

"Yes; they gave me a most elaborate outfit. Gent's Jaeger dressing-gown, and everything."

"Put on the dressing-gown and come along."

We turned out Nigel's light, and I led him, pleasantly intrigued, to the far end of the passage. Here I knocked softly.

"Who's there?" asked Corrie's voice immediately. Evidently she had been lying awake—and no wonder!

For answer I unlocked the door and opened it a few inches.

"It's all right," I whispered. Then to Nigel: "Is her light on?"

"No."

I led him in, and closed the door.

"Two gentlemen to see you," I announced. "May I turn up the light?"

"Half a minute!"

I heard a creak and the patter of bare feet on the boarded floor. Apparently Miss Lyndon was supplementing her present attire. Then came another creak, as she climbed back into bed.

"All right," she said; and I turned on the light; then turned it off again suddenly.

"Why the mere glimpse?" asked Nigel.

"The window: I'd forgotten it. It looks into a courtyard, and people opposite might see the light, even through curtains. We'll sit in the dark, if you don't mind, Corrie."

"Mind? My dears, I'd sit in the coal-cellar with you gladly. Make yourselves comfortable. There's a little chair beside the bed, Nigel. Barry, hop up here."

Presently I found myself perched on the edge of the bed. Nigel took the chair, and in the gross darkness of that silent house we held a council of war. It was the first time we had been able to exchange a word since our meeting in the ambulance that afternoon.

"Corrie, how have they treated you?" I asked at once.

"Quite well. I even have a maid; at least, a woman brought me some supper and gave me some night things."

"Was she an ordinary servant?"

"No. One of the house-party, I fancy. Quite snappy. You should see the nightie I have on!"

"Did she say anything?" I asked.

"No; and I said nothing to her. I was feeling too mad to trust myself. Who is looking after you?"

"Our friend Mike. He was not communicative either. He simply informed me that I would find food on the table and night attire on the bed, and left me."

"Same here," said Nigel. "Now, what about it? What does all this mean? Why the movie stuff?"

"First of all," I suggested, "let us tell one another how we got into that ambulance. I'll give you my sad story first. Nigel knows it, but you don't, Corrie." And I recited my rather humiliating tale. Then I asked Nigel:

"What happened when you found the ambulance?"

"I'm not very clear on the details. It was standing there, outside Grosvenor Gate. There was no one on the box, but Mike was waiting at the back, with his hand on the door.

"'Step right in,' he said. 'We got the young lady here.'

"He half opened the door, and I walked straight into the arms of Pucky, the chauffeur, who was waiting inside. He held on to me like a grisly bear, while Mike got in beside us and closed the door after him. After that they must have got busy with the chloroform."

"They had given me mine already," said Corrie. "That was why I didn't yell for help."

"But how were you lured into it in the first place, Corrie?" I asked.

"The same way as you—only the other way round."

"You mean, they told you something had happened to me?"

"Yes. I was with Arturo. We were standing in Park Lane, watching the procession go by, when a man came over to us—"

"Mike, I suppose?"

"Yes—and said that you had had a bad accident, and were being taken to the police station over by the Serpentine. He said that you had some very important information for Sir Gavin, which had to be delivered at once, and Sir Gavin had better hurry, or else— That got Arturo out of the way. He jumped into a taxi and drove off to fetch his father, while I went with Mike."

"Was Mike in St. John Ambulance uniform?"

"No. I took him for an ordinary friendly bystander. It wasn't until Arturo had gone that he mentioned the ambulance and took me to it. It was standing in a little street off Park Lane, right behind the Marble Arch Picture Palace. I walked straight into the trap—to be frank, Mike pushed me in—and in two minutes found myself tucked away on that cute little shelf, with my feet tied together and my eyes blindfolded, feeling pretty mean and mortified."

"Were they rough with you?"

"No—just businesslike. When they got me on the shelf a foreign voice said: 'You smella that!' I found myself sniffing chloroform from a handkerchief. Just a whiff, but it was enough. I passed out: not unconscious, but— you know!—all in. Sick, to be frank. There were two men in the ambulance, I think. One was the foreigner, the other the man in the uniform."

"I think his name is Flawn. What happened next?"

"Flawn went off—to round up you two boys, I suppose. Mike came in, and he and I and our private automobile moved down Park Lane a piece, and waited."

"It was a neat job," I said, "to pick us up in two different places like that, and so avoid attracting too much attention at one."

"They had it all doped out," said Nigel.

"'Doped' is right," assented Miss Lyndon feelingly.

"But how did they *know*?" I asked. "We didn't decide to go to the Park until just before lunch."

"That girl Edna Butterick knew."

"I'm sure she had nothing to do with it. Some one in Kensington Gardens must have been listening in on us. I expect we have been shadowed—"

"Never mind about that," said Corrie. "We're here, and that's the real news. But where are we? Can anyone tell me that?"

"Old Barry thinks he knows," said Nigel.

"Then put a poor curious girl out of her pain. Barry, where are we?"

"We are in Bramleigh Chase."

"The name sounds familiar."

"I mentioned it to you once before. It was where I came during the war—to learn how to be a blind man. I know every angle and corner of the place. I have been in this room scores of times, and I slept for six months on the very bed I was in tonight."

"But it's a miracle!" whispered Corrie.

"It's Providence, I think."

"But are you quite positive? How did you come to recognise the place so quickly?"

"I began to suspect long before we got here. We drove through Isleworth and Staines to Sunningdale—"

And I told my tale—so simple to me, so miraculous to people gifted with the power of vision.

There was a long silence. Outside a clock struck three.

"The stable clock," I said—rather proudly, I am afraid.

"Tell us all about this house," commanded Corrie. "We may need to know."

"It's an old Tudor mansion, with additions. Roughly, it forms a hollow square. This room, with the others in the passage, looks down into a courtyard, which has a grass plot and a little fountain in the middle."

"Yes, I saw it before darkness set in. On the right of the courtyard were tall, churchy-looking windows."

"The chapel once; a general lumber-room now. The only way in and out of the courtyard is from there. Opposite to us the ball-room runs the whole length of the ground floor. There are big guest chambers above. On the left, opposite the chapel, are servants' quarters, with the windows all looking outward and not into the court."

"They brought us in through a big square hall," said Nigel.

"Yes; that lies on the other side of us. The house is much thicker at the front than the back, so to speak. There was a gallery all round the hall, with a big staircase leading up, wasn't there?"

"Yes."

"These rooms of ours lie between the back of the gallery and the courtyard. If we went down our passage now, through the curtains at the end, and turned left, we should be looking down from the gallery into the hall."

"I'll take your word for it," said Nigel. "I was in too much of a doodah to notice anything in particular when I was imported."

Suddenly in the darkness Corrie's hand was laid impulsively in mine.

"Listen," she said. "Instead of telling us all about the house, why not take us for a tour around it?"

It was an utterly mad suggestion; but it was in keeping with our situation, and we adopted it unanimously. We took certain elementary precautions, however. Nigel was instructed to go along the passage to the gallery, where he would find a switch controlling an electric light spray at the foot of the staircase. He was to turn this on, and then wait five minutes for results. If there were none—if Bramleigh Chase persevered in its unjust slumbers—he was to come back and report. Meanwhile I would wait in the passage while Corrie dressed.

Nigel and I slipped out of Corrie's room, and Nigel left me. I heard a distant click, and knew that he had found the switch. The ensuing five minutes seemed like five hours, but he returned at last.

"All absolutely clear," he announced.

"Put on your clothes, then," I said. "There's just a hope that we may find a way out of this place."

II

The tour lasted half an hour, and left us divided between disappointment and interest.

First, the disappointment. We tiptoed down the great stair and across the hall, where Corrie and Nigel examined the front door. It was locked and bolted, and every visible window was shuttered and barred. A doorway under the staircase, which I knew led to the back premises, was locked, too. That left only the dining-room and drawing-room—the former on the left, the latter on the right of the hall as one stood facing the front door.

Here the interest began. We tried the dining-room first. I knew it well. Some twenty or thirty of us had messed there—quite literally—for many a month. We closed the door behind us and turned on a light.

"What does it look like now?" I asked.

"It's a vast barn of a place," said Nigel, "and not too tidy. Packing-cases and things lying about."

"Is there a big mahogany table down the middle?"

"Bless you, no! There's hardly any furniture. But there's a table with a green baize cover in a sort of alcove on the left, with eight or ten chairs round it. It looks as if someone had been holding board meetings there."

"In the alcove?" I said. "Aha!"

"What is the sudden thought?" asked Corrie.

"Nothing," I said. But the thought was there, all the same.

Nigel broke in:

"There's a pretty good-looking wireless outfit—a big valve-set with a loud-speaker—fixed up on a shelf in the alcove."

"I expect they have a bedtime story during the board meeting," I said. "A pretty thought. Anything else of note? A rack of saxophones, or anything of that kind?"

"No, but there's a strange-looking contraption over there in the right-hand corner of the room. A sort of roofed-in cubicle, with a padded leather door."

"It may be a sound-proof chamber," I said. "I suppose it's not a telephone box, by any chance?"

"It's far too big for that."

"Perhaps someone is sleeping there," suggested Corrie.

"I'll go and look," announced Nigel.

"Don't be a young fool," I said, instinctively lowering my voice. "By the way, are the windows shuttered? We mustn't show a light to people outside."

There was silence. Then Corrie said:

"That's funny. This room hasn't any windows."

"But there ought to be two, at the far end."

"There's nothing now, except a pair of big double doors."

"They must open on to the lawn, then. Are they locked?"

Nigel went to the far end of the room and tried the doors. Then he came tiptoeing back.

"They don't lead on to the lawn," he whispered. "Somebody must have thrown out an extension. There's a light through the keyhole, and I can hear something going on beyond."

Corrie took my hand, and we crept to the doors. They were of stout undressed pitch pine and smelt new. I put my ear to the keyhole. A low steady vibrating hum greeted my senses. It was a dynamo. The "extension" beyond the doors was a power-station of some kind, and someone within was charging accumulators. Could it be Alf Noseworthy? And could this be the legendary "Studio," of which we had heard so much and knew so little?

At this moment a footstep was distinctly audible just on the other side of the doors; and a man cleared his throat, suddenly and stunningly.

With one accord we turned and crept out of the dining-room....

"Are we going anywhere else," I inquired, when we found ourselves at the foot of the staircase again, "or do I now put you two infants to bed?"

"Let's give the drawing-room the once-over first," said Nigel, "while we're about it."

"Come on, then."

Very cautiously we opened one of the high double doors on the other side of the hall. We were greeted by a smell of dust, damp, and general mustiness.

Nigel switched on a light.

"No social activity of any kind in this messuage or dwelling-house," he announced. "The drawing-room has been closed up for months. Furniture covered, and everything. We might as well leg it for bed."

"Just a minute," said Corrie. "There's a door there on the left—a new door. It is like the new doors in the dining-room, only smaller."

"Another extension, perhaps," I said. "Has this door got a keyhole?"

"There's no need. It's standing open. Come along."

Corrie led me across the room.

"One step down," she said to me. "Switch on the light, Nigel."

Nigel obeyed.

"A garage," he announced.

"A very small one," added Corrie, "with just one car in it—our own private ambulance!"

"A car of any kind is an odd thing to keep practically in the drawing-room," commented Nigel.

"It's a very handy spot," I said thoughtfully. "This may be an emergency exit. I wonder if—"

"H'st!"

Corrie's hand tightened on my arm, and I heard a hasty click as she turned out the electric light. From the gravel outside came the crunch of a substantial pair of boots. There followed an eager snuffing under the outer doors, then the growl of a dog. A harsh voice addressed the animal, in a foreign language. The snuffing ceased, and the footsteps died away.

We stood as still as death for a full three minutes, then turned and proceeded upstairs, carefully closing all doors behind us. No one spoke again until we reached Corrie's room.

"It rather looks," observed Master Nigel, "as if our real troubles won't begin until we succeed in busting out of this hydropathic establishment."

III

"But what is Comrade Manoukian going to do with us, now he has pinched us?" continued Nigel presently.

"Yes," echoed Corrie. "What?"

"I can't bring myself to take this business very seriously," I replied lightly. "After all, we are living in the twentieth century, in times of peace, within twenty-five miles of London. If we were in Central Africa or Chicago one might feel different; but here—well, that sort of thing sounds simply silly. Besides, Manoukian isn't of the murdering sort. He's an unscrupulous blackguard, but I think he has a kind of idea that he's a gentleman. That may cramp his style, particularly where Corrie is concerned. I suppose he will just hold us for ransom, or something of that kind."

But I said all this without much conviction. In my heart I was mortally afraid—especially for Corrie.

It was Corrie herself who rounded off the discussion.

"Still," she said, "I shall be obliged if you two boys will form yourselves right away into the Ancient Order of Chaperons—with one of you always on duty!" Her voice was cheery, but in the darkness her hand touched mine. It was deadly cold.

Five minutes later I had locked my two colleagues into their respective chambers, and was lying in my own, with the door wide open—on duty. On the whole I was a trifle happier than I had been an hour or two ago. At least we knew the geography of the place in which we were to fight out this dim, groping, underground battle of ours.

CHAPTER 13

A PASSAGE OF ARMS

When the birds outside began to chirp I tapped softly upon the wall. Presently Nigel answered me, indicating that he was wide awake and ready to take his turn as chaperon. Then I undressed and went to bed properly. I was asleep in two minutes.

About nine I was awake again, roused by the entrance of Mike, with a tray which rattled.

"Good morning, Judge!" I said.

Plainly Mike was a little shocked by this levity.

"You got your nerve with you, ain't you?" he asked.

"Usually. What's the programme today? Third degree, or the electric chair?"

Mike set down his tray with a clatter.

"Say, where did you get that stuff?"

"I got most of it in the United States."

"You bin there?" Mike was plainly interested, despite himself: it might be worth while to conciliate him. No American can resist asking you what you think of his country, and if you answer wisely you may reap great profit thereby. I would try.

"Sure," I said. "In the Great Middle West, and then some. Chicago, Denver, Butte. That's the country!"

"D'jever know Cicero?"

I realised that Mike was referring, not to the father of forensic oratory, but to a particularly tough township in the State of Illinois.

"Of course I know Cicero. A grand place, and wonderful people. It'll make Chicago look like thirty cents one day."

"My home town!" said Mike huskily.

I gave him a minute or two wherein to master his emotion, and then asked:

"Now, what are you going to do with us, Mike?"

"You gotta see the Boss this afternoon; he'll tell youse. He ain't arrived yet."

"I rather thought not," I said.

"You ain't here to think."

"Talking of 'here,' where am I, exactly?"

"You'd like to know, wouldn't you?"

"Yes; that is why I am asking."

"Well, don't you try to pull any of that stuff on me. Nobody don't know where this place is. You don't know, and that swell Jane and the kid next door don't know, because we blindfolded them on the road. I don't hardly know myself. And listen—the bulls don't know neither! So if you think there's going to be any kind of rescue staged for you, brother, you've got another think coming. S'long!"

And Mike left me. Not altogether dissatisfied with the results of my little excursion into his psychology, I consumed my breakfast and went to sleep again. It was obvious that we could do little by day.

Mike woke me with another meal, and this time I got up. After dressing I sat smoking, as patiently as might be. I deemed it wiser to make no attempt to communicate with the others. Conspicuous helplessness was the line indicated for me.

At five o'clock Mike appeared again, and, taking my arm, led me along the passage and down the staircase. Arrived at the foot, we turned left and entered the dining-room. I was conducted to the alcove, and, stumbling up the single step which led thereto, found my hand laid upon the back of a chair.

"Sit down," said Mike.

I obeyed him, gropingly; then drew the chair up to the table.

"Hallo, Barry!" said a cheerful voice beside me. It was Nigel.

"Hallo!" I said. "Is Corrie with you?"

"The gang is all here. Make a curtsy to the gentleman, Corrie."

"Good afternoon, Barry," said a calm voice on my other side.

"You can cut that out," Mike instructed us, as usual.

Further courtesies were frustrated by the entry into the room of a number of people. I heard them sit down upon the chairs round the table. Then the voice of Manoukian addressed us—suave and agreeable, but with the little sing-song inflexions which always betray the European of Oriental extraction.

"Good afternoon, Miss Lyndon, and gentlemen. Let me introduce my colleagues. On my right is Captain Flawn, whom you have seen before; beyond him, Mr. Michael Moran, whom you also know. On my left is the Countess Mazarieff; beyond the Countess, Mr. Jadassah. Beyond Mr. Jadassah, Signor Puccini."

I listened to this remarkable catalogue with some interest. It revealed the extremely representative character of Manoukian's distinguished Council of Action, or whatever they called themselves. Friend Flawn, assuming that he was British-born, which I rather doubted, was the link which bound our own unhappy country to the chariot-wheels of International Upheaval. Mr.

Michael Moran (in whom I recognised my sentimental friend Mike) was an ordinary Irish-American gunman, of the type imported into Ireland so freely during the black years which followed the Armistice. Mr. Jadassah was a Bengal *babu*, and presumably spoke for his downtrodden brethren of the Indian Empire. Countess Mazarieff, whom I knew by reputation as a monomaniac of a particularly unpleasant kind, apparently represented hysteria in general. But:

"I thought Puccini was dead," I remarked.

"Not the musician, my dear Captain; someone more eminent still. Comrade Puccini is our Consulting Engineer."

"And Honorary Anæsthetist!" said Nigel feelingly—from which I realised that Puccini and Pucky were the same person.

Manoukian laughed. Evidently he was in high good humour.

"I am delighted that you take everything in such excellent part," he said. "It makes the apology which I am about to offer all the easier; and I really do apologise, most sincerely. But—what else could we do with you?"

"I will answer that question," I said, "when you have told me what you are up to."

"A perfectly justifiable attitude, Captain. Well, to a certain extent I can gratify your curiosity. To put the matter quite concisely, you know too much; 'such men are dangerous!' Miss Lyndon, unfortunately and accidentally, knows too much, too. The pair of you might have presumed upon our chance encounter at Le Touquet to intervene in the very delicate mission with which I have been entrusted here. My only course was to remove you from all possible temptation in that direction until such time as your intervention could avail nothing. Your detention will only last for a day or two. After that I hope to send you safe home again."

"And what do you think we're going to do after we get home?" inquired Nigel. "Send you an illuminated address?"

"A delightful idea. But where will you send it? Answer me that, young gentleman."

I scented a trap. The man was trying to find out how much we knew of our whereabouts. Fortunately my left heel was resting lightly upon Nigel's right instep. Nigel winced, then remarked politely:

"There, I admit, you have the bulge on us."

"Exactly. You don't know where you are—north, south, east, west. You haven't the slightest idea! You may be anywhere within a radius of fifty miles from Charing Cross, and if my mathematics are correct that means anywhere over an area of seven or eight thousand square miles. I should advise you to accept the situation until we can safely send you back."

"What about Alf Noseworthy?" I asked suddenly. "Does he go back too?"

I had created a sensation this time. There was dead silence for a moment. Then Manoukian said pleasantly:

"I congratulate you, Captain, upon your really remarkable knowledge of our *personnel*. And I congratulate myself—on having arranged for your silence!"

"Don't you think your self-congratulation is a little premature?" I asked. "If I know that Alf Noseworthy is here, perhaps other people do. Perhaps the police do. What of that, Mr. Manoukian?"

Manoukian laughed softly.

"A good bluff, Captain. Have you any real cards to play?"

"If I have I am not going to play them at present. But I want to remind you that the arm of the law in this country is long, and that the penalties for conspiracy, abduction and forcible detention are rather painful. Seven to fourteen years' penal servitude will be no picnic for any of you."

Manoukian laughed again.

"First catch your hare, my dear Captain. I do not think that your excellent Sir Gavin will run us to earth too easily."

"I'm not so sure," I said, for I was determined to make someone's flesh creep if I could. "An ambulance will not be difficult to trace."

"There is some truth in that, but it cuts both ways. We chose the ambulance because an ambulance gets through traffic easily. Your police are so sympathetic to sick and injured persons. On the other hand, you are right in suggesting that once out in the country an ambulance is rather a conspicuous object. But I do not think that ours will be traced—not for some time, at any rate."

"Why not?"

"Because after today your admirable Scotland Yard authorities will be much too distracted by other events to trouble about tracing ambulances. Listen!" Manoukian suddenly dropped his bantering tone, and the voice of the mob-orator came through. "Tonight, at midnight, a universal, nationwide strike of forty-eight hours' duration comes into operation—as a gesture of protest on the part of the workers and thinkers of this country against your capitalistic rulers' cowardly treatment of that apostle of world freedom, Emanuel Spargo."

"We will now join," announced Nigel suddenly, "in singing 'The Red Lead-Swingers' Anthem'!"

There was a savage snarl from all round the table; but Manoukian, quite unperturbed, silenced it.

"I understand your feelings, Countess," he said, "and yours, my dear Comrade Jadassah; but we must be indulgent to our young friend. After all, he is entirely uneducated, and pitifully class-conscious into the bargain."

I think Master Nigel would have made some rather risky rejoinder to this, for he possessed the fearlessness if not the *finesse* of his distinguished father; but my heel functioned again, and he restrained himself.

"Mr. Manoukian," I asked, "are you really going to try another General Strike—after last time?"

Manoukian was quite ready for me.

"The strike of a few years ago, my dear Captain, suffered from two little weaknesses—it was not general, and it lacked the element of surprise. This time these two conditions will not arise. The Government have been caught napping; and what is more, they are approaching the end of their term of office and have long ago exhausted what popularity they enjoyed, even among their own hired supporters. And this time the strike will be really general. The workers are solid: the Spargo outrage has closed their ranks. Listen to me. Tomorrow, when your bourgeois John Bull rises from his bed, he will find no gas to heat his geyser or to cook his breakfast, and not a bus, taxi, train, or tram to take him to his business. If he succeeds in walking to his office, he will receive neither letters, telegrams, nor telephone messages all day; and when he gets home at night he will find his house in darkness and his larder empty. This state of affairs will continue until midnight on Wednesday, after which we shall automatically relax our hold and allow the normal life of the country to be resumed—for the time being. But we shall have shown our power and given the capitalists fair warning of what we can do—"

"And will do!" the Countess broke in.

"And will do—if Emanuel Spargo is not set at liberty."

"Bet you a hundred to one he isn't!" said Nigel. "Pounds, dollars, francs, marks, roubles, piastres, or marbles!"

"I am afraid you will lose, young gentleman," rejoined Manoukian. "Your so-called Government will be powerless. You see, we can cut them off from all communication with their supporters. There will be no newspapers, no—"

"What about wireless—broadcasting?"

There was a triumphant murmur all round the board. Evidently Nigel's query was about to rebound upon him. Manoukian gave a little gratified cough.

"It is curious that you should have asked that," he said, "because we in this house are in quite a unique position to answer you. You may remember that during the General Strike the capitalists, owing to their control of all broadcasting facilities, were able to issue false but reassuring reports to their dupes; and this to a great extent weakened the solidarity of our cause. Naturally, we have taken steps to ensure that this shall not happen again. We have established a British Wireless Publicity—or, if you prefer it, Anti-Publicity—Bureau. You are in the presence of its Executive Council now—Countess Mazarieff, Captain Flawn, Mr. Moran, Mr. Jadassah, Signer Puccini, and my humble self."

"Couldn't you have managed to co-opt an Eskimo somehow?" asked Nigel.

"And we are gathered here," pursued Manoukian, ignoring this legitimate thrust, "because this building is our headquarters—our transmitting station."

"What building is it?" I asked carelessly.

"I will tell you this much about it. It stands in a slight hollow on the top of a hill, and is invisible from the surrounding country. A few years ago a company—with which we had nothing to do—was formed to convert these premises into a country club, and work was started upon a large concrete and steel annexe which was intended for a swimming bath. The enterprise failed, and the entire property fell into our hands. The annexe had been completed, with the exception of the roof. From the summit of two of its opposite walls two vertical steel girders projected into the sky, just clearing the surrounding trees. These have been a familiar feature of the landscape for more than two years. They have long been regarded as part and parcel of a derelict skeleton."

"And you have converted them into wireless masts?" I said.

"Exactly; and the annexe itself into a power-station. In Comrade Puccini we have a formidable expert in these matters; under his inspired supervision our preparations were completed some weeks ago. How powerful are we, Comrade?"

The Italian spoke for the first time.

"I will not giva you complications of voltage," he said, "but we are ver' powerful indeed. Not so powerful as Daventry, but much more powerful than 2LO."

"Who did the work?" I asked Manoukian.

"Some of our constructional staff came from abroad, others from your Scottish Clydeside. They have all gone home now. The station is under the charge of Comrade Puccini. He had an assistant, a most competent electrician, a compatriot of his. Unfortunately he is no longer with us; he attended a meeting of international Crusaders in the East End of London, and foolishly allowed himself to be drawn into a brawl with the police. He is now spending six weeks in Brixton Prison. That was why we had to co-opt—as the young gentleman over there would say—your friend Mr. Alf Noseworthy."

"And what are you going to do with your broadcasting station now you have got it?" I asked.

"I will tell you."

Suddenly Mike broke in.

"Say, Boss, what's the idea in putting these guys so wise?"

"What can they do with their information?"

Mike considered.

"I guess they can't do nothing but choke on it. But why *tell* 'em?"

"Because I want to impress them all—Captain Shere, his young friend here, even Miss Lyndon—with the completeness of our power. I want to help all three of them to acquire the virtue of—resignation, shall we say?"

I stirred in my seat; I had suddenly realised that all this was really to the address of Corrie Lyndon. Manoukian continued:

"Above your head, Captain, is an ordinary wireless receiving set, with a loud-speaker. The hour is five o'clock. Let us hear what 2LO has to say to us."

There came a faint buzzing from the wall above me, and a pleasant voice announced that London was calling, and that Miss Harriet Grubb would now give a Garden Chat.

"Not much foreboding of trouble to come there!" commented Manoukian, switching off the apparatus. "You see, the country is not taking tomorrow seriously. So much for our receiving apparatus; now let me draw your attention to an apparatus of the opposite kind. Through those doors at the end of the room is our power-station—our dynamos, our accumulators, our valves. They are of purely technical interest, and I shall not enlarge upon them, except to say that they form a very formidable combination. That boxed-in space in the corner over there"—I pricked up my ears: this was evidently the "cubicle"—"is our broadcasting chamber. In it hangs the microphone through which we communicate with the outside world; or, rather, through which we shall communicate; its existence is a secret at present. When the right moment comes to speak to the homes of England we shall tune in on the same wave length as 2LO or Daventry and get to work. In this way everyone who listens to that particular station will also have to listen to us! Simple, isn't it?"

"What form is your propaganda going to take?" I asked.

"A very elementary form, in the first instance. Would you like to hear some of it?" There was a malicious snigger from Flawn: evidently Manoukian had some exquisite jest up his sleeve.

"I am sure we should all be delighted," I said politely.

Manoukian turned to Puccini.

"The power is not switched on, I suppose, Comrade? We don't want to be premature."

"No; da circuit is open."

"Good. Then listen, Captain, and note what happens when I press this button by my side."

From the chamber in the corner there came, muffled but strident to our ears, the prolonged screech of a Klaxon motor-horn. Then there was silence again.

"That," announced Manoukian, with a satisfied little chuckle, "will be our sole propaganda for the next few days."

"It sounds more convincing than usual," said Nigel.

"I assure you, Mr. Dexter, it not only sounds convincing but is convincing. Nothing else can compete with it. We switched it on experimentally for a couple of minutes last night, and it fairly smothered the official programme of 2LO! They issued an explanation this morning—atmospheric disturbance, and so on—and undertook that it would not occur again. I am afraid they will be disappointed."

Happy laughter rippled round the board. Manoukian pushed back his chair and rose. We did the same.

"That is all, I think," he said. "Once more, let me assure you of my desolation at having to treat you like this. I can only endeavour to make your period of detention as comfortable as possible. Will you do me the honour, all three, of dining with me tonight? Countess Mazarieff will be glad to lend you a frock, Miss Lyndon."

"I will dine in my own room, thank you," replied Corrie composedly.

"I will dine in mine, too," I added—"always providing that the police do not arrive before then."

"Your invitation, Comrade"—it was Nigel summing up—"is turned down all round. It isn't that we are really class-conscious, but one has to draw the line somewhere. Sorry."

Manoukian, to do him justice, received these rebuffs without rancour.

"You are my guests," he said; "you must act as you please." Then he added: "Is there anything else that I can do for your comfort?"

"Yes," I said suddenly, for an idea which had been floating vaguely in my mind for nearly twenty-four hours had at that moment crystallised. "You must give us the opportunity of fresh air and exercise."

There was silence. Then:

"Most reluctantly," replied Manoukian, "I must say no—in your own interests. The grounds round this house are not very safe. We keep some rather fierce Alsatian dogs."

"Is there no quiet enclosed spot," I asked, "where the dogs cannot reach us?" And, ever so gently, I touched Corrie's hand with mine.

In a moment she divined her cue.

"I saw a kind of courtyard from my window this morning," she said. "Couldn't we walk round that for an hour or two?"

Manoukian appeared to consider. Then:

"You ask that from me, as a personal favour, Miss Lyndon?" he inquired. "I do."

"Then it shall be granted," announced Manoukian; and I have no doubt that he made a magnificent gesture as he spoke. "The courtyard," he explained, apparently in answer to a whispered protest from one of his colleagues, "is quite secluded; it is only accessible from the old chapel. The chapel itself can be reached from the passage in which your rooms are situated. There is a door at the extreme end of the passage, which I will have unlocked. Through it you will find a spiral staircase, which leads down into the chapel itself. From tomorrow morning the courtyard is your property, Miss Lyndon. I shall certainly join you there for a stroll, sooner or later. *Au revoir!*"

CHAPTER 14

THE PRIEST'S HOLE

Knowing that I might be busy later on, I went to bed directly after my evening repast, and slept until midnight. Then I rose, dressed, and tapped on the wall again. I had arranged a simple code of signals with Nigel. Two taps from him meant that the light in the passage was out, and that I might safely embark upon my duties as turnkey. Three taps meant that it was still burning, and that I must bide my time.

To my signal of inquiry Nigel answered with an emphatic negative. I was not altogether surprised: I had rather expected that the arrival of Manoukian would lead to a general tightening up of prison rules. Last night had been an off night: tonight we were under real discipline.

Well, so long as Manoukian kept out of our passage, I did not much mind. Corrie was all that really mattered. I opened my door wide, lay down on my bed, and devoted myself to meditation.

First of all, how many people were there in the house? There were no servants, or Mike and the Countess would not be performing the duties of waiter and chambermaid respectively. Evidently Manoukian had gathered round him a select and compact band, each of whom could be trusted entirely. He and his "Executive Council" numbered six. There was at least one man outside, in charge of the dogs: more probably there were two or three, disguised as gardeners and lodge-keepers. Then the power-house: what sort of staff would that employ? Alf Noseworthy was there: presumably, since he was there against his will, there was someone with him to look after him and keep him up to his duties. Alf himself had said something to me weeks ago about a pair of "stout country lads" to help him in assembling the dynamo. Doubtless the lads were there still, and doubtless they were stout; but I was not too sure what country they came from.

Then, again, Manoukian had asked us to dine with him. Had he a *chef*, or were those duties performed by the versatile Mike? No, probably there was a cook—a burly gentleman capable of doubling the parts of cook and butcher.

Taking it all round, it seemed likely that the establishment strength of Bramleigh Chase was at least eleven or twelve. Some of them, of course—Jadassah and the Countess, for instance—might almost be ruled out as ineffectives. But the rest? What chance would a blind man and a stripling of twenty have against them? Even though we succeeded in enlisting the help of Alf Noseworthy, the odds were overwhelming.

Yet the attempt must be made. It was a forlorn hope, but the only one. Nigel and I had decided this very night to penetrate into the power-house and find Alf. If he, Nigel, and I could overcome the immediate opposition—Puccini and the two country lads, probably—or at least take their weapons from them, we might possibly get Corrie away. In the garden we would have to run the gauntlet of the dogs and the outside watchers; but—what else was there to do? One fact outweighed all others in my mind, and that was that the longer Corrie stayed within the walls of Bramleigh Chase the more dangerous, the more terrible, her situation would become.

Manoukian was showing himself far too patient, far too accommodating: even allowing for the Armenian strain in him, he was turning the other cheek a little too persistently. And I guessed why. I recalled Sir Gavin's words to me only a fortnight before. "Barry, the General Strike was intended to be the prelude to a revolution. The country didn't know it; the strikers didn't know it; the respectable old gentlemen who preside over the trade unions didn't know it. But the crowd who are holding on to the tail of the dog knew it—and meant it!" Now they were making a second effort, and this time they were confident of success. That was why Manoukian had been so suave with me, so long-suffering with Nigel, so—abstemious—with Corrie.

Feverishly I rose, and strode to the open door. Would the people below never go to bed?

I walked straight into the arms of Mike Moran.

"Kind of restless tonight, ain't you, brother?" he inquired. And, pushing me into my room, he closed the door and turned the key on me.

Furious at my own thoughtlessness, I sank upon my bed. If I was to be locked up at night as well as the other two, good-bye to our hope of getting into touch with Alf. With my head in my hands, I concentrated desperately upon an alternative scheme.

II

Next morning Mike announced to me that he had unlocked the door at the head of the passage leading to the chapel, and that we were at liberty, within the hours prescribed, to avail ourselves of this route to our exercise-ground.

"Thank you," I said. "We may take a stroll there later. What sort of day is it?"

"For England, great. It ain't raining—yet. You better have an hour out on the courtyard before you eat lunch."

"Is your General Strike started yet?"

"Sure. Midnight last night."

"How is it getting along?"

"Fine and dandy. No trains, no newspapers—nuth'n! I'll be along about twelve." And Mike departed, locking the door again.

But it was not Mike who came at twelve: it was Manoukian himself. He passed my door and went straight to Corrie's room. I heard him turn the key and enter. A quarter of an hour elapsed. Then I felt my way to the fire-place and discovered an iron fender. Holding this in the position of a battering-ram, I advanced towards my door. Almost at the same moment the door opened, and my senses told me that Manoukian stood before me. He was in his most playful humour.

"Hallo, Captain! Are you dissatisfied with the present arrangement of your furniture?"

"No," I said. "I was coming to kill you."

Manoukian laughed.

"I congratulate you, my dear Shere. A man who can strike the heroic note in the middle of a prosy, humdrum, political-industrial dispute has my admiration."

"You can drop all that," I said. "I give you fair warning now. If you hurt a hair of her head I will never rest until I get hold of you; and when I do that, as there's a God above us, I'll kill you with my own hands!"

But a man as sure of his own bearings as Manoukian is not to be ruffled by stage thunder—and I had realised as soon as I uttered it that it was stage thunder, of the most banal description.

"You were quite right in what you said last night," he remarked thoughtfully. "You need exercise: the liver must be stirred up; the vapours blown away. *Mens sana in corpore sano*—isn't that one of your favourite English proverbs? I have come to set you free for the day. The courtyard is yours to stretch your legs in; and the chapel too, if it rains, as it threatens to do. I will now unlock our young friend, and he shall take you along. Miss Lyndon has gone down already—and you will find her *coiffure* intact!"

With that he left me. It was only the second time that we had met alone—and, as it turned out, it was the last.

III

"Take one of my arms, each of you," I said to Corrie and Nigel, "and walk me up and down the courtyard. Is anyone watching us?"

"Not as far as I can see," said Corrie. "And I don't think anyone can hear us, anyway."

"Good! Still, we will walk with bent heads, looking dejected. Nigel, register acute despondency."

"Righto! My head is bowed, but not with years. Spill the news."

"I will. When I asked for leave to walk in this courtyard, I was reaching farther than I intended to grasp. The chapel was my real objective."

"And what is the big surprise hidden in the chapel?" asked Corrie. "An underground passage to the nearest police headquarters?"

"No such luck. Still, something. Have you ever heard of a Priest's Hole?"

"No. What is that?"

"The hiding-place of the priest who used to be smuggled into Catholic houses long ago, in times of Protestant persecution. He arrived at night, and slept in the Hole; then celebrated Mass or ministered to the sick members of the estate next day; then stole away when his job was done, to risk his neck somewhere else."

"Stout fellow!" commented Nigel. "But I suppose these Holes have hidden other people beside priests?"

"Oh, yes. Charles the Second slept in one for a night or two after Worcester. White Ladies, I think the place was called."

"And there is a Priest's Hole in this house?"

"Yes—one of the most famous in England. Fortunately this gang of heathens are not interested in ecclesiastical history."

"Do you know where it is?"

"Yes. It used to be one of our favourite stunts, when we were learning to be blind men, to find the entrance and crawl in without help."

"And the entrance," said Corrie, "is in the chapel. Am I right, sir?"

"You are."

"This is great," said Nigel, all agog. "How big are these places, as a rule?"

"They are pretty slim. Generally they are constructed in the thickness of a wall; otherwise, priest-hunters with measuring tapes might have spotted them. Ours is a bit more roomy. It starts with a little passage-way leading out of the chapel, and that brings you to the Hole itself—a chamber about eight feet long and five feet high."

"How wide?"

"Six feet or so. But the last two feet have no floor—just the plaster underneath. And where do you think the place is situated?"

"Where?"

"Over the alcove in the library! What's more, there is a little spy-hole in the plaster which looks right down on to the table at which we were sitting yesterday afternoon."

"We must listen-in at the next board meeting," said Nigel busily.

"Of course; we may pick up some interesting information—something that will help us to get out of this place. Failing that, we may overhear something that will be useful to your father and his merry men—afterwards."

"Then what are we waiting here for? Let's go there now."

"I think we had better wait until this afternoon. After all, we asked for fresh air and exercise: we must prolong our constitutional to a convincing length. Keep on walking, Felix—and Felicia!"

"Could we all three get into the place?" asked Corrie.

"Yes; there is just room. I see your idea. We could lie low there for days, if necessary, until we had a chance to get clean away. We should have to come out at night, of course, to forage. We had better start laying up a small supply of food and water there now—especially water."

"This is going to be lots of fun," said Nigel. And he honestly meant it.

With bowed heads, we continued our promenade.

IV

In the afternoon fortune did us a good turn: it began to rain. We beat an ostentatious retreat from the courtyard, where we had been sitting gloomily round the fountain back to back, and took refuge in the chapel.

"Now, follow me," I said briskly. I felt my way along the dusty oak panelling until I came to the south-west corner. Here, built into the wall, stood a stone font. I stooped down and busied myself with a section of the carved scroll-work at the foot; then, inserting my fingers into a well-remembered crevice, gave a stout tug. Corrie uttered a little cry of astonishment, for the font swung bodily out from the wall, like a door, which indeed it was. They had done their work well, these long-dead artificers, for it came as easily as the door of a modern safe.

"Can you see the entrance?" I asked.

"We can; we can!" gabbled Corrie and Nigel in unison.

"It opens into the passage; the passage leads up to the space over the alcove. We mustn't make a noise; the board of directors may be in session. I'll lead the way. Who follows? Do you, Corrie? You'll have to go on your hands and knees, I'm afraid. What about those Sunday stockings which I presume you are wearing?"

"I stay here," said Corrie. "My stockings don't matter; but a fair captive clothed in dust and cobwebs might arouse unworthy suspicions, even in the simple soul of a Manoukian. Besides, somebody has got to stay out here and watch."

"You are right," I said. "Nigel and I will go. If you hear anyone coming into the chapel, get inside the passage yourself and pull the font to after you. Whatever happens, we mustn't give this secret away. I'll be back directly."

I crawled up the chimney-like tunnel, with Nigel hanging on to my right heel. Presently I drew myself over a stone sill, and we were in the Priest's Hole itself. It had a boarded floor, thick with the dust of years. I crawled to the edge of it. Here the boards ceased, and, cautiously groping, my hand descended upon the rough plaster which formed the moulded ceiling of the alcove beneath. By this time Nigel was beside me. We lay close together, parallel with the edge of the flooring.

"Is there any light?" I whispered.

"Yes; it's coming through a little hole in the plaster."

"That's the spy-hole into the alcove. Listen!"

A nasal voice, surprisingly clear, rose suddenly from below us.

"Say, Boss, is that blind lobster as blind as he looks? I caught him breezing out of his room just now slicker than Nurmi doing a Marathon."

"He's blind enough," replied Manoukian's voice; "I can answer for that. I think he is just a little agitated at present, about—something. Where's Pucky?"

"Here he comes."

"There's no need for both of us to stay," I whispered to Nigel. "I'm going back to Corrie. Listen to all they say, and report. And whatever you do don't roll off these boards, or you'll fall slap through the plaster on to the committee table!" With that, I clambered cautiously over the prostrate form of my companion and crawled away down the passage.

V

Corrie was sitting patiently on the steps of the font. I sat down beside her, and she welcomed me by taking my arm, in her friendly fashion.

"Nigel is listening in," I said, "as happy as a king. You and I will now go into Committee of Ways and Means. First of all we must arrange for your safety, in case things go wrong."

Corrie gave a little chuckle.

"Hasn't anything gone wrong yet?" she asked.

"Well, things are not so bad as they might be. You have not been molested, so far; I have been lucky enough to find myself in a house which I know backwards; and we have this secret dug-out to retire to as a last resort."

"Then why," inquired Corrie unexpectedly, "are you worried to death?"

"Am I?"

"Yes."

"How do you know?"

"The blind have few secrets, as you yourself once told me, especially from people who—pay attention." She turned upon me accusingly. "Barry Shere, you may be able to fool Nigel and Manoukian, but not your Aunt Corrie. Confess, now; you know there is far more at the back of this Two Day Strike than Manoukian allowed, or more than you would allow when you were trying to comfort us two children the other night!" She sat up. "What do you know? Tell me! It will do us both good."

So I told her. Her arm lay in mine as I talked; once or twice the soft muscles grew suddenly tense, but for the most part she gave no sign either of emotion or of fear.

"This is my belief," I said, "and each succeeding event has borne it out. When Spargo came over here a fortnight ago and got arrested, he meant to get arrested. That arrest was a necessary step in a deep game. Spargo is President of the Dodekadelphi—I think I have told you about that sweet crowd—and his arrest was calculated to stir up the Intelligentsia generally, and so create a dust behind which real business could be done. And that real business is now well in hand. The house we are in at this moment and all that is going on inside it are sufficient proof of that. In other words, the real storm-centre is here and not in Hyde Park or the industrial areas."

"The real puzzle is Manoukian and not Spargo?"

"Exactly. Look at that polyglot Council of Action of his in the next room. They have been mobilised here from three continents, to smash up the British Constitution under cover of an ordinary Labour and Capital scrap. Capital and Labour—or the Community and the Strikers, or whatever we like to call them—are both being equally bamboozled. While they are barking up the tree which contains Spargo, the real plot is being hatched under this roof."

"But what *is* the plot?"

"That we don't know," I said. "But I'm afraid Manoukian and his friends, if things turn out as they hope, may hand an unpleasant surprise to the British nation, genuine Labour and all, on Thursday morning. Anyhow, that was what Manoukian's demeanour conveyed to me yesterday. What did you think?"

Corrie's arm suddenly stiffened in mine.

"Barry," she said, coming closer to me, "you're right. That man was too easy with us! Look how fresh Nigel was with him, and he never got mad one little bit! Look how he took our refusal of his invitation to dinner, purring and smiling! He is playing cat and mouse with us, and I don't mind admitting to you that I am scared—badly scared!"

"Cheer up!" I said, with a confidence which I was far from feeling. "We've got to remember two things. In the first place our friends are probably searching for us, and they may arrive at any time; in the second, if Manoukian gets too enterprising, especially where you are concerned, we have got the Priest's Hole to retire to. He can't know of its existence, or he would never have allowed us into the chapel. In any case, we're immune for a day or two: he can't show his hand before Thursday. So keep up your courage! You've been wonderful so far."

With such poor words I tried to comfort her. She did not answer, but she took my hand in hers and leaned more heavily against my shoulder....

"I wasn't really scared," she said presently. "It was just the idea of being left alone, or separated from you. And Nigel, of course," she added.

"You shan't be," I assured her.

"Then I don't care—any more."

Her head drooped upon my shoulder, and in a moment she was asleep. I could hear her soft breathing—feel the regular expansion and contraction of her young body. Very carefully I placed my arm round her, and held her from falling. I, too, did not care any more. But I realised, with a sudden pang of love and pity, how dreadful was the strain under which she must have lived for the last two days. Probably she had not slept since we entered the house.

I do not know how long we sat in that ghostly, dusty, heavenly spot. I kept very still, to avoid rousing her, speculating dimly as to what the immediate future held for us. Not that I minded particularly. If this were captivity, who would be free?

Then Master Nigel came scrambling down the tunnel—and we both woke up.

CHAPTER 15

S.O.S.

Nigel had not much to report. He had listened in to a brief conference between Manoukian, Mike and Flawn, but had learned little that we might not have guessed for ourselves.

The strike was completely effective, and the country was paralysed. There were no trains, trams, or buses; no posts or telegrams; no gas, no electricity; even the telephone had ceased to function. Sentimental affection for the martyred Spargo had done its work, and moral suasion—they had called it peaceful picketing last time—had done the rest. London was completely isolated from the provinces, except through the medium of aeroplanes and wireless. The Government were keeping in touch with the military centres by means of the former, and the latter was to be employed officially in the evening, the B.B.C. having announced that the Prime Minister would deliver an official statement—in other words, a reassuring speech—at six o'clock. Meanwhile, a state of emergency had been declared, and it was hoped that transport and a milk supply would be organised within the next twelve hours.

"I wonder why Manoukian didn't jam all that information," I said.

"He let it go through quite deliberately. He is waiting until the Prime Minister really gets down to it tonight, and then he means to come in good and proper with his little motor-horn. The whole country will be listening in then, and the surprise will be more generally effective. I am bound to say old Manoukian does think of things."

"Did any other news come through?"

"I should rather think it did! There's a hue and cry for us! We are on the front page at last!"

Corrie and I stood up excitedly.

"How do you know?"

"2LO broadcast our names and description ten minutes ago. 'Lost, Stolen, or Strayed, from Hyde Park last Sunday, a tall blind ex-officer with a fair moustache; a real she-girl from the Great North-West; and a distinguished-looking gentleman in a grey flannel suit. Dirty work feared! Five hundred pounds reward!' I tell you, it was a great moment."

"And the gang round the table didn't even jam that?"

"No. Most of them got considerably windy about it, but Manoukian was firm. He said there was no indication that the Government connected our disappearance with them, and that to block the message would only rouse suspicion."

"He's quite right. By the way, did the message mention the ambulance?"

"Yes. It said that we had probably been carted off by such a vehicle, and if anyone had noticed one proceeding furtively in any direction on Sunday afternoon would he report to his local police station?"

"That sounds hopeful," I said.

"Yes; but I fancy the local bobbies are too busy with other matters to follow up clues about wandering ambulances at present."

"Still, it's better than nothing. Have you anything else to tell us?"

"No, except that there's to be a full session of the Executive Council, or whatever they call themselves, at half-past five. Additional assassins are coming down from town to join the glad throng. Bramleigh Chase Club *and* Ground, I fancy."

"Did you hear their names?"

"Yes; rather rum ones. One was called Laxley Spooner, and the other Bunghole, or something of that kind."

"Aynho, I expect. They represent the Dodekadelphi. Anybody else?"

"Adam Cargill. Who is he, if anything?"

"He is one of our native Communists—from Scotland, I fancy. Not a bad old chap; more of a dreamer than a fire-eater."

"That is what Manoukian said, only he didn't put it so nicely; in fact, he was rather fed up about Cargill being sent down at all. Said he would cramp the style of the rest of them, and that what they needed was a man with some stuffing in him. However, Flawn reminded him that probably all the real tigers were fully engaged in the virile north, flapping the gallant old Red Flag, and what not. Cargill was as good goods as could be expected at the moment. That's all, I think."

"What is the time?" I asked.

"Nearly half-past five."

"Has the rain stopped?"

"No."

"Good. I shall go into the Priest's Hole now. You two had better stand in the doorway of the chapel and watch the rain, disconsolately. That will establish some sort of alibi for our side if anyone is observing our movements. As a matter of fact, I expect everybody will be at the five-thirty meeting."

But I was wrong. Even as I spoke heavy steps were audible descending the spiral staircase. It was Mike.

By the time he found us we were sitting on a dusty bench opposite the open chapel door. My head was bowed, and Corrie and Nigel were drearily surveying the rain-spattered courtyard. The font was back in its place against the wall in the corner.

"You birds has got to get back to the coop," Mike informed us. "I know it's early, but I expect to be busy by and by. Your eats are waiting for youse."

Five minutes later he had locked us all up in our respective bedrooms—for the night.

* * * *

I sat beside my untasted supper. The house was absolutely still. A solid curtain of silence and oblivion seemed to have descended between us and the outside world—between us and life itself.

Yet not completely. Suddenly the silence was broken by a faint, distant, mechanical screech, penetrating the thick stone walls. It was a Klaxon motor-horn. The Prime Minister of England was broadcasting a message to forty-two million of his countrymen—and a handful of assorted aliens seated round a table in a country house in Surrey were howling him down, with none to prevent and none to punish them. We seemed to have touched bottom.

CHAPTER 16

THIS WOMAN BUSINESS

The next day was one of the longest that I have spent in my life. In the world outside, great and critical events were in progress, with gathering momentum. It was possible that the fate of our country was being decided for the next hundred years; but so far as three poor captives were concerned, all was limbo and outer darkness.

Yet we had not been entirely forgotten, as the broadcast inquiry for us indicated. And here it is permitted to anticipate a little.

II

We were first really missed—so we heard afterwards—about seven o'clock on Sunday evening, when Nigel and Corrie failed to return to Hyde Park Gardens for dinner. I say really missed, because suspicion so far had been vague. Sir Gavin and Arturo had arrived hot-foot at the Serpentine Police Station about five, to find that they had been made the victims of what seemed to Arturo a pointless hoax. But Sir Gavin was not so sure; and when Corrie and Nigel failed to answer the dinner-gong, he was certain. By nine o'clock the Special Branch at Scotland Yard was humming like a hive, and every policeman who had been on duty in or around Hyde Park that afternoon was questioned. Had any officer observed a blind gentleman in difficulties of any kind—or even a blind gentleman in no sort of difficulty at all? This brought in our affable friend from Grosvenor Gate, who deponed that he distinctly remembered, about the hour of 4 s, observing a blind gentleman in close proximity to a waiting ambulance which—so the chauffeur, a foreigner of some kind, presumably French, had informed him—contained a young lady who had been injured in a street accident near Marble Arch, and was now asking for the blind gentleman aforesaid. The gentleman had got into the ambulance, accompanied by his guide, and the vehicle had then moved off in an orderly manner towards Hyde Park Corner and St. George's Hospital. The officer had not taken a note of its registration number, having no cause to regard the incident as unusual. The blind gentleman's guide was not dressed in a grey flannel suit—of that he was certain. He was a St. John Ambulance man.

Here at least was something to start on. Sir Gavin had no doubt in his own mind that Corrie, Nigel, and myself had been trapped, probably at different points, by Spargo's associates, and conveyed in the ambulance to the frequently mentioned and highly mysterious Studio in Essex.

Accordingly, all the best part of Monday was occupied in an entirely fruitless search throughout the length and breadth of that considerable county.

With Monday midnight came the Lightning Strike and its attendant distractions and preoccupations. The police now had other work to do. It was not until Tuesday afternoon that my uncle, realising that he could expect little help from his expert henchmen until the critical forty-eight hours had elapsed, and knowing full well that such a delay might mean death or worse to at least one of us, bethought him of the good offices of the British Broadcasting Corporation. Hence the appeal for information concerning us, which Nigel had overheard. And hardly had the same been planted in the ear of the British public, than it yielded fruit of the most valuable kind from an entirely unexpected quarter.

III

That very evening Sir Gavin was informed, on returning home for a hasty dinner, that two ladies (anonymous) were waiting to see him. They proved to be Maudie, Hal Horner's wife, and Lil Montgomery. Lil, it appeared, had information to impart, and Maudie had come along with her, partly for purposes of moral support and partly in the rôle of Aaron to Lil's faltering Moses.

Maudie, assisted by tearful promptings from her companion, set to work at once.

Miss Montgomery, she explained, had been engaged to be married for some months past to a Captain Percy Flawn. The pair had originally been brought together through a common interest in the arts, Miss Montgomery being a revue actress of distinction, and Captain Flawn a pioneer in the promotion of All-British Films.

"Under the managing directorship," interpolated Sir Gavin dryly, "of the saintly Emanuel Spargo."

"How did you know that?" asked Lil, in a startled voice.

"It is my business to do so. It will probably save you two ladies a good deal of superfluous exposition if I say that I know all about Spargo and a good deal about Captain Flawn. For instance, I know that Captain Flawn and yourself, Miss Montgomery, spent Easter at Le Touquet in company with a rather notorious individual named Manoukian, and that there was an angry encounter—a scene, in fact—between Manoukian and Captain Barry Shere, one of the three missing persons for whom we are inquiring. Let me reassure you, Miss Montgomery"—Lil was on her feet by this time, trembling violently—"as to your position. I know nothing against you at all, and I have a feeling that the information which you are now about to give me regarding Captain Flawn and his colleagues will more than counter-balance any—stigma, shall we say?—which you may have incurred by your association with him."

Lil Montgomery responded to this delicate invitation by bursting into tears.

"I don't want to tell you any more," she sobbed. "You might go and—"

"The fact is, sir," explained Maudie, patting Lil with a large and motherly hand, "the poor girl is still very fond of this Flawn, and she doesn't want to get him into trouble, badly though he has treated her. And I must say—"

"Then why has she come here?"

"Well, she wants to get back at him, in a manner of speaking. It's partly her conscience, of course, but it's mainly jealousy. You see, sir, she's a woman." With this perfectly adequate explanation Maudie resumed her narrative.

The course of Miss Montgomery's true love, it seemed, had not run smooth. Flawn was of an inconstant disposition, and, moreover, was frequently absent from London, on alleged business at the "Studio," for days at a time. Lil suspected a rival and decided to have her affianced watched and his movements traced.

"I suppose he had never told you where the Studio was, Miss Montgomery?"

"No; except that it was somewhere in Essex."

"That was just his artfulness," said Maudie. "I soon found that out!"

"How did you come into the matter at all, Mrs. Horner, if it isn't too personal a question?"

"Well, sir, Lil couldn't follow Captain Flawn herself, or he might have seen her; so, as he didn't know me by sight, Lil asked me to watch him for her."

"I see. Well, how did you set about it?"

"I waited outside his office one Saturday morning in a taxi, and when he came out with a suitcase, I told my taxi to follow his. My idea was to follow him to Liverpool Street Station and then stand by him at the ticket window and hear what station in Essex he booked to."

"Admirable. And what station in Essex did he book to?"

"He didn't go to Liverpool Street Station at all!"

Sir Gavin looked up sharply. "Ah! Where, then?"

"Waterloo, sir."

"Waterloo! Go on, please!"

"I followed him quite easily right up to the window. There were a lot of people taking tickets, it being Saturday morning, but I managed to squeeze into the queue just behind him. In fact, I had a few words with a couple of young girls about it—"

"And where did he book to?" asked Sir Gavin patiently.

"Sunningdale."

"You are certain of that?"

"Quite, sir. It's not an easy name to mistake."

"And it all happened last week?"

"Last Saturday week."

Sir Gavin turned to Lil.

"And how did you utilise this information when you got it, Miss Montgomery?"

"She didn't utilise it at all, sir," replied Maudie. "She couldn't make up her mind whether to go down to Sunningdale, and poke about there and see what she could find out about this woman, or wait here in London and have it out with Captain Flawn when he came back; or what. You see, she was very upset, poor thing, and couldn't bring herself to face things. Then, while she was still worrying, this Labour trouble came along, and the Strike, so she decided to wait until that had blown over. But the broadcast message this evening—we heard it in Hal's dressing-room after the *matinée*—well, it fairly made up Lil's mind for her. Of course, it didn't mean a thing to Hal and me, except that our friend Captain Shere was missing: but it gave Lil a real turn. As soon as she heard it, she jumped up and said she knew where they all were; and even if it got Percy into trouble she could never rest until she had told what she knew. You see, she had always liked Captain Shere, from the time—"

But Sir Gavin had heard all that he wanted, or all that Maudie could tell him. He rose, shook hands with both ladies, and conducted them to the street door in person.

"You may have saved three lives," he said; "and for all I know you may have saved your country."

Then he called for his car and was driven furiously to Whitehall. His course of action was clear enough now. Flawn did not matter; neither, for the moment, did Nigel or I. Corrie was the true objective. Where Corrie was Manoukian would be, and where Manoukian was there would be revealed the real inwardness of the conspiracy which was threatening to wreck that slow creation of a thousand years, the liberty of the British People. Well, Corrie and Manoukian both were hidden somewhere among the Surrey Hills, in the neighbourhood of Sunningdale. Manoukian had been mixing up business and pleasure again—not for the first time in his interesting career. But this time, please God, it would be the last.

CHAPTER 17

PLAN B

The stable clock chimed ten. I could bear the suspense no longer. I felt my way to the fire-place, and once more armed myself with the fender. Then I returned to the door, and attacked it. At my third frenzied blow the stout oak splintered. I laid down my battering ram and listened fearfully at the broken panel. Perfect silence reigned throughout the house. I had not been heard: Mike and everyone else was at the all-important meeting of the Council.

I put my hand through the door and reached down. The key was in the lock. I turned it, and was free. Next moment I was in Nigel's room. He was lying on his bed, but not asleep.

"I am going to the Priest's Hole," I said. "I *must* know what is going on round that table tonight. Let Corrie out of her room and bring her along. I feel there is going to be a crisis of some kind: we may have to act on the spur of the moment, and act together."

Then I fairly raced down the spiral staircase.

II

Five minutes later I lay stretched along the dusty planking of our listening post, straining my ears for the conversation below. Manoukian was speaking. There was nothing suave or diplomatic about his utterance now.

"Listen to me, my man. At midnight you will be ready to get on the air, or whatever the technical term is—forgive me, Comrade Puccini, but I am a child in these matters—in order that we may broadcast a message to the country at large. You say that your batteries are charged and your valves adjusted?"

"That's right." As I expected, it was the voice of Alf Noseworthy which answered. But I barely recognised it, so weak and attenuated had it grown. Poor little Alf had evidently been having a rough time of it.

"Good! Now go back to your power-house and stand by for further orders."

"I got something to say first," announced Alf, faintly but resolutely. Evidently his fox-terrier spirit was unbroken. "It's this. I was brought here in the first place—"

A hand fell softly upon my shoulder. It was Nigel, kneeling in the dust beside me.

"Corrie's staying down below," he whispered, "keeping *cave* by the old font. Let me go next to the edge of this bit of floor. I want to look through the peep-hole. You'll still be able to hear." And with that he rolled over me and wriggled into place.

"Can you see anything?" I murmured.

"Wait a minute; I'll take a squint." He lowered his head into the shallow chasm beside him. I held him round the waist to prevent him from rolling bodily on to the frail plaster and adding involuntarily to the number of the committee below. Presently he came up to breathe again.

"Manoukian's at the head of the table," he said in my ear. "Flawn is on the one side of him and fat Pucky on the other. There are a lot of other people, but most of them are bending over the table, reading reports, or taking notes, or something. Manoukian is talking to a little man in an overall, who is standing down on the floor a few feet away from him."

"What does he look like?"

"The little man? Nothing on earth."

"Has he reddish hair and a waxed moustache?" (I remembered about the moustache: Edna Butterick had been very proud of it.)

"Reddish hair, but no wax about the moustache that I can see. No wax about him anywhere. He looks all in. Who is he?"

"Alf Noseworthy. You've heard of him. Let's listen to him."

Alf was still addressing the Board, shrill with righteous indignation:

"You bring me here for to learn me"—shades of Homer P. Keedick!—"to be a movie actor. That was your first bit of funny business, and, like a mug, I fell for it. Next, you tell me that I've got to do an electrical job—a wireless job—set up an outfit for broadcasting adverts of your Studio. 'Granted,' I says, 'on condition I gets to London now and then, to see my young lady.' What do you say to that? You tell me right out that I don't leave this here moated grange until the dynamo is assembled, and the accumulators charged, and the valves tuned up, *and* the microphone fitted. When I reply that I'm an Englishman and won't be treated like a lackey, what do you do to me then? Put me in charge of a couple of greasy foreigners with orders to watch me by turns and cut short my rations if I show fight! And they done it on me all right, all right! I tell you, I'm 'alf starved; and I won't go on until I gets a square meal—so there!"

"Who's this felly?" inquired a heavy and entirely unfamiliar voice, directly underneath us.

"Just a poor, non-class-conscious piece of cannon-fodder, Comrade Cargill," replied Manoukian—"a wage-slave of the military oligarchy of this country." (Despite myself, I had to admire the unfailing way in which the fellow handed out the patter.) "I was compelled to bring him here to replace a tried comrade of ours who fell by the wayside. He has been refractory, but you may safely leave him to me."

Then he turned to Alf again.

"Get this!" he barked. "Those who will not work, shall not eat! Go back to the power-house, and attend to your duties. Tonight I have no time to waste upon you; but tomorrow—! Take him away!"

I heard a slight scuffle, as of someone offering resistance; a few words of indignant protest, a dragging sound—and silence.

"What happened?" I asked Nigel.

"A big bruiser hauled him off by the collar."

Doubtless one of the stout country lads, I reflected. But Manoukian was calling the meeting to attention.

"Comrades will now answer to their names," he announced. "In addition, the outside delegates will communicate to me, in a whisper, the password for the day. A precautionary measure; a spy once found his way into one of these conferences."

The voice of Flawn now recited a string of names, each of which was answered by its owner. It was a superfluous piece of mummery, for all present must have been well known to one another and their leader. But they enjoyed it; one could realise that from the unction with which most of them answered the roll. Secret orders and brotherhoods, even the most august, are all alike in this respect; they love make-believe and unnecessary ceremonial.

Most of the names—and, indeed, the voices—were by this time familiar to us. But two or three were new.

Adam Cargill spoke the broad and not unattractive Doric of the Clydeside. Laxley Spooner, whose fluent pen and uncanny instinct for self-advertisement had raised him to the position of Sir Oracle among the motley horde of "pink" revolutionaries who infest some of our more intellectual suburbs, answered his name in a high, reedy, piping tone—a revealing blend of inherited Cockney and acquired Chelsea.

Desmond Aynho, on the other hand, replied to his name with the impressive aplomb of the practised public speaker. I knew him for a far more dangerous man than Spooner. He was a Public School and Oxford product, who, having failed to make friends in his own class—for the sufficient reason that his own class had to draw the line somewhere—had announced himself a convert to the doctrines of Karl Marx, proceeding thereafter to acquire a comfortable fortune by lecturing in America upon the approaching disintegration of the capitalistic British Empire. With the possible exception of

Flawn, whose origin was wrapt in mystery, these were the only two English-men present.

Then the outside delegates—"furtive-looking blighters with suet faces," so Nigel confided to me—answered their names and communicated the pass-word. After that they made their reports in turn, and for the first time Nigel and I had first-hand information of the progress of the Strike.

They spoke of a "blackleg" tram-car service closed down in Glasgow; of moral suasion brought to bear upon scabrous persons caught discharg-ing food-stuffs from a ship in Hull; of a party of clerks and girl typists tri-umphantly ejected from a motor-lorry and compelled to tramp five miles through the rain in North London.

And there was, to us, more ominous news than this. A train run by staff engineers and volunteer conductors had been derailed and burned. There had been a determined attack on an electric power-station, and two policemen had been killed. Evidently imported hooliganism was trying out its hand al-ready.

"This will never do!" remarked Cargill.

"Why not?" snapped the Countess. "Capitalistic hirelings!" Apparently her Excellency referred to the deceased officers of the law.

"I agree with Comrade Cargill," said Manoukian. "The execution of the policemen was a blunder, because it was no part of Plan A."

"What is Plan A?" asked a voice.

"I will explain that in a moment. Meanwhile, comrades, I think we may congratulate ourselves. We have made good. You remember our slogan of last week: 'Not a wheel shall turn, not a chimney shall smoke, not a wire shall spark, till Spargo goes free!' Well, transport is at a standstill—"

"Aye; but has Spargo gone free?"

It was a disconcerting question, and it came, as might be expected, from Adam Cargill. I suddenly realised that this old gentleman was going to be thoroughly unpopular by the time the meeting was over, and my heart warmed to him.

I had followed his political career for many years, and always with re-spect. Adam Cargill was one of Nature's philanthropists. He had been born in a Glasgow tenement nearly seventy years ago, in one of the worst housing districts in the world, and from that day had lived solely to destroy the system which had rendered his own upbringing possible. He loved his fellow-men, and to him a system under which a single one of them suffered was an im-possible system, to be scrapped and forgotten. His dream was a new heaven on earth, where all would share alike, and there would be no more war, and no more alcohol, and everyone would attend an approved place of worship on Sabbath. But his trouble was that he could not wait. He might have been an asset of price to innumerable generous and enlightened schemes of social amelioration; but his only cure for an imperfect world was to turn it upside down. Revolution! Bloodless revolution, of course—but Revolution! And it was characteristic of the man and his simple faith in humanity that he honestly believed a bloodless revolution under leaders like Spargo and Manoukian to be possible.

Evidently Manoukian shared my anticipations, for he went out of his way to conciliate Cargill.

"A fair question!" he said affably; "and it shall have a straight answer. Spargo has *not* been released. He is still at Southampton, confined on board the ship which was to deliver him to his enemies."

"*Was?*"

"Yes—*was*! The crew are staunch. Deckhands, firemen, stewards—all are standing fast. The ship has not sailed."

"And shall not sail!" cried the Countess.

"Sister," said an approving and familiar voice, "you spoke a mouthful!"

But Cargill was not satisfied.

"Has the Capitalist Government no taken ony steps?" he asked.

"Yes, they have. They sent a destroyer over from Portsmouth this afternoon. They are going to employ their Navy to do their dirty work. Emanuel Spargo sails for America tomorrow morning under their cursed White Ensign!"

There came a cry from round the whole table.

"Then the Strike *has* failed!"

But Manoukian's voice rose high above them all.

"The Strike has *not* failed!" he cried. "Plan A has failed, as I knew it would. It is for us to retrieve the situation—with Plan B!"

"What is Plan B?" asked Cargill. "I never haird of it. I doot some here will know it already—but not all of us. Tell us!"

"Yes, tell us!" cried several voices.

III

And Manoukian told them. Long before he finished I realised that Plan A *had* been a blind—a mere sop to the Moderates. The real plan was being revealed now; the tail, as Sir Gavin would have said, was wagging the dog at last. Stark red rapine and destruction were to be let loose upon the deep peace of our ancient land.

Manoukian was adroit enough in his recital, for he knew that he had a mixed and contrary team to drive. He began by enlarging upon the futility of setting an advertised time-limit to remonstrance. He had consented to the Two-Day Strike because the Workers' leaders (upon whom be peace) had desired it. But what did such a gesture amount to? Nothing! What, in effect, had the Workers done? Rung a door-bell and run away! At least, that was what would be said. It would be useless to point out that the Strike was intended

to be a mere demonstration in force—just a stern hint of greater power behind—and that it had never been proposed to press this fight to a finish.

"The Capitalist Government will say they have beaten us," he concluded, "and their kept, subsidised Press will back them up. And what will be the
effect upon the Workers themselves? Demoralisation! Despair! Refusal to try
again! That is the situation, comrades. There is only one thing left to do, and
you know it. What is it?"

"Go on!" They were all shouting at once now.

"Very well, then. The Strike is dead! Long live the Strike! *A l'outrance!*
Plan B!"

He could do what he liked with them after that, and they settled down
with avidity to absorb the details of the new, real programme.

"Under Plan B," Manoukian began, "Capitalism goes, once and for all.
It goes tonight at midnight, when we signal to our agents, who are waiting all
over the country, to put the Plan into operation."

"What form will the signal take?" asked Aynho.

"A very simple one. As you know, we are tonight in wireless communication with all the patrons of Daventry. In fact, we have taken the liberty of
sharing Daventry's wave-length! Our microphone chamber is in that corner
over there. The preconcerted sign is a bugle-call, to be broadcast by Comrade
Moran here." (What an all-round man Mike was!) "Many will hear it, but
only the chosen few will understand it—and act on it. Of course, until they
hear it, and unless they hear it, they will do nothing."

"But Plan B? What does it amount to, briefly?" Laxley Spooner asked
the question: evidently there was an outer ring present who were not in pos-
session of the inmost secrets of the Council.

"Briefly, to this. So far we have merely interfered with the comfort and
convenience of the Bourgeoisie; now we are going to make their flesh creep.
It will be a progressive, psychological assault. First of all, each section of the
country is to be kept in complete ignorance of what is going on in the other
sections. (London, of course, has already been entirely isolated from the
provinces.) That will breed uncertainty, and uncertainty will breed rumour;
and rumour, properly controlled, will breed panic. (We have people attending to rumour everywhere.) Secondly, we will attack the Bourgeois stomach.
Starvation, though familiar enough to the Workers, will be a complete and
compelling surprise to them. Besides, shortage of food supplies always en-
genders a suspicion that someone is profiteering, and that, of course, will
create an atmosphere additionally helpful to us. Thirdly, propaganda must be
concentrated upon the waverers—in the Army, for instance. Reports in that
quarter are already favourable."

"I *don't* think!" murmured Nigel; and he was unexpectedly supported in
his view.

"Are you no sure that you are taking ower much for grantit there?" inquired the indefatigable Cargill. "Ye mind what happened oot in China, only the other day, to yon felly of ours that was sent to convairt the British troops in Shanghai? They listened to him fine for the inside of a week; then, one afternoon, they took him and gave him hauf an hour tae learn the words of that Capitalist doggerel, 'God Save the King.' After that they stood him on his heid in the barrack square, and made him sing it!"

It was a story which had made all England laugh a few months previously, and possessed the additional merit of being true, but it was received upon this occasion in chilling silence. Evidently tact was not included in Adam Cargill's many qualities of heart and head.

"That one didn't go with much of a swing," whispered Nigel to me.

"The troops in question," explained Manoukian glibly, "were of a regiment recruited from a particular class and accorded special privileges by the capitalists. The poor cannon-fodder of the British county units are of a very different calibre. After all, why should men receiving a few pence a day in return for the life of a convict refrain from helping themselves to what Revolution has to offer them?"

Personally, I was unable to share this rosy view of the case, but apparently the company below did, for they forgot Adam Cargill and settled down to listen again.

"Now," continued Manoukian cheerfully, "we come from theory to practice, from promise to performance. Our agents fall naturally into two groups—those sent to take external action against certain vital spots in the enemy's defences, and those who are already working for us within the walls."

"What vital spots in particular?" asked Aynho.

"I have a list of them here. In London we have Buckingham Palace, Scotland Yard, and the Bank of England, to name only a few. These must be the subject of direct action: we have found it practically impossible to introduce our agents into any of them. In the provinces—"

He read on—a methodical tale of telegraph cables to be cut, power-stations to be wrecked, banks to be raided, viaducts and reservoirs to be destroyed. The recital occupied some time, for nothing seemed to have been forgotten.

"Of course," he added, "in many of these places comrades are already working for us on the inside—in positions of trust which give them access to valuable secrets. Woolwich Arsenal, for instance, and the Admiralty and War Office, and the great petrol-storage plants at Thameshaven and Avonmouth. The latter are particularly important. Petrol has been our chief enemy so far. It is easy enough to paralyse a railway system; a rail or two torn up here and there is sufficient; but motor transport is a real problem. Almost anyone can drive a car, and it is impossible to barricade all the roads. With Thameshaven and Avonmouth out of action—burnt out, to be explicit—local stocks, in London and the Home Counties at any rate, will be exhausted in a few days, and then the transport standstill will be complete."

There was a gratified buzz.

"What about the Navy?" asked Spooner. "Can't we prevent that from interfering?"

"Certainly. Arrangements have been made for the destruction of the great wireless station on the roof of the Admiralty. That should prevent any kind of harmful co-ordination for at least three days; by which time we are sanguine enough to hope that the Naval oligarchy will be willing to accept a *fait accompli*."

I became conscious of a gradual sinking sensation in the pit of my stomach. Manoukian might be over-sanguine, but no one could say that his scheme suffered from lack of organisation.

"Now to sum up," he said. "*Divide et impera!* First, isolation—uncertainty—rumour! Then, shortage of supplies, the threat of starvation, and the suggestion of profiteering on the part of the Capitalists. Then the awakening of the unruly element—rioting—the homes of the wealthy looted! Next, universal panic, and repudiation of the capitalistic regime! Then a nation-wide cry for leadership—leadership of any kind! A *coup d'état*, and the establishment of a provisional Government! Then the instant re-establishment of communications, and the setting-up of local Workers' Committees! Promise of immediate relief—supplies—personal security—law and order once more! Public confidence restored—the Press permitted to function again, on carefully defined lines—general and joyful acceptance of the new era—and the millennium has dawned! *En avant!* Plan B!"

The last words were drowned by a roar of excited applause. Chairs were pushed back; men appeared to be dancing about the room.

"They're kissing each other," Nigel reported. "An excitable lot, these foreigners!"

Presently the hubbub died down, and Manoukian graciously inquired if there were any obscure point which he could clear up.

"Is it permitted," inquired the voice of Aynho, who seemed now to have appointed himself interlocutor on behalf of the outer ring, "to inquire what form the *coup d'état* will take?"

"Certainly. It will take the form of the simultaneous apprehension of all the members of the Cabinet, and their replacement, at the head of their respective departments, by more worthy representatives. The thing has been done more than once, quite successfully, in modern history. You have heard of the 18th Brumaire, in 1799? Louis Napoleon, too, as recently as 1851—"

But Adam Cargill was not interested in European history.

"What are ye gaun' to do to the members of the Capitalistic Cabinet when you get them?" he asked bluntly.

"They will be retained in custody," replied Manoukian, "until the time comes to bring them to account for their actions. One or two of them have monstrous records. Examples must be made."

"Shoot the lot!" suggested that amiable visionary, the Countess Mazarieff; and Jadassah squeaked assent. But Adam Cargill spoke again—with the voice of some old giant, suddenly aroused.

"There shall be no bloodshed," he said steadily, "among high or low!"

"There need be no bloodshed," replied Manoukian, taking him up quickly, "if—"

"Can you guarantee that? No, ye canna! And that is why I resist your plan. All over the face of the land you have organised violence and burnings and destruction. I held my peace while you read oot the tale of them, but now I will speak. This is not bloodless revolution. I warn you, you are gaun' aboot things the wrong way. There will be no blessing on such doings; and more than that, the innocent will suffer with the guilty!"

"As I said," Manoukian reiterated patiently, "there need be no bloodshed—if we adopt Plan B. Plan B involves the employment of the only two factors which will save bloodshed—simultaneous action, and complete surprise." He rose to his feet. "Comrades, it is within a few minutes of midnight. All over the country our agents are waiting for your signal. Are they to have it? Is Plan B going through?"

"Yes!" shouted a chorus of excited voices.

"No!" roared Adam Cargill. "Not without further guarantees!"

"The Ayes have it!" said Manoukian. "Comrade Cargill, you are in a minority—a minority of one—and minorities must suffer. The greatest good of the greatest number—that must be our slogan now! Comrade Moran, go to the microphone. Sound the call, and let Freedom wake!"

This well-timed oratorical climax was greeted with another roar. But that practical assassin Mike inquired:

"Has that little guy turned on the juice? There don't seem to be much use of my serenading a dead microphone."

He was answered, with staggering suddenness, by "the little guy" himself—Alf Noseworthy, in full voice again, transformed and transfigured by patriotic wrath. He was speaking, or rather bawling, from the far end of the room, by the power-house doors.

"No, he ain't turned on the juice, and he ain't going to turn it on! You dirty dogs! You lousy 'ounds! So that was the game all the time! You and your moving pitchers! You and your broadcast adverts! I always thought this show of yours was a fake of some kind, and as soon as I set eyes on your dials round that table an hour ago I was certain of it! Well, I been doing a bit of listening in on my own since then, and I know what you're up to. But you're not going to do it! I won't let you! I've been a soldier of His Majesty the King, and I won't let you! I'm not afraid of you: I've put a belt of machine-gun bullets through a bigger crowd of 'ogs than you before breakfast! I ain't got no machine-gun now, but I've got this three-inch spanner; and if anyone tries to push past me in 'ere, I'll serve him the same as I've just served those two fat Dagoes that was told off to take care of me!"

He was drowned by a roar of execration.

"Can you see him?" I asked.

"No," muttered Nigel. He was shivering violently, and I could hear his teeth chatter. He was in the grip of some violent emotion; but it was not fear.

"And another thing!" roared Alf. "I'm an honest trade unionist, and if I wants to 'ave a scrap with my boss, or a strike, or a lock-out, or any kind of row at all, I'll do it on my own, see? with my own mates to 'elp; and we shan't require no advice *nor* assistance from a set of lop-eared, slab-sided, pig-eyed, foreign murderers! That's what you are—foreign murderers what's jumped your bail and come over here to make us worse than what you are yourselves!"

A thunderous voice came to his support.

"By God, the laddie's richt! That's what ye are! Murrderrerrs!"

It was a grand word for a Scot to finish on. It fairly caught me by the heart.

"Nigel, Nigel," I whispered, "what can we do to help those two?"

Nigel made no answer. He was leaning down, shaking harder than ever, and peering through the spy-hole. Suddenly I felt his lithe young body stiffen. Then:

"Put down that gun, Flawn, you beast!" he yelled. "Put it down! Oh, I can't stand this!"

And, without the slightest warning, he shook off my encircling arm and rolled off the edge of the planking. Next moment, with a rending of lath and plaster, he had crashed through the flimsy ceiling of the alcove and projected himself upon the heads of the petrified mob below.

At the same instant Flawn's revolver went off.

IV

I rolled away from the newly-created abyss to the far side of the Priest's Hole, and lay listening excitedly to the turmoil which now ascended free and unmuffled from the room beneath. My first concern was for that young idiot Nigel; next, for Alf Noseworthy. Presumably Flawn had been covering the latter with his revolver when Nigel intervened. Had Nigel descended in time to divert Flawn's aim? At present there was too much noise to decide. There were sounds of a general struggle, and Nigel's voice uplifted in furious ejaculation; then comparative silence. Presently Manoukian's voice rang out authoritatively:

"Tie him up," he said, "and leave him for the present. It is close on midnight. Stand by, Comrade Moran. Comrade Puccini, we must fall back on you. Will you test the switches and valves in the power-house, and satisfy yourself that all is in readiness?"

"*Si, signor.*"

"Comrade Flawn," continued Manoukian, "you will accompany Comrade Puccini to the power-house, and keep that demented little creature covered until Comrade Puccini has tested the plant."

There came a sound of receding footsteps, as Puccini and Flawn went about their work. I breathed a sigh of partial relief. Evidently Flawn had missed Alf the first time, and Alf had retreated into the power-house.

"Ready with that bugle, Mike?" asked Manoukian, dispensing with ceremonial as the crucial moment approached.

"Sure!" Mike blew a soft low G, to demonstrate his preparedness.

"Then get to the micro— God in Heaven, what was that?"

From the direction of the power-house came a piercing shriek—a shriek of mortal agony and terror:

"*Santa Mar-i-a! Pieta! Pieta! Santa—!*"

Almost simultaneously Flawn's revolver rang out. In a flash I guessed what had happened: Alf had gone for Puccini with the spanner, and Flawn had shot him.

Shouts and confusion followed, and I heard men running to the far end of the room. Then came a horrified, frozen silence. Presently:

"Well, I guess that fixes Pucky," drawled Mike's voice. "The chair at Sing-Sing couldn't have fixed him no better. Twelve thousand volts! Gee!"

Apparently I had been wrong in my conjecture about the spanner.

But once more Manoukian's voice was uplifted. Nothing seemed to shake him.

"The dead must look after themselves. Get to the microphone, Mike!"

I heard Mike open the door of the microphone cabinet. Then he said:

"The red bulb ain't shining: Pucky didn't get that juice turned on. Is the little guy too far gone to do it?"

"I shot him in the stomach," said Flawn's voice calmly. "He's rolling about on the floor of the power-house."

"Then kick him on to his feet," commanded Manoukian, "and threaten to—"

"You filthy swine!" It was Nigel speaking, apparently from the corner where he lay trussed up. "Let the poor devil die in peace! He's a better man—"

Some one struck him a blow—in the mouth, presumably; for he stopped suddenly. But they had forgotten Adam Cargill.

"Would you threaten a dying man," he roared—"a man that's gaun' tae his Maker? I'll no permit it! I'm a Scotsman first, and I'll see the lot of ye in muckle hell before—"

But he never finished. From the power-house came the sound of a sharp detonation. It was followed by the splintering of wood and the crash of glass. Then came voices—a roar of voices—English voices—then a rush of heavy boots across a concrete floor, and a shriek of terror from the polyglot crowd beneath me, as the burly owners of the boots and voices burst in upon them....

A scattered shot or two rang out—doubtless some of the defenders were "heeled"—but the policemen were well into the room now, and came with a rush. The fight was on. I even detected amid the din a joyous view-halloo which in my whirling brain I associated with Arturo....

We had been discovered, and were going to be rescued. How it had all happened I did not know or care at the time. All I realised was that immediately below me honest British truncheons were thudding reassuringly down upon Bolshevik carotid arteries; that the signal for Plan B had *not* been blared forth, and that the Revolutionary Council of Action had just gone into automatic and frenzied liquidation.

Nigel and poor little Alf were—or would be—in safe hands now. My immediate concern was to get back to Corrie, and conduct her to a place of security until the present turmoil was past.

Stiff and sore after my long vigil, I rolled over on to my hands and knees and, turning my back upon the Priest's Hole for the last time, crawled down the tunnel to where I had left Corrie Lyndon.

She was not there.

CHAPTER 18

EMERGENCY EXIT

"Corrie," I cried passionately but echo answered.

I found my way to the spiral staircase and ran up it to the passage above. I reached Corrie's room; the door stood open. Again I called:

"Corrie! Corrie! Corrie, my dear!"

There was no reply. I made my way to the bed, and touched it. It was empty.

Manoukian?

I sat down on the bed, and tried to think. What would Manoukian do? What would I have done had I been Manoukian during the last ten minutes? When the police broke in, would I have set my back to the wall, or would I have run for it?

I decided at once that, valuing as I did my own skin above all the lost causes in the world, I would have run for it; and further, that as director of initiative in the recently dissolved board of assassins, I should have had sufficient extra intelligence to get out of the room before any of my colleagues had realised their danger.

What next? Obviously I would leave the house at once, by some unlikely and possibly unguarded exit, and do my best to get clean away.

No, I would not. I was Manoukian, and Manoukian was accustomed to mix up business and pleasure. I would find Corrie and take her with me.

And then, suddenly, I remembered the garage—the little garage which opened out of the empty drawing-room, with the ambulance in it.

Next moment I was hurrying along the passage, towards the familiar curtained entrance and the hall.

At the top of the great staircase I paused, and ran my finger along the row of switches which controlled the lights below. They were all down, not up. Good; the place was in darkness. Swiftly I descended. I could hear the sound of furious tumult behind the closed door on my left; evidently the fight was still in progress. This was not altogether surprising, for I suppose not five minutes could have lapsed since I had left the Priest's Hole.

I was at the tall double doors of the drawing-room now, on the opposite side of the hall. They were closed. Very gently I turned the handle of one of them and entered; then closed it behind me, and listened.

Across the room, through the musty silence, there came to my ears the steady hum of a running engine. Manoukian *was* in the garage—and where Manoukian was Corrie would be.

Que faire? Oh, for my sight again—for two minutes—one minute—one second—that I might see to get my hands on him!

Well, there was just one chance—one condition that would put us on equal terms. I groped my way through sheeted pieces of furniture to the little door in the outer wall. As I expected, it was closed. I turned the handle and opened it stealthily for perhaps two inches. I was greeted by the acrid, noxious fumes of a motorcar's exhaust; the whole atmosphere was heavy with them. Naturally, Manoukian would not open the outer doors of the garage until the last moment.

The electric light switch, I remembered, was just inside the door, to the left. Very carefully I extended a hand and touched it. Oh joy, it was down; the light was out. I might have known it, for Manoukian would not be likely to advertise his presence more than was necessary. For the same reason his car-lights would be out, too. If that were so, then my prayer had been answered, and he and I were alone in the dark together—alone in the country of the blind. And in the country of the blind the St. Dunstan's man is king.

Very carefully I slid through the door, closed it, and stood with my back to it, with the switch close on my left. Then I waited. I was tormented by an intense desire to cough, for the reek of the exhaust filled the place; but I fought it down.

The ambulance was facing inwards, towards me: the running engine was only a few feet away. Manoukian would have to back out: that fact might be helpful.

Suddenly I heard his voice—the voice he used towards women. It came from the other end of the little garage, and sounded hollow and muffled. Probably he was speaking into the body of the ambulance, through the doorway at the back.

"I must leave you alone for the present, my dear," he said. "I expect to be rather occupied for the next ten minutes or so. I don't *think* there is anyone waiting outside for us, but in any case my defence scheme is arranged. Now I will get these garage doors open, and we'll be off. Don't be alarmed if our conveyance bumps a bit; I shall not be utilising the carriage drive. I am going to run you through the plantations to a place where I keep another car—*not* an ambulance this time! When I have got you transferred to that, our difficulties should be over. *A bientot!*"

He closed the door of the ambulance, and I heard him rattle the pivoted horizontal bar which held the doors of the garage in position. Presently he gave an impatient exclamation, then left the door and began to feel his way in my direction. My heart quickened, for the thing I was hoping for was happening. He could not find the catch which held the bar in place, and was coming to turn on the electric light.

I had decided exactly what to do. Manoukian was feeling his way along the off-side of the car, on my left. I stood bolt upright, hardly breathing, with my back against the little door and my left hand poised just by the light switch, palm upwards.

He reached the corner of the garage, turned—I could smell him now—and came towards me. Next moment he had laid his groping right hand in my open palm!

Then he gave a piercing yell—a yell of panic and pain—for I had crushed his loose, unsuspecting fingers in mine. I heard them crack. At the same moment I got my right hand to his throat, with a grip that I meant never to relax so long as both of us remained alive. This was to be the final trial of strength between us, and I knew that my only chance was to make it a strangling match. So I gripped.

But, to do him justice, this fellow had courage. The first shock of surprise and fear had passed, and he was his powerful, brutal, aggressive self again. His disengaged left arm came round like a flail, with his doubled fist at the end of it. It struck me only a glancing blow, for which I had to thank the darkness. My head sang, but I stuck to him; I had his right hand twisted behind his back now, and with the purchase which I could exert on his fingers he was helpless in that quarter. His left hand came again, but this time it came slowly, feeling its way. Now he had me by the throat, and I, having no hand to spare, could not prevent him.

Then the struggle began in earnest. I do not know how long we stood there together, choking, squeezing; squeezing, choking. His hand was larger than mine, but that mattered little; for, perhaps in compensation for my blindness, I had developed exceptional muscular strength during the past five years, especially in wrist and finger. Then he receded a step: owing to my superior hold with my other hand I had been able to bend him backwards. This weakened his balance and probably saved my life, for he could not get his great weight behind his efforts to choke me. I followed up this small advantage hard: I wanted to get him to the wall and beat his head against it. I had no scruples or qualms, for I knew that if ever I let him from my grasp he would kill me—kill me without compunction and without difficulty. So I gathered him to my bosom as another blind man once gathered the pillars of the house at Gaza, and heaved and strained until I thought my heart would crack.

Then, suddenly, he did what he should have done before: he stopped trying to kill me and tried to shake me off. Such a manœuvre was all in his favour, for, once free, he could re-engage on terms completely advantageous to himself. He took three rapid steps backward, right across the garage. I was taken unawares. My left hand, slippery with sweat—chiefly his, for he was an oily customer—relaxed its grip upon his right. In a flash he had wrenched it free, and with his open palm gave me a staggering buffet in the face. That tore my hand from his throat, and he was gone!

For a moment I stood reeling; then recovered myself and sprang blindly back at him. I landed with a crash against the bare garage wall. Luckily my hands arrived there a fraction of a second before my head, or I might have brained myself. As it was, the sudden shock was horrible. I heard a mocking laugh on my right: Manoukian was working his way along the side of the ambulance, towards the other end of the garage.

"Now catch me, Captain!" he panted.

The taunt was his undoing, for it enabled me to locate him. I did the only thing possible, if I was to live. I leaped forward in the dark like a Rugby football player, in the direction of his voice, and tried to tackle him low.

And I just got him! It was a terrible leap to make in such surroundings: probably only a blind man, inured to knocks and bumps, could have faced it. My right hip struck the off-side rear mudguard of the ambulance, and my forehead encountered the concrete floor of the garage almost simultaneously. But I got Manoukian! In another moment he would have been round at the back of the car, out of reach again. Then, I suppose, he would have slipped round by the other side, turned on the light, and murdered me at leisure. But I got him: I got him by the ankles as neatly as an international full-back. Down he went, with a thud and a rattle against the wooden double doors of the garage, and in a moment I had jerked myself on top of him.

Then began the final struggle. We rolled, we punched, we hit, we scratched. Above all we squeezed—each trying to squeeze the life out of the other. Sometimes we were up against the doors, sometimes under the back of the ambulance. I was getting desperate, for my strength was failing. The atmosphere was heavy with the products of petrol combustion, and I began to feel sick and faint. We were under the car for the tenth time. Close beside me I was conscious of a steady, purring, pulsing noise, and a hot, mephitic jet of vapour discharging almost into my face.

Then, by the grace of Heaven, I suddenly realised how I could win this fight.

With one supreme contortion of my entire frame I rolled on top of Manoukian again, got his throat with both my hands, and planted his head, with a resounding bump, just underneath the mouth of the car's exhaust. Then, with my shoulders braced beneath the rear step, I held him there.

How he fought! How he shrieked, roared, gurgled, choked! I clung on; he could not budge me now without lifting the car off its axles. It was only a matter of time—if I could last out. My head was whirling: I held it as high as possible, for I knew that the choking carbon dioxide which was oozing from the orifice below me was a heavy gas, and was spread over the floor in a pool.

I had only one chance to live, and that was to keep Manoukian's head below the surface of that pool and my own above it.

His struggles grew fainter; his grip on my throat began to weaken. I myself was nodding and swaying; once or twice my head sank down almost into the invisible river of death below me. But I held on, somehow. There were noises in my ears: someone seemed to be calling my name; and just above my head I could hear a hammering and wrenching sound, as if a prisoner inside the ambulance were trying to break out of it. Then, dimly, I recognised the voice. It was Corrie's. Bless her!

That was about the last thing that I remember, for at this moment Manoukian, with one final, convulsive heave, collapsed limp and inert beneath me. His great arms fell to his sides, and he was still, still as death—for the most compelling of all reasons.

I rolled over beside him. I was conscious, but far too faint and exhausted to move a finger. I knew that the gas would have me directly, for I, too, was below the surface of the pool now. I had beaten Manoukian—beaten him in fair fight—but Death was going to beat us both.

Then, through my stupor, close beside me, I heard a light footstep. Next came the sound of someone wrestling desperately with the bar that held the garage doors. Then a clash, as the bar went down. Then the sweet night breeze, blowing through the open doorway.

Later on I was aware that someone was half carrying, half dragging me out on to the gravel. I tried to walk, but my feet would only trail. Then, suddenly, we were on grass—a soft, mossy grass-bank. I sank down on it, and went to sleep like a child, with Corrie's arms round me.

CHAPTER 19

THIS ENGLAND

So ended my participation—and Corrie's—in the epic of Bramleigh Chase. Its concluding passages, and they were stirring enough, were played out without us, and we were well content.

And so, simultaneously, ended the great Spargo Strike. Next morning the British Workman, having loyally complied with the instructions of his appointed leaders, returned to his job, refreshed and invigorated by two days' unexpected holiday and an agreeable measure of liveliness in certain industrial centres. The fact that but for a couple of people he had never heard of—a blind ex-officer and a little Cockney seeking escape from insignificance—he might have had no job to return to was unrevealed to him, and still is.

But we must go back a little.

The raiding party consisted of a mixed force of Metropolitan and Surrey police, headed by Sir Gavin himself, with Arturo attached as honorary and voluntary A.D.C. They had arrived in Sunningdale early upon the second morning of the strike—Wednesday. (It was on Tuesday evening, you may remember, that Lil Montgomery had volunteered her all-important statement.) Sir Gavin knew that there was no time to be lost, for he was positive that the Two Day Strike, if it went well, was intended to be a mere prelude to a far more ambitious scheme, which scheme would probably come into operation by Thursday morning at the latest. That scheme must be stamped to pieces before midnight.

And then Fortune, who perhaps considered that Manoukian had had a long enough innings, began to favour our side. In the first place she moved the local Superintendent of Police to make a most sensible suggestion.

"If the ambulance turned up the Chobham Road," he said, "the gipsies must have seen it. There's a lot of them gathering there for Ascot, on their usual pitch just below the monument that marks the place where the old Queen reviewed the troops after the Crimea. I'll tackle them."

"It's not easy to make gipsies talk," said Sir Gavin.

"They'll talk to me," replied the Superintendent.

And he was right. His persuasive methods, coupled with the mention of the proffered reward, promptly produced evidence of capital importance.

A nomadic gentleman with one eye, hereinafter referred to as Black Ben, came forward and announced not only that he had seen the ambulance on the day in question, but its driver on several other occasions in charge of another vehicle. The said driver's personality had been impressed upon Ben's notice by the fact that he had some days previously run over and killed Ben's dog, without even stopping to apologise. Instead, he had accelerated and disappeared round a corner. The corner in question was situated in Chobham village, by the tobacconist's shop, and the episode was witnessed by none save Black Ben himself, it being early morning—about 4 A.M., Ben coyly admitted. As he had obviously been returning from a poaching expedition, the correctness of his chronology was not disputed.

Grieved by the loss of his faithful slave, and eager to exact reparation for the same, Ben had devoted the next two days to patrolling the route which the canicidal Puccini had taken, and was rewarded by seeing the car again, going in the opposite direction this time. It was a wet, muddy morning, and Ben, by dint of following its wheel-tracks backward as far as he could trace them, and then lying in wait for its return, had succeeded at last in identifying the car's connection with the high, locked lodge-gates of Bramleigh Chase. He had not set eyes upon Puccini again until last Sunday afternoon, when that asterisked dog-slayer had driven past Black Ben's Ascot quarters in a white ambulance, going towards Chobham, and bound presumably for Bramleigh Chase.

Further questioned, Ben admitted that he had, three days after the murder, penetrated into the grounds of Bramleigh Chase by a route known only to few, in the hope of encountering the criminal and "setting about him." He had met, not Puccini, but an inhospitable person accompanied by two mastiffs, and had not stayed to prosecute further inquiries.

Here, then, were three pieces of luck—the Latin indifference of Puccini to the lives of the humbler creation, the outraged proprietary instincts of Black Ben, and the sound common sense of the Superintendent, all combining to give Sir Gavin the clue that he was groping for. His plans were soon laid. Bramleigh Chase and its surrounding terrain were cautiously reconnoitred and picketed, and arrangements were made, with Ben as guide, for a raid in force that evening.

The rest is history—secret history of a particularly interesting kind—and secret, for reasons set forth below, to this day.

II

"I gather there has been nothing in the papers about our recent adventure," I said to Sir Gavin.

"No," he replied, "and there isn't going to be. So if you are craving for limelight, my boy, you will have to go somewhere else for it."

A week had elapsed, and I was out of bed for the first time that day, more or less myself again, but still stiff and sore from my recent and frequent encounters with various unyielding surfaces of concrete, metal, and timber. My throat, too, felt as if it had recently been imprisoned in a vice—as indeed it had—and bore marks which confirmed that impression. I was in my own home, but the doctor had promised that if I behaved well my mother and I might proceed to Le Touquet in a couple of days now. Nigel was there already, with his sisters, none the worse for his recent experiences. (Arturo was once more wallowing in the *Swallow*.)

Corrie was at Le Touquet, too. Poor child, she had had a bad shaking, but her last letter, which my mother had just read to me, was reassuringly cheerful. Apparently her vigorous young spirit had suffered no permanent ill.

"No, we're going to keep quiet about the whole business," continued my uncle—"and for the usual reasons."

"Which are, that you don't want to tell the country a story which the country won't believe, and also that you don't want to manufacture any more martyrs than you can help."

"Your recent adventures seem to have sharpened your intelligence," said Uncle Gavin approvingly. "We must try bumping your head on a garage floor a bit oftener. But there's another thing. There is nothing like keeping your enemy in the dark. Do you remember how in the War, whenever we destroyed a German submarine, not a word was said about it, even to our own people. Brother Boche never knew whether his property had run on a rock, or been sent to the bottom by us, or gone to glory through some technical defect in its own construction. He did not even know where the disaster had happened: all he knew was that nearly two hundred of his U-boats never came back. You can imagine the effect on the *morale* of the German Navy. They fairly had to push the crews on board the last few months of the War. Well, that's the effect we are out to create on Brother Bolshie. All he will know this time will be that someone has thrown a monkey-wrench into the machinery of one of the grandest plots he ever hatched. He won't know how the thing was discovered, or how we got wise to Bramleigh Chase, or what has become of Manoukian. Only you know that—and Corrie—and one or two of Us."

"But what about the rest of the troupe—the people you rounded up? Are they to go free?"

"Free? Not by a long chalk!"

"But aren't they entitled to a public trial before being—?"

Sir Gavin chuckled.

"They are, and they're going to have one. But not on this charge! Fortunately there are plenty of others available. Their history-sheets are known to all of us, and in some cases we have quite an embarrassing selection of indictable offences to choose from. Some of the gang, of course, can be counted out already. Spargo arrived in New York yesterday: I don't think we need worry about Spargo any more. Manoukian is dead, and so is Puccini."

"Who accounted for Puccini? Was it Alf?"

"Yes. It was during that final unpleasantness in the power-house. Puccini tried to switch on the power which would have made it possible to broadcast the signal for revolution. Alf, although he was covered by Flawn's revolver, suddenly went for him. They closed, and Flawn couldn't fire for fear of hitting Puccini. Alf was trying to shove Puccini up against the live switchboard, and Puccini was trying to throttle Alf. Suddenly Puccini tripped over the bed of one of the generating machines. Alf shook himself clear just in time, and Puccini tumbled backward against the brush gear of the machine, which electrocuted him on the spot. It was Mike who told me about it: he said it was a real snappy ending. Puccini's shriek was a thing to remember."

"Thank you, I heard it! A bit of an artist in words, Mike. What has become of him, by the way?"

"He has been forwarded to Chicago. He's wanted there on about fourteen different charges."

"I'm sorry for him, almost. He had bowels of a rudimentary sort. I suppose he's dated up with the chair now, as he would say?"

"He guessed not. He said that there were fifty-seven different varieties of bail to be had in Chicago, if you were one of the right set, and when you had used them up you could go on appealing till all the judges were dead. No, I think Mike is going to have an easier time than the rest of them."

"And Flawn?"

"We found ourselves in a bit of a difficulty about Flawn. By rights he ought to have got seven years' penal servitude for the attempted murder of Alf Noseworthy. (Alf, by the way, is now out of danger.) But his trial on that count would almost certainly have brought out the Bramleigh Chase story. So we rooted around for something else. We had no difficulty whatever. Comrade Flawn has a sweet record. He has lived on women since he was eighteen, and the law of England has an ugly name for people like him, and an unpleasant remedy for their activities. Fifteen strokes of the cat and two or three years' hard labour, followed by deportation! (He is an Argentinian, by the way.) That's Flawn's probable future. I expect he would rather have done the seven years."

"Poor Lil!" I said. Somehow Flawn did not seem to matter so much. Then I asked:

"What about the rest of them? The Countess, for instance."

"The Countess is a lunatic, and has been for years. Her colleagues would be only too pleased to see her put away; she is a perpetual blister to them. So we are going to leave her at large. Spooner and Aynho, too. We gave them a slap on the wrist and told them to run away and be good boys in future, or else—! That was enough! I have never seen two men in such a pitiable state of funk. That's the worst of your Intellectual Revolutionary; he's such a physical poltroon, as a rule. I fancy the Dodekadelphi will sing pretty small for some time; I shouldn't be surprised if they disbanded altogether.

"Let me see—any more? Oh, yes, Jadassah and Adam Cargill. Jadassah is a venomous little brute. We let him go, but we told him that he would be kept under observation, and that if there was any trouble with him in future he would be sent back to his native Bengal. He would hate that, because he has quite a good time of it here, spouting in Hyde Park and being petted by white women at Communist tea-parties.

"But Adam Cargill was the supreme joke. We thanked him, very formally and seriously, in the name of the British Constitution, for the gallant fight he had put up at the meeting on behalf of Law and Order, and the Union Jack, and so forth. Then we shook him by the hand and bowed him out. The old fellow didn't know whether he stood on his head or his heels: he just faded away, glowering. I fancy he'll have some home-truths to tell his organisation when he gets home, though."

"And that's that?"

"Yes. Taking things all round, we've knocked the bottom out of foreign interference with our national liberty for another ten years or so. We made a wonderful haul of documentary stuff at Bramleigh Chase: lists of names, plans of campaign, and everything. Of course, the latter are of little value, because they'll be automatically scrapped; but the names will be useful. And for all these blessings, my boy, we have mainly to thank you and Alf Noseworthy—you because of the way in which you handled the tactical situation while a prisoner in Bramleigh Chase, and Alf because he prevented the signal for general revolution from going out."

I was silent for a while. Then I said:

"I wonder!"

"What do you wonder?"

"Whether the signal would have brought about all that it was intended to bring about. Demoralisation—panic—collapse."

"That means, you think it wouldn't?"

I nodded.

"I can't help feeling," I said, "that you set too little store by our national character. We are a stubborn race, not easily stampeded, especially by those who don't understand us. It seems to me that there lies the chief obstacle in the way of people who set out to destroy us from the outside. You can't demoralise a nation any more than you can demoralise an individual unless you understand its habit of mind and point of view; and that is where your Spargos and Manoukians will always come to grief in the end. They haven't the faintest beginning of an idea how an Englishman thinks. Some of them believe he doesn't think at all."

"I know, I know! The stupid English!

"Their psychology is bovine, their outlook crude and raw;
They abandon vital matters to be tickled with a straw;
But the straw that they were tickled with—the chaff that they were
    fed with—
They convert into a weaver's beam to break their foeman's head
    with!"

"Our Rudyard usually has something pithy to say on these occasions, if one knows where to look. And you, too, believe that our national peculiarities constitute a sufficient shield against external attack?"

"To this extent. I believe that if ever the British Commonwealth crumbles, it will be from within."

"That's what I'm afraid of, too, my boy. We're so cursedly apathetic."

"Still—are we? We are fond of telling one another that our character is apathetic, but you might describe it with equal truth as the character which knows how to sit back and do nothing until the right moment. It lies below the restless surface of our national life like a deep reservoir. Sometimes we are tempted to forget its existence. But it is there all the time, and at times of crisis it has a way of rising in a spontaneous flood, right over the level of party feeling and class prejudice, and of swamping a lot of perfectly good plans for its own destruction. And usually it gives someone an awkward surprise as well. It did that in the days of Elizabeth of England and Philip of Spain. It did it in Napoleon's day, when we, left alone out of all Europe, beat him single-handed. It did it in August, Nineteen-Fourteen, when the German Intelligence Headquarters had assured the Kaiser that we were far too deeply involved with trouble in Ireland, and trouble with Labour, and trouble with the Suffragettes, to intervene in a European war. And it did the trick once more in that May of a couple of years ago. Without a ripple on its surface it just overflowed its banks and drowned out the General Strike. That's how I feel, Uncle. I know you function differently. Your life has been one long battle for your country against treachery and sedition. But after all, treachery and sedition are exceptional things in this England of ours. Don't you think that one may sometimes be tempted to mistake an exception for a rule?"

"You seem to have devoted some consideration to the matter, Barry."

"Yes. I think about these things a lot; perhaps because I have exceptional opportunities for thinking a lot. I sometimes feel that we who sit in darkness have a clearer conception of the light than you, whose vision is so concentrated upon passing clouds as to make you a little oblivious of the blue sky that lies behind them. Anyhow, I trust this people—all the time."

Then I was suddenly silent, for I had spoken with more intensity than I intended. Sir Gavin rose to his feet.

"Perhaps you are right," he said soberly. "I hope so." He shook hands. "And God bless you, old man," he added suddenly and unexpectedly—"and give you good luck."

CHAPTER 20

THE FOURTH RESOLUTION

Corrie Lyndon and I were back in our old nest—the warm hollow of soft, running sand in the side of the hillock that looks down on the fifteenth green at Le Touquet. It was the season of what the French call Pentecost, and the links had been crowded all day. However, it was now past seven o'clock, and the tide of after-tea mixed foursomes was beginning to run slackly. A family match, consisting of Enid, Vivien, Nigel, and a young gentleman from Cambridge University, who had succeeded in scraping acquaintance—not one of the labours of Hercules—with Vivien at a Casino fancy-dress ball the night before, had just halved the fifteenth hole in an argumentative eight, and the sisters Dexter had both put their partners into the *forêt* from the sixteenth tee. The quartet had departed in a mist of back-chat and recrimination, and Corrie and I were alone. Corrie had dispatched the faithful Marie Thérèse to the refreshment shed at the eleventh tee, to fortify herself with *limonade* and milk chocolate. All was peace. I had only arrived from London that afternoon, and I had a vague feeling that I was in heaven—in heaven without a ticket of admission. But for the moment I was content to ignore that uncomfortable fact. When Corrie had sailed again for Canada—an event which I knew had been fixed for the end of next week—I would see about facing the chucker-out with what philosophy I could muster.

"It is just six weeks," said a demure voice at my side.

I started.

"Six weeks since what?" I asked.

"Since you and I became acquainted."

"So it is," I said. "Easter, wasn't it? Of course!" Then I added heavily: "A good deal has happened since then, hasn't it?"

"Yes," agreed Corrie; and was silent again.

"A good deal more than you think, perhaps," she added presently.

I did not relish the turn which the conversation was taking. I would change the subject.

"I paid a visit to Alf Noseworthy just before I left London," I said. "He is mending every day, and he and Edna are full of plans. Hal Horner has got him a job in a pierrot show, at a remote watering-place in Wales. 'The Lips that Touch Kippers' is to be released on August Bank Holiday. What do you think of that?"

Apparently Corrie thought nothing at all of it. She sighed patiently. Then:

"Do you remember showing me round Le Touquet?" she pursued. "Paris Plage and the Normandie, and those sandhills by the Channel?"

"Rather!" I said.

"And the talks we had, and all the questions I asked? I was a bold young thing, I fear. I'm not feeling so bold today."

I turned to her quickly.

"I hope you're not still feeling the effects of—"

"No, it's not that." Corrie sighed again.

"It's a difficult world for us women," she remarked.

"Can I help?"

"I doubt it. Do you remember what we talked about, out on those sandhills?"

I shook my head.

"It was about some resolutions of yours," she reminded me.

"Yes, I remember now."

"You said you had made three of them. You told them to me."

"I have an impression that you told them to me."

"So I did! And I said I knew there was another one, a fourth. I never told it to you, though. Shall I, now?"

"I can't prevent you."

"No; that is my only chance. It was: 'I never can and never will ask a woman to marry me.' Am I right, sir?"

There came a long pause. Then:

"Why do you make me talk about these things?" I was speaking very low now.

"Because I—" Corrie broke off with a sudden quavering little laugh. Then she asked:

"Barry, do you remember another thing? That day when you asked if you might touch my face?"

"You know I do."

"Well, if—if you were to—to do the same again—you would find a difference. Feel my cheek for a moment."

She took my hand and led it to her face. It was burning hot.

"Now do you understand?" she said. "I'm blushing! I'm all upset! And it's your fault!"

"Corrie!" I whispered; "do you mean—"

"Yes, that's just what I do mean—and you're a brute to make me say it first. You are resolved never to marry—even a girl whom you love as much as you love me. You do love me, don't you?"

"God help me, I do! But I thought you didn't know. I prayed you didn't know!"

Corrie's two hands were holding mine now.

"Then the only course left open to a poor girl," she said, "is to ask you herself. Barry Shere"—her voice quavered again—"will you marry me?" She gave a little choking laugh. "There, I've said it! Will you?"

I released my hands and sat immovable. But, deep down in my soul, I let myself go just for a moment. After that I hardened my heart and spoke.

"It would be all wrong," I began resolutely. "You—with your glorious youth, and beauty, and vitality—tied—tied—"

"Barry," she said gently, "I am asking you to marry me. I'm not doing it well, because I've never done it before. But I love you, and I've got to have you. There, I've said it; and I know how you feel. You can just nod your head if you like."

She slipped her hand into mine again. There came a discreet cough from the crest of the hillock, and the hand was hastily withdrawn. Marie Thérèse was with us once more.

I turned to her.

"Marie Thérèse," I said, "shall I marry this lady?"

"Kwah kwee!" replied Marie Thérèse resignedly.